Straight, Bent and Barbara Vine

NOEL BUTCHER

Garry Disher grew up in South Australia and now lives near the Victorian coast. He began writing short stories as a break from his history MA, and on the strength of these was awarded a creative writing fellowship to Stanford University, California. He later taught fiction writing to supplement his writing income, and helped design the Victorian TAFE system's professional writing course, before turning to full-time writing in 1988. His award-winning fiction titles include novels, short-story collections, thrillers and children's books.

May, 2001.

Straight, Bent and Barbara Vine

short stories by

Garry Disher

To Virginia,
with best wishes,
Garry Disher

ALLEN & UNWIN

First published in 1997 by
Allen & Unwin
9 Atchison Street, St Leonards NSW 2065 Australia
Phone: (61 2) 9901 4088
Fax: (61 2) 9906 2218
E-mail: frontdesk @ allen-unwin.com.au
URL: http://www.allen-unwin.com.au

National Library of Australia
Cataloguing-in-Publication entry:

Disher, Garry, 1949- .
Straight, Bent and Barbara Vine : short stories.

ISBN 1 86448 524 8.

I. Title.

A823.3

Set in 11/14pt Garamond Book by DOCUPRO, Sydney
Printed and bound by Australian Print Group,
Maryborough, Victoria
10 9 8 7 6 5 4 3 2 1

Contents

Acknowledgments

The author and publisher wish to thank the publishers and editors of the anthologies in which these stories first appeared: 'Wyatt's Art', 'Old Ground', 'Threshold' and 'Trusthouse' in Stephen Knight (ed.), *Crimes for a Summer Christmas* (1990), *More Crimes for a Summer Christmas* (1991), *A Corpse at the Opera House* (1992) and *Murder at Home* (1993), Allen & Unwin, Sydney. 'Scrapings' in Jennifer Rowe (ed.), *Love Lies Bleeding*, Allen & Unwin, Sydney, 1994. 'Stalking Moon' in Jean Bedford (ed.), *Moonlight Becomes You*, Allen & Unwin, Sydney, 1995. 'The Two-Hundred Dollar Picasso' in Stuart Coupe and Julie Ogden (eds), *Case Reopened*, Allen & Unwin, Sydney, 1993. 'My Brother Jack' in Robert Hood and Stuart Coupe (eds), *Crosstown Traffic*, Five Islands Press, Wollongong, 1993. 'Love and Grudges' in Helen Daniel (ed.), *Expressway*, Penguin Books, Ringwood, 1989. 'Airship' was first published in *Fine Line*, 6, 1989, and later appeared with 'Early Warning' in the author's third short story collection, *Flamingo Gate*, HarperCollins, Sydney, 1991.

Author's note

You could say that I wear three fiction-writing hats—'literary', crime and children's—but in *my* head the three are indistinguishable from each other in terms of worth, writing craft and hard work. Labels like 'crime writer' seem to exist to marginalise writers and what they write, and to acknowledge the existence of conventions. I hope you're entertained by the stories in *Straight, Bent and Barbara Vine*. I can't deny that they employ some of the conventions of crime fiction, but I also hope they bring the genre in from the margins a little by demonstrating its artistic possibilities and complexities. Indeed, I can truthfully say that crime fiction has taught me how to write.

From time to time I'm invited to talk on 'mystery' fiction or review a 'detective' novel. I wish those terms could be abolished. All fiction is mystery fiction, and these days few detectives walk the mean streets of the genre. I prefer the term *crime* fiction, for it is fiction dealing with the perpetration, investigation, reasons for or effects of a crime, and my taste is for contemporary crime novels, which work on three main levels—as mysteries, critiques of society and accounts of character.

The classical murder mystery has 1) a mysterious but unlikely and uninvolving death; 2) a closed circle of half-a-dozen suspects, each improbably with motive, means and opportunity; 3) a police or amateur detective, generally an outsider, a keen observer who solves the puzzle logically from the clues supplied but who is devoid of personality; 4) a staged setting (for example, an English manor house on a stormy weekend); 5) a murderer who must be compatible with half-a-dozen other suspects; and 6) a puzzle about time, place and opportunity, so that the question being posed is *Who-dunit?* rather than *What-manner-of-person dunit?*

Motive and personality are secondary and characters two-dimensional in classical whodunits. We can't engage very far with murderer, victim or investigator. Social attitudes are conservative, loose ends are neatly tied up and the puzzle often depends upon a deception of the locked room, obscure poison or ice-bullet kind.

The private eye novel is another classical form. It has slightly more relevance to the late twentieth century but the traditional hardboiled *hero*, with his down-at-heel office, desk-drawer bourbon bottle, solitary habits, indestructible skull, misogyny, deep cynicism, unshakeable honour, blonde heiress clients and apparent lack of mother, father, siblings, wife, children or friends, has become unconvincing and irrelevant.

Contemporary crime fiction takes in the police procedurals of Ed McBain, the black comedies of Carl Hiassen, the forensic whodunits of Patricia Cornwell, the crime-from-the-inside approach of my own Wyatt novels, the apparently right-wing cops of James Ellroy, the very human, doubting and fallible policemen of John Harvey and Tony Hillerman, female investigative journalists, gay and lesbian police officers, medieval monks, lawyers, psychiatrists—even cats. It engages with the role and influences of modern technology such as computers, bugging devices and forensic tools, and may tackle social justice issues. Many successful 'literary' novels are crime novels. They include E. L. Doctorow's *Billy Bathgate*, Peter Hoeg's *Miss Smilla's Feeling for Snow* and David Guterson's *Snow Falling on Cedars*.

The stress now is on character, rather than tricks and clues. We learn something of the hero, the victim and the villain. The hero is flawed, not a super-reasoning machine, and the forces driving the villain may be explained, if not forgiven or condoned—childhood sexual abuse, for example.

Gay and lesbian crime novels are enriched by their examination of concealment, prejudice, sexual passion, love, workplace tension and particular kinds of vulnerability and courage. There is a great demand for psychological thrillers, which take us into the minds of apparently normal people, plotting their gradual disintegration, madness, depravity or criminality. In accidental hero novels, ordinary people stumble upon a crime, are the victims of one, or are accused of one. They find their capabilities tested. Those in some of Elmore Leonard's novels may sit on the fence for a while, then suddenly adopt the tactics of the bad guys and so unexpectedly level the contest.

There can be a strong element of contradiction and moral blurring in contemporary crime fiction: corrupt cops and good criminals, criminals framed for crimes they didn't commit, hitmen who kill the wrong person, vicious criminals unhappily in love, cops who fall in love with suspects. The modern reader is impatient with superheroes. We've come a long way from the stereotypes of an earlier era, those effete aristocrats, tough guys and gentlemen police inspectors with first-class degrees from Oxford. Not that contemporary crime novelists aren't capable of inventing new stereotypes, for the sake of difference or effect or political correctness, but it would be a cynical act if I were to create a gay Aboriginal police inspector.

And the puzzle factor evolves from character. Modern writers tend not to set up intellectual puzzles for the sake of it. If there is a murder—and we could argue that there must always be a murder—then it may be the fallout from another, more compelling or deeply buried crime, such as blackmail. For example, the real issue at the heart of Ruth Rendell's novel, *The Gunner's Daughter*, is not the horrifying massacre of a family but an inner corruption that had been at work within that family. (The family as a structure may have a lot to answer for, according to the psychological thrillers of Barbara Vine and Minette Walters.)

Why do we read crime fiction? Why do I write it?

One, it entertains. One reader's stirred martini is another's hemlock, of course, but if fiction does not entertain then it fails, regardless of whether it's driven by action, character, experimentation or ideas.

Two, it tells a story. Story is sometimes seen as unfashionable, but humankind's need for story, for wanting to know the solution to a mystery, or what happens next, is undeniable. The style, formal structure and ideas of Michael Ondaatje's *The English Patient* may be dazzling, but they would fail to satisfy if they weren't also married to an absorbing mystery story.

Three, we are beguiled by puzzles. The promise of a solution keeps us turning the pages. As apparently random fragments of information accumulate, we try to make sense of them, try to order them into a pattern. We negotiate with the information; we read actively, not as a sponge. But all good fiction writers pose puzzles, stay a step ahead of their readers, anticipate their questions, subvert their expectations, delay gratification. And so they hook us. And so we read on.

Four, there is the appeal of the hero. We identify with quirky senses of humour, sardonic attitudes, vulnerable traits and messy private lives on the one hand, and admire heroic qualities on the other. Heroes act where we fear to tread, at the edges of the law, morality and respectability. They have some excitement in their lives. We envy them their physical and mental abilities. If they are paralysed or hampered by doubts and scruples, or intimidated by authority figures, it's only briefly, to remind us that they are not so different from us, and then they get on with the job. This is a vital factor in the success of crime fiction by and about women, in which readers meet characters who are powerful role models yet resemble them in fundamental ways. Sara Paretsky's V. I. Warshawski depends upon a community of women friends and is given to examining her conduct in personal and private matters. But ultimately she must act alone. It's a rule of thumb of crime and children's fiction that the solution must lie with the hero, not the cavalry.

Five, there are vicarious pleasures: the threat of violence, the exciting chase, the heart-stopping reversal, the absorbing stages of the detection in a novel like Thomas Harris's *Red Dragon*.

Six, good crime fiction stimulates the senses. All writing should 'make pictures in the head', and in crime fiction we can smell the toxins, taste the thermos coffee on a midnight stakeout, feel and hear the grit under our shoes. It's this richness of sensory detail that helps account for the appeal of James Lee Burke's Louisiana bayou novels.

Seven, some of our finest stylists are crime writers. Content, character, setting, mood and a relentless focus condition the edgy lyricism we hear in the prose of Burke, Elmore Leonard and James Ellroy.

Eight, many crime novels and stories are distinctive for their humour. In Robert B. Parker's Spenser novels, we strike the sly asides, mordant wit, wisecracks and pungent observations of an unimpressed mind.

Nine, crime fiction tells us about the world we live in. It satirises institutions, personality types, lifestyles and tastes. It can act as a barometer of prevailing tensions and social forces in the community, point to injustices, and articulate the attitudes of those who are overlooked by 'city hall'. Crime fiction is also more likely than the latest grunge or *caffe latte* novel to tackle the big issues of the age. Sara Paretsky's novels have dealt with official corruption, pollution and the American healthcare system, for example.

Ten, it's reassuring. With all those random forces acting upon us, we look to crime fiction to restore order and right wrongs, even if the method and the solution should happen to be morally ambiguous.

Finally, why do we law-abiding writers and readers find murder fascinating, the pathology of a dark mind engrossing, bank heists exhilarating, revenge satisfying? *We imagine.* We must be able to acknowledge our darker side in order to appreciate crime fiction—indeed, *any* fiction.

Like all writers, I'm often asked where my ideas come from. Several of the stories in this book were commissioned for anthologies, most of which were theme-based. 'Trusthouse' for example, appeared in the fourth volume of Allen & Unwin's popular Crimes for a Summer Christmas series, the editor, Stephen Knight, asking for stories on the theme of 'murder at home'. Even so, a theme is not an idea, and every story in *Straight, Bent and Barbara Vine* had to come from somewhere.

The fact that these are crime stories is immaterial. I used no special source of ideas but drew from my general well of characters, incidents, observations and plotlines. I incorporated experiences (my being stalked suggested the background of 'Stalking Moon'), landscapes from my past ('Old Ground', 'Trusthouse', 'Scrapings', 'Early Warning' and 'Airship'), actual events '(Trusthouse' is based in part upon the disappearance of the Beaumont children), and newspaper clippings ('The Two-hundred Dollar Picasso' and 'Wyatt's Art').

I brainstormed an image to find the storyline of 'Threshold'. The editor of the anthology in which the story appeared had supplied each of the contributors with a description of a woman found dead on the steps of the Opera House in Sydney. The obvious questions were: Who killed her? Why? How is the Opera House important? Who shall tell the story—the killer or the investigator? I answered these, tested the answers and asked further questions until the story evolved.

In the case of 'Old Ground', I simply borrowed a conventional situation (an investigator returns to his home town after a long absence to look into a mysterious death), but I also knew the *ending* first (the location of a body) and worked back from there. In most cases, however, I start with a *beginning*, which, in the words of Sean O'Faolain, will incorporate a character, a situation and a promise. All I knew before I started writing 'Wyatt's Art' was that Wyatt was in Europe, on the run from the law, but wanting to come home. Then I read an article about smuggling and the Customs Service, and the story took off.

I never jettison old notes or scraps of manuscripts. My latest novel, *The Sunken Road*, is based on notes and false starts going back almost twenty years. It could be said that I hadn't known enough about the character, place and way of life that I was describing, but I was also in want of a key to unlock the material, and it came serendipitously, my noticing the words 'the sunken road' in three different war histories. 'Trusthouse' and 'Scrapings' were once the beginnings of novels that I'd abandoned after many months and many thousands of words. In resurrecting them as stories I simply refined the central issue—which may indicate that many of the novels we read should have been short stories.

Sometimes a sense of disquiet or irritation is useful. 'Airship' and 'Early Warning' are from *Flamingo Gate*, my response to the gentrification of the inner Melbourne suburb in which I lived—the burglar alarms, police helicopters, syringes in the gutter, fancy townhouses and general 'white noise' of consumer images, fear and self-absorption.

The stories in the second section of *Straight, Bent and Barbara Vine* grew out of my interest in the writing process itself. At about the time I was writing the early drafts of *Kickback* (the first Wyatt novel) and 'Wyatt's Art', Helen Daniel invited me to contribute a story to her influential *Expressway* anthology, a collection of responses to the Jeffrey Smart painting, 'Cahill Expressway'. Crime was in my head, and so 'Love and Grudges' is a (kind of) crime story, but, as I'd been making a botch of the early *Kickback* drafts, it's also about clichés of story and character, and the sorts of plotting decisions that writers make.

'My Brother Jack' and 'Cockeyed at High Noon' extend the notion of the creator and his creation, and take a tongue-in-cheek look at genre conventions. 'My Brother Jack' was commissioned for *Crosstown Traffic*, a collection of hybrid crime stories, and grew out of my dismay that some interviewers and readers had assumed that I had a criminal past. (I don't.) It's good to know that Wyatt and his adventures are convincing, but I began to think about the link between author and character, and so we find Garry Disher with a criminal brother called Jack, alias Wyatt. And in thinking about the conventions of genre fiction over the years, I've seen parallels between Wyatt and loner Western characters. In 'Cockeyed at High Noon' we see Wyatt reborn as an outlaw who rides in from the badlands one day, intent upon hanging up his guns and his spurs and finding true love.

And so the structure of this book: *Straight* stories (a murder mystery, a private eye investigation, a heist, a betrayal-and-revenge thriller), *Bent* stories about genre conventions and the writing process, and psychological mysteries along the lines of those written by *Barbara Vine*, pen name of Ruth Rendell.

Crime short stories are more difficult to write than crime novels. By tradition, both are linear in shape, involving set-up (the beginning), conflict (the middle) and resolution (the end), but where novels can be relaxed, expansive and discursive, short stories should create a single, focused impression. Stories tend to cover a smaller canvas than novels and have fewer characters, a more contained situation and limited setting changes. The problem for the writer of a short crime story lies in introducing a compelling mystery quickly and solving it neatly, without recourse to tricks and shortcuts but using the acknowledged techniques of variable pacing, carefully placed surprises, delaying tactics, finely judged turning points and the factors of causality that underpin and govern the plot.

These are demanding conventions. I can't employ them effectively unless I plan in close detail, balancing plot and character and keeping the tone fresh rather than mechanical. I don't use filing cards, whiteboards or butcher's paper pinned to the wall but simply make scrappy notes, beginning usually with the crime, the main players and the broad plot stages, before spending days, weeks, revising, fleshing out, discarding, always testing the story in terms of *character* (What is motivating him? Given who she is, would she respond like this/do that? What if he did X instead of Y?). If my instincts lead me in a different though plausible direction, I'll restitch the plan. I envy Raymond Chandler, who quipped that he had a man walk through the door with a gun in his hand whenever he wrote himself into a corner, and Elmore Leonard, who says he doesn't plan, and Agatha Christie, who waited until the whole story was in her head before sitting down for the six weeks it took her to write a novel. Then again, James Ellroy wrote a 211-page outline for *L.A. Confidential* and Sara Paretsky threw out 300 pages of *Tunnel Vision* because it was 'kind of meandering and it didn't have a shape'.

The *thinking* approach varies, depending upon the type of suspense that needs to be generated. The Wyatt novels and stories are crime-from-the-inside. The questions that drive them are, 'Will he get away with it?', 'Who betrayed him?' and 'Will he get his revenge?'. With whodunit mysteries the author must decide upon the real truth (what really happened and why, revealed at the end), the truth that is apparent to the reader and the hero (the layers of deception, the false truth, that make up the bulk of the story), and the method by which the hero will uncover the truth. Psychological mysteries deal not with criminals but with ordinary people and what might make them break. Minette Walters's novel, *The Scold's Bridle*, grew out of the question, 'What would happen if the members of a family were repressing one another?'

But perhaps that's all it boils down to—asking the 'What if . . . ?' question.

Further information

The following publications and organisations are useful:

Delys Bird (ed.), *Killing Women: Rewriting Detective Fiction*, Angus & Robertson, Sydney, 1993

Marele Day (ed.), *How to Write Crime*, Allen & Unwin, Sydney, 1996

Mean Streets magazine, published quarterly, available from newsagents or What Goes On Pty Ltd, 214 Hat Hill Road, Blackheath, 2785, Australia.

Sisters in Crime exists to discuss and promote women's crime fiction and further the careers of women crime writers. The Australian chapter (branches in each state) offers membership open to all (men are 'brothers in law'), a newsletter three times a year, regular meetings, talks and competitions, and an annotated bibliography of crime fiction by women writers. Write to: Sisters in Crime, GPO Box 5319 BB, Melbourne 3001, for details.

Crime Writers' Association of Australia exists to promote Australian crime writers and their work, and organises the annual Ned Kelly Awards. Write to: c/- 24 Bennett Road, Granville, 2142, for details.

There are similar crime writers' and readers' organisations in the USA, Canada, Europe and the UK. Many have an Internet home-page. In the UK, the *Crime Writers' Association* may be contacted c/- PO Box 172, Tring, Herts., HP23 5LP.

for:

Liam
Frankie
Tony
Kathy
Marcus
Debbie

STRAIGHT

Old Ground

A hazardous switchback road plunges down the northern slope of Isolation Pass, so my first glimpse of Mawson in twenty years was interrupted by guardrails and rockface. Mawson is one of those drowsy wheat and wool towns on a treeless plain, a place where they know the cost of everything and the value of nothing. It's named for Governor Mawson's son, who in 1841 set out from Adelaide to survey the range that now shelters the town and the merino stud properties, failed to return, and was found a year later with a spear pinched between two bones of his rib cage. That was about the first thing they taught us at the primary school. Later I learned how the sheepmen replaced the Aborigines, but I didn't learn it in Mawson. I was only going back there because my brother had expressed some doubts about a death.

The road straightened and I accelerated. Before long I could make out MAWSON painted on the roof of the pub, a landmark for the buyers who fly in from New South Wales for the ram sales. I could also see the cemetery, a dusty patch of gum trees and gravestones on a rise beyond the Elders-GM saleyards. The cemetery was somehow linked to why I was coming back.

I slowed at the outskirts of the town. For a moment I had that old sensation—Broken Hill to the north, Adelaide to the south, Mawson at the centre—but shook it off to concentrate on the present. The first few houses had not changed—walls of local stone; low, broad verandahs; golden cypress hedges; TV antennas twenty metres high. The RSL hall where Mick and I used to dump empty bottles for the annual Legacy drive was still there. The changes began in the main street. The craft shop was new, and so was the coffee shop, called the Copper Kettle. Every façade had been renovated in late colonial styles and there wasn't a Coke or Marlboro advertisement in sight. I knew what it meant: Mawson had got itself a conservation-cum-historical society.

I angle-parked outside Mick's office. 'Michael Ryle: Taxation and Accountancy Services' was painted in old-fashioned script on the main window. I knocked and went in.

The woman at the reception desk didn't acknowledge me, but I recognised her all right. There is a mulish family named Clancy in Mawson. Clancys never leave the place but marry into struggling sharefarming families, drive trucks for the district council and populate the convent school and the football team. This was a Clancy. She had the same bulky jaw and affronted air.

'Is Mick in?'

'Mick?' she said.

A Clancy, all right. I said, 'The man who pays your salary. Is he in?'

She resumed chewing her gum and flicked on the intercom. 'Mr Ryle, someone to see you.' The speaker crackled and she looked at me and said, 'He wants to know who.'

'Tell him his brother.'

She did, and Mick stepped out of his office. He wore a tweed jacket, a shirt and tie, and grey trousers, all of them wrinkled-looking. He didn't come forward but gestured. I nodded at the Clancy woman and went by her into his office.

He closed the door and we shook hands warily and said things like, 'How have you been?' These days we see each other only every couple of years, usually on Christmas Day and never in Mawson.

'Sit down,' he said, and we settled into a couple of old club chairs on either side of a faded rug. We regarded each other for a few seconds, looking for an opening. Mick seemed to be tense. He held his thin body stiffly and his hands worried each other.

'I'm glad you could come,' he said at last.

I nodded encouragingly. I like to let people explain things in their own way, in their own time.

He jerked his head, indicating the outer office. 'I couldn't explain on the phone.'

We both grinned. When we were kids, all our conversations had been coded with Clancy references.

Mick grew sober again. 'You remember Geoff Lyle?'

I did. We'd been contemporaries, but where my family had drifted into the district after the Second World War, his had been there for generations. As a child he'd been a bully. As an adult he was thrusting, vigorous and successful. 'Took over his old man's undertaking business,' I said.

'Right. Well last Friday he wrote himself off coming down the Pass. They buried him yesterday.'

I said nothing.

'I handled his insurance,' Mick said.

Apart from genes and Mawson, all Mick and I had in common was Eagle Provident. He was their agent in the mid-north; I investigated fraud for them from time to time.

'Go on,' I said.

'About two months ago he tripled his life cover,' Mick said, and he looked at me and waited.

'Who benefits?'

'Who else? Lisa.'

Another contemporary. Lisa Heinrich had been called Lisa Acres by the farm kids because the first thing she ever asked them was how much land they had. Being a railway ganger's son, I wasn't even in the running. Then Geoff Lyle inherited his father's business and she hauled him off to the altar.

'People increase their cover all the time,' I said. 'It doesn't mean anything's wrong.'

Well, it often does, but I wanted to hear what Mick had to say.

'It's a bit more complicated,' he said.

I waited.

He sighed. 'The thing is, the Lyles had a big development scheme on the drawing board.'

He handed me a glossy brochure from the coffee table next to him. The hype was about what I expected from the Lyles:

There is one certainty, even in this time of recession: people die. G. & L. Lyle Funerals are proud to announce The Pines, a development offering landscaped grounds, Mercedes-Benz hearses, chapel with soothing piped music, and the latest in crematorium technology from the United States of America. All types of interments catered for, from a simple plaque to a family vault. Serving the entire mid-north of the state. Invest now!

'I gather work hasn't started yet.'

Mick shifted uncomfortably. 'And it's not likely to.'

I watched him. 'How much are you in for?'

This time his whole face twisted. 'Seventy-five.'

'Thousand?'

He nodded. 'If I don't get it back, I'm stuffed.'

It had taken us a while to get to this point. I've stopped being surprised. Some people have an innate love of suspense, some are hesitant, others are fearful. I said, 'What makes you think you've done your dough?'

'The first dividend payment was due last week. It didn't come. The next day Geoff Lyle ran off the road.'

'Payments like that are often late.'

'Consider this, then. Two weeks ago Lisa came in here all apologetic and said they wouldn't be needing me any more, they'd decided to hire a full-time accountant.'

I stared at the pattern in the rug for a while. I said, 'Who else did they sting?'

'I hoped you'd be able to find out. You know people here, you know how the place ticks.'

'If there *is* a problem here, how do you see it?'

'Geoff Lyle leaves Lisa well-provided for—insurance,

investments salted away somewhere—then commits suicide.'

'Was he ill? Cancer?'

'I hoped you'd find that out too,' Mick said.

Mick's wife and I don't get along so I booked into the motel. By then it was midday. I rang the Mawson clinic and arranged to see Rob Turner after lunch, then wandered down the street to buy a sandwich. A little sign in the window of the Copper Kettle said, 'Breakfast and lunch served all day'. I went in.

It was a curious place. The decor suggested art-and-craft, sidewalk-cafe bohemia, and the food consisted of croissants, Devonshire teas, open rye sandwiches, eggs-all-styles and good coffee. I nodded at a farmer dressed in a tweed jacket, moleskin trousers and R. M. Williams boots. An Akubra hat on a hook above his table accounted for the stark white forehead above his creased, sun-browned cheeks. When last I'd seen him he'd been wearing a school uniform. The other customers represented a fair cross-section of the district: shopkeepers, townspeople, kids from the high school. There hadn't been anything like the Copper Kettle in my day.

At 1.30 I walked to the clinic, which is on the eastern edge of the town, next to the hospital. A brass plate named the town's two doctors. Rob Turner had returned to Mawson after graduating. The other was Alison Smart. For all I knew she'd lived in the town for twenty years, but she wasn't what the locals called 'a local'.

It was 2.00 before my name was called. The first thing I noticed about Turner was his new confidence.

At school he'd always hovered on the edge of things, hot-faced and envious and disapproving. Now he thrust a pudgy, dampish hand into mine and pumped it weakly and said, 'Long time no see.'

We went on in that vein for a couple of minutes, Turner telling me about the clinic and his tax write-off farm, and then I showed him my card and said, 'I was wondering if Geoff Lyle was your patient.'

Turner's lips narrowed and he seemed to sniff. 'He was.'

'Was he in good health?'

'You're asking me to betray a confidence.'

'He's dead, Rob.'

'Even so . . . '

'Put it this way: did he have a major illness of any kind?'

'I'm starting to find this offensive.'

'I'll put it another way. Had he heard anything from you that would make him want to take his own life?'

Sometimes you have to push. It puts people's backs up, but in the process they might give you an answer. Turner got out from behind his desk, held the door open and said, 'There was nothing wrong with him. I think you've got a bloody nerve, Ryle, coming back and sticking your nose into the lives of people you grew up with.'

You can't operate in my game without a system of favours owed and owing. I went back to the motel and called investigator contacts in the Securities Commission, the Corporate Crime Squad and the fraud department of the Lyles' bank. Then I went about sticking my nose into the lives of the people I'd grown up with.

After some coaxing, the local bank manager said that The Pines account had been closed and the funds transferred, but he wasn't prepared to say where, or to comment on the extent of local investment. The editor of the *Mawson Weekly* let me look at her file on the Lyles, but it didn't tell me anything new. I spoke to other people too, but, in general, everyone seemed to be wary and reluctant to say anything about the Lyles or The Pines scheme.

But when you push, something generally gives or pushes back. I was walking to the Copper Kettle for breakfast two mornings later, having decided that Clancys cooked the motel's breakfasts, when Lisa Lyle pulled up alongside me in a dusty white BMW. She turned off the engine, leaned across to open the passenger door, and said, 'I want to talk to you.'

I got in and settled my shoulder against the door. She looked angry, her glossy hair tossed back, her patrician nose at an angle, her eyes flashing. It was a look I remembered from primary school.

'I don't like sneaks,' she said. 'If you want to know about Geoff, ask me direct.'

I watched her for a moment. Any one of a dozen people might have told her what I'd been doing. 'All right,' I said. 'Was he in trouble financially? Had he been suicidal?'

'No to both questions. You're incredible, thinking you can come back here and poke about when we're all still mourning him.'

'Where's the money, Lisa?'

'What money?'

I said, 'Will you stay in Mawson, or have you got other plans?'

Her fine head tipped back another inch. 'You always were pathetic.' She started the engine. 'If you're finished, I've got work to do.'

I got out and watched her drive away. It's the same in every country town: Clancys at the bottom; a middle rung of people like Mick; and Lisa Lyles at the top, who have wealth and privilege but no intellect at all, a combination that can baffle the best of us.

I unwound with strong hot coffee in the Copper Kettle. It had been an odd couple of days, discovering the present and rediscovering the past. A voice, a gait, the hot-wood smell of a verandah post—these had aroused powerful memories of school days, weekends, idle vandalism, boredom and longing. I'd felt the same hostility or indifference toward some people, the same affection for others.

And the same desire. Rose came into the Copper Kettle, said, 'Give us a kiss,' and threw her arms around me.

We disentangled and she stepped back, her clever face lively and assessing. 'A few grey hairs,' she said.

'But distinguished. Coffee?'

She joined me. 'Been a while since we did this,' I said.

'I don't recall that we ever did this. We spent all our time behind Dad's woolshed in the back seat of your father's car.'

I grinned. Soon after I had learnt to drive, the word 'discothéque' had reached beyond the cities. I hadn't been alone in combing my hair forward, driving fifty miles to pick up a farmer's daughter, then another fifty to dance to a Beatles look-alike band at a country hall, then back again, finally getting home as the sun was rising, feeling tossed and edgy after a few mostly unconsummated hours under a tartan rug somewhere.

'I always knew you wouldn't stay in Mawson,' she said.

I couldn't think of an answer to that. Twenty years ago I'd been on the edge of staying, but Rose had seen something in me she didn't want and I didn't know was there, and she'd chosen someone else. I said, 'How's Ken?'

She looked at me, faintly troubled. 'Didn't Mick tell you? Ken died five years ago. Cancer.'

'Oh. I'm sorry.'

'I run the business now.'

A grain and seed firm. After a while I said, 'Bad luck about Geoff Lyle.'

Rose looked instantly wary and alert. 'Yes.'

'Do you think Lisa will stay on? Be a shame if The Pines fell through.'

Rose had never been slow. She dropped her voice and said, 'Good old Andy Ryle, back after twenty years. But not for old time's sake. If you want to know if I've got money invested, that's none of your business. If you want me to say Geoff Lyle was a shit, I won't do it. He was my friend.'

And she got up and walked out.

I went back to work. By late afternoon I'd taken the investigation as far as it would go. I sensed that many locals had invested in The Pines, but if they were anxious they weren't letting on. They had an automatic regard for the Lyles and felt that my questions were in bad taste.

Time to check with Adelaide. I learned from my contacts that the Lyles' new accountant had a history of moving money sideways and off-shore. Also, owing to heavy borrowing and recent losses by an investment company associated with The Pines project, the bank was about to issue the directors with a 'please explain' notice.

I asked for details about the directors. The fax came through to Mick's office for me at 5.00. The directors were Lisa Anna Lyle, Geoffrey Paul Lyle—and Robert Anthony Turner.

There was no indication that Turner was a doctor. He'd listed his occupation as 'farmer'.

Eagle Provident has plenty of clout. By Friday we had an exhumation order.

'So when The Pines went bust,' Mick said, 'Lisa and Rob killed Geoff for the insurance. Shouldn't be hard to prove.'

It was a few days later and we were on our way to the Council Chambers behind the Memorial Hall. The chambers had been set aside for the coroner after it was discovered that the RSL hall had a rotten floor and exams were being held in the high school assembly hall.

'That's up to the police,' I said, 'and they won't act unless the coroner finds that Geoff died as a result of foul play instead of the car smash.'

But things didn't go like that. The first to give evidence was King, the forensic pathologist, a fussy man with clean, slender fingers, and he said immediately: 'The deceased man is not Geoffrey Lyle.'

He held up two large buff envelopes. 'A simple comparison of X-rays establishes that. This X-ray of the deceased man reveals an old pelvic fracture. This one of Geoffrey Lyle, taken recently for a chiropractor treating him for sacroiliac pain, reveals no pelvic fracture.'

He paused. The coroner, a smiling, lazy-lidded man, said, 'Any other discrepancies?'

The pathologist seemed to recite: 'The deceased is a male Caucasian aged about fifty-five. The body weighs seventy kilograms and is 170 centimetres in length. The lungs indicate that he was a heavy smoker. The teeth are crooked, worn and heavily filled.' He coughed. 'Geoffrey Lyle was'—he paused significantly—'or is, forty-two years old, and is both heavier and taller. He is a non-smoker. According to his dental records, his teeth are in excellent condition.'

The coroner said, 'Put simply, the man who drove to his death in Geoffrey Lyle's car was not Geoffrey Lyle.'

That was when the pathologist dropped his second bombshell. 'Correct. Except that he didn't die in the crash.'

The coroner blinked. So did I. 'Go on, Dr King.'

'The face and hands were burnt beyond recognition, and the head, trunk and pelvis were badly traumatised—all consistent with the injuries one might expect when a car crashes and burns. However, not all of these injuries showed signs of bleeding, and there were massive internal injuries that are not consistent with a car smash. In addition, the lungs, throat and nasal passages revealed traces of dust. Now, if death had been instantaneous one would not expect to find traces of smoke from the burning wreck, but there were dust traces, and these—together with the other injuries—seem to point to death by crushing, possibly in a landslide.'

His opinion was supported by Alison Smart, Rob Turner's partner. She looked tired, and revealed in a subdued voice that around the time Geoff Lyle's car went over the cliff, she had treated a prospector injured when a mine shaft had collapsed on him. Accidents like this were not uncommon, she said. Every couple of years someone was injured or killed in the arid gold-bearing country east of Mawson.

'He died without regaining consciousness,' she said, 'and I signed the death certificate.'

She paused. The coroner said, 'The body, Dr Smart?'

'Normally we release a body to the deceased's family, but this man didn't have any, so we obtained authorisation to assign the body to the local undertaker for burial in the Mawson cemetery.'

Well that made us sit up. The coroner said, 'You are satisfied that the man who died of injuries sustained in the collapsed mine is the man found in Geoffrey Lyle's car?'

'Yes. I assisted Dr King with the autopsy, and matched his X-rays with X-rays I took when I treated the man.'

Then Rob Turner was called. His confidence had disappeared. He looked anxious, and immediately began to stammer explanations and apologies.

The coroner held up his hand. 'Dr Turner, please, we are not assigning blame here. Simply tell us what happened when the body from the crashed car was brought to the hospital.'

Turner gathered himself. 'I was on duty when the body was brought in. I examined it and signed the death certificate. I'm sorry, it was my fault, I just assumed it was Geoffrey Lyle. It was his car and we found his wallet.'

'The clothing wasn't burnt?'

'Scorched. It was a woollen suit.'

The coroner assessed him. 'You admit that you based your identification of the body on superficial evidence?'

Turner winced. 'The face and hands were unrecognisable, but everything else seemed to point to its being Geoff Lyle.'

'He was your patient?'

Turner raised a twitchy pale face. 'He was also a friend. I suppose I was too upset to see beyond the car and the wallet.'

Then Constable Lovell gave evidence. The Mawson policeman was a sandy-coloured man with a half-amused manner. He did not refer to notes and, mercifully, did not use police-speak. 'The dead man was Karel Pavek, a Czech who migrated to Australia in 1954. He had no friends or relatives here or in Czechoslovakia. I learnt all this from his partner, who was only slightly injured and managed to raise the alarm at Anlaby Station homestead. He's gone back to the mine and wasn't interested in claiming the body.'

That left Lisa Lyle. She looked pale and drained of energy. The skin was tight over her cheekbones but pouchy under her eyes.

'Mrs Lyle,' the coroner said, 'who took delivery of Mr Pavek's body?'

'My husband, the day before he disappeared.'

'Speak up, please, Mrs Lyle. And he took responsibility for the funeral?'

'Yes. A simple burial.'

The coroner nodded, thinking it through, along with the rest of us. 'Did you witness this burial?'

'No.'

'Where were you?'

'Taking care of the laundry. The business generates more than you'd expect.'

'I see.'

Lisa said heatedly, 'I didn't see my husband bury an empty coffin. I didn't see him put poor Mr Pavek's body in his car and stage the crash.'

'Mrs Lyle,' the coroner said mildly, 'you are not on trial here. Getting back to the burial—wouldn't cremation have been easier and cheaper?'

Lisa looked down at her hands and muttered, 'We don't have a crematorium.'

Then her manner changed. She looked challengingly around at us. 'We were going to build one,' she said. 'Our friends, our neighbours, they all had money invested. At first I thought we were victims of the recession—that's what Geoff said. I didn't know he was stripping the company.' She broke down. 'He even cleaned out our joint savings account. There's nothing left. He's run off with everything.'

'They'll be happy at Eagle,' I said later. 'No body, no payout.'

'Poor bloody Lisa,' Mick said. 'From ogre to victim in the space of a week.'

'She's not the only victim.'

He nodded gloomily. 'They'll never find the money.'

'They'll never find Geoff Lyle.'

We were in the motel's licensed bar. They didn't have Clancys working there: the glasses were clean and no-one was wiping a greasy rag over our table. We were discussing the coroner's findings, which simply implied what we all knew: Geoff Lyle had staged his own death and run off with the investors' money.

'You think he's overseas?' Mick said.

'I'm positive. But his real name won't show up on the computers. He'll be using a false passport.'

Mick sighed. Then someone opened the door, admitting noise and a band of sunlight. It was Lisa Lyle. She crossed the room to our table. When she spoke, her voice was throaty with accumulated emotions.

'I owe you an apology for the other day.'

'Forget it,' I said. 'Will you join us for a drink?'

'Scotch,' she said, sitting opposite me.

Mick went to get it and I said, 'It's me who should apologise. I thought you were somehow behind everything.'

She seemed to shiver. 'I can't get over how calculated it all was, even to arranging for increased life insurance so I'd be provided for. He must have had some feelings left for me.'

I didn't respond to that. If it gave her comfort, let her think it. I said, 'What will you do now?'

Her face twitched bitterly. 'I've got no money, the

business is about to fold, the town hates my guts. What would *you* do?'

It was true that the town hated her guts. After the hearing had closed I'd been approached by half-a-dozen locals who'd invested in The Pines. All were angry. All wanted me to find Geoff Lyle.

I said none of this. Suddenly Lisa grabbed my wrist. '*I want you to find the bastard.*'

'I don't have the resources,' I said reluctantly. 'And the trail is cold, and when people don't want to be found, and have the money to create a new identity, it's not easy finding them.'

She left without waiting for her drink. She looked desolate. I didn't envy her. It was all waiting now, and she might wait forever.

The next morning I packed my bags. Karel Pavek's grave was being exhumed later, but I couldn't see any point in hanging around to look at an empty coffin.

It was Friday, a market day, so the Copper Kettle was busy. I perched on a stool at the counter and waited to be served. The air was fragrant with the smell of fresh coffee and warm croissants. Dishes clattered in the kitchen, voices discussed the coroner's findings and the little bell above the gingham-curtained door pinged as people entered or left the room.

Then Rose came in. She looked tense. I felt a tug of emotions and turned away to face the counter hoping she wouldn't see me.

A moment later she was standing at my elbow. 'I need to talk to you,' she said, and just stood there waiting.

I said, 'Morning,' or something like it, marking time.

'I need to talk to you,' she said.

I looked at her, taking in the stubbornness and agitation. 'Go ahead.'

'Not here.'

All the conversations dropped to a murmur as we crossed the room. This was a small community and it wanted to know our business, but it was also essentially well-mannered, and the conversations started up again as we reached the door.

On the footpath outside I said, 'What's this about?' but all Rose would say was, 'Not here. Your motel.'

A few minutes later, the door to my room closed behind us, I said again, 'What's this about?'

'You're all so bloody satisfied. You're all so convinced he did it.'

I watched her for a moment, then counted on my fingers. 'One, he faked his death. Two, he's disappeared. Three, a million dollars of investors' money has disappeared with him.'

'No-one's seen him, though.'

'He's travelling on a false passport, living it up in some tropical paradise.'

Rose smiled then, and it was hard and glittering. 'Did you know he recently applied to have his passport renewed?'

I nodded warily. 'The police told me. What are you getting at?'

'Has anyone seen the new passport?'

'No, but that doesn't mean anything. He probably chucked it away.'

'Then why apply for a new one?'

'Part of the general smokescreen.'

Even as I said it I wasn't convinced. If he wanted people to think he was dead, he wouldn't go to the trouble of renewing his passport, especially as he couldn't risk travelling on it if the ruse failed.

The doubts showed on my face. Rose pressed her advantage. 'It doesn't add up, does it?'

I said, 'Come on, Rose. Spit it out.'

She said nothing. She opened her handbag, removed something and flung it on the bed. It was a passport.

'Aren't you going to look at it?' she said.

I picked it up. It had been issued a month earlier. The face in the photograph was Geoff Lyle's: there was no doubting the vigorous jaw and mocking eyes.

'Where did you get it?'

'He gave it to me,' Rose said. 'He also gave me these.'

She tossed two airline tickets onto the bed. They were return tickets to Auckland, first-class. I looked at her.

'We're lovers,' she said, using the old-fashioned term unselfconsciously. Her eyes filled with tears. 'Or were—I think he's dead.'

I waited. I didn't think she'd want me to touch her.

'It's impossible to hide things in this town, so every year we slip away for a holiday together. Last year Fiji, Bali the year before that. Only for a few days, but still worth it. I can't believe he'd go to the trouble of renewing his passport if he was meanwhile working on some elaborate scheme to stage his own death and run off using a false passport. It doesn't make sense.'

'What about the missing investments?'

'The business may have been going under, but if I were you I'd ask his co-directors.'

I watched her, thinking about it. 'How come you've got the passport and tickets?'

'So Lisa wouldn't find them.'

'How strong was it between you and Geoff?'

If she said Geoff had sworn undying love and was intending to leave Lisa any minute now, I was going to say 'Pull the other one.' But she didn't. She shrugged and said, 'Strong enough, but no-one was promising anything and I wasn't in a hurry to get married again. I think Geoff's long-term plan was to wait until The Pines was running profitably so he could sell out to the others and try something new.'

I digested this. 'Lisa and Rob . . . ?' I said, leaving the sentence unfinished.

Rose smiled coldly. 'Lisa would rather be a doctor's wife than an undertaker's wife.'

'Was anything said?'

'We were all playing a waiting game. Except someone stopped waiting and it wasn't me and it wasn't Geoff.'

I watched her carefully. I said, 'Why did he increase his life cover?'

'Oh Lisa made him do that. He said she went on and on about the recession, what if he died tomorrow, etcetera.'

'You don't like her much.'

'Geoff told me he'd wake up sometimes and she'd be lying there watching him.'

I felt my skin prickle as she said it.

A runaway wheat truck had killed my father, and my mother had died of heartbreak, and they're buried together next to a gravelly path in a boxthorny corner of the Mawson cemetery. I could feel the pull of their headstones but I didn't go to look. I was with the coroner, Constable Lovell, Lisa Lyle and a scattering of others, watching two Clancy cousins digging up Karel Pavek's coffin.

We were a cheerless lot. A gritty wind was blowing, the Clancys were surly, everyone else looked bored. As far as Lovell and the coroner were concerned, today was routine. They expected to find an empty coffin.

I didn't. I glanced at Lisa. A complicated expression passed across her face—part tension, part irritation, and, when she met my gaze, part challenge. I was asking myself why she hadn't taken advantage of a fifteen hours' head start, when the coffin appeared. 'Let's get this over with,' she said.

It was a cheap varnished coffin. The Clancys didn't waste any time. They prised off the lid. Lisa stepped forward before anyone else, looked in, turned triumphantly and said, her voice ringing out: 'Empty. Now perhaps you'll all put your energies into tracking down my husband.'

Empty, all right. I don't deny that I was disappointed. The coroner said, 'Thank you, Mrs Lyle, we're finished here,' and he walked back to his car, accompanied by Lovell. Lisa gave me another complicated look, told the Clancys to fill in the grave again, and hurried away after the coroner.

I stood for a while, looking at the hole in the ground,

while the Clancys sat on the coffin and smoked cigarettes. I heard one of them mutter, 'Bitch.'

I said, 'Did Geoff Lyle supervise this job?'

'Pardon?'

'Was Geoff Lyle here when you buried this coffin?'

Kevin Clancy took his cigarette from his mouth long enough to say, 'We'd of known it was empty, wouldn't we. Wouldn't of weighed anything.'

It was my turn to say, 'Pardon?'

Bevan Clancy spat on the ground. 'Wasn't us what buried it. The boss rings on the Thursday, says there's this unclaimed body to bury, but when we get here on the Friday *she*'—he jerked his head—'says don't bother, it's been buried. A bloke could of slept in.'

'So who buried it?'

'Wouldn't have a clue. Lisa did, for all I know,' Bevan said.

'But weren't you suspicious?'

'Mate, she's the boss.'

'She gave you something for your trouble?' I asked.

Kevin winked. 'Might of.'

'I'd like you to do me a favour,' I said.

That alerted them. Five minutes and fifty Eagle Provident dollars later, their spades struck something soft and yielding and coated in what looked to be lime.

I was about halfway up the torturous road over the Pass before I found where Geoff Lyle's car had plunged over the side. New posts and rails marked the spot. The place and the means had become so strongly associated with his death that I wondered how long it would take before the locals adjusted to the actual place and means.

According to the autopsy report he was heavily doped but still alive when dirt and then the coffin and then more dirt had been dumped on top of him. When the coroner heard that, he said, half-admiringly, 'If there had been no inquiry, the wife and Turner stood to get the insurance on top of everything else. If there was an inquiry, suspicion would fall on the husband. Either way they'd get to keep the invested money. Smart plan.'

Yes and no. I've encountered smarter. Right now I want to believe I'd have seen through the plan and Lisa's greed much earlier if time, place and memory hadn't got in the way, but only a chance conversation with a pair of Clancys had helped me, and that's a cruel realisation.

Wyatt's Art

He could go home now. The heat would be off him. Not that he was risking a computer check of the passenger list: this morning he had paid eight hundred guilders for a passport with the name Ross on it. His own photograph, though, now that he'd made some slight but convincing alterations to his face.

The problem was money. At 2.00 Wyatt walked to the post office on the other side of the canal and spent the remainder of his money calling Melbourne. It was night there, late, but late was the only time you'd catch Milne.

Wyatt didn't give his name: Milne would know his voice. He said, 'I'm in Amsterdam.'

'Yes.'

'I'm coming home.'

'I see,' Milne said.

'I need the fare,' Wyatt said. A moment later he said, 'I'm prepared to work for it.'

Milne was silent. Interference crackled softly on the line. Finally he said, 'Where are you staying?'

Wyatt gave the address and phone number of his *pensione*.

'Someone will contact you in a few hours,' Milne said. 'Don't go out.'

'There are jobs I won't do,' Wyatt said.

'I'm aware of that,' Milne said.

Wyatt returned to the Duyfken and asked Wilhemina for his key. 'I'm expecting a telephone call,' he said. 'It's important. I'll be in my room.'

Wilhemina shrugged. It was nothing to do with her. The Duyfken was a place where strangers stayed a short while and muttered on the telephone and slipped out at night. She said, 'Mr Ross, you must pay for your room.'

'I'll pay,' Wyatt said, turning away from her.

He went upstairs to his room. It was at the front of the building, its smeared window overlooking the street and the canal. Two-thirty. The sun was high, flooding the houses beyond the canal with light. Most had their shutters closed; red geraniums spilled out of every window box. Respectable people lived there. Wyatt saw them buying croissants in the mornings and breadsticks in the evenings and he imagined their lives, their decent narrowness of range. He had nothing against them. He knew them—here and in Melbourne and everywhere else on the globe. They read newspapers that sniffed around crime like eager dogs. Men like Wyatt thrilled and appalled them.

He turned away and stretched out on the bed. He was well known in Melbourne now, but it hadn't always been like that. Just ten months ago, life had been sweet for him. High-fliers in Brighton, Doncaster, South Yarra, finding themselves short of cash, would contact Milne, who hired Wyatt to burgle their homes for a percentage of the insurance or the reward money. Everyone was happy. But they had been relying on a bent assessor and a bent cop, and when the Fraud Squad eventually set up a job, Wyatt found himself in the frame. He shot and wounded a cop to get out of it. He couldn't stay in the country after that. Now it was time to go back. Milne had helped him get to Europe, Milne would help him get home again.

He was dozing when Wilhemina tapped on his door. He followed her downstairs to the grubby coin telephone in the hallway next to the reception desk and picked up the receiver. 'Yes?'

A hectoring man's voice said, 'You will be in your room at five o'clock.'

'Have you got a ticket for me? And I need cash.'

'Five o'clock,' the voice said.

At 4.30 Wyatt walked out to one of the sidewalk cafe tables next door to the Duyfken. He sat where he could watch the *pensione*. Behind him three backpackers were consulting a Baedeker, and an elderly Englishwoman at the next table smiled at him briefly over her Nicolas Freeling. Wyatt stretched out his legs and ordered lager from the waiter. A tourist launch grumbled by on the canal. Somewhere a scooter howled through a back street.

At five o'clock a black Mercedes crept past the Duyfken. It was chauffeur-driven and two men were in the back seat. Wyatt watched as it slowed for the next side street, hugging the kerb as though the driver intended to pull over as soon as he'd turned the corner.

He remained seated until a man appeared at the corner and approached the Duyfken. He was about forty, carrying a briefcase, an overweight, balding pink man obviously distressed by the heat.

Wyatt waited for the man to enter the *pensione*, then he crossed the street to the path by the canal and sauntered along it until he could see into the side street. The black Mercedes was parked fifty metres down from the corner. The driver was slouched behind the wheel. The second passenger was outside the car, leaning on the boot, smoking a cigarette. Wyatt automatically fixed the man in his mind: a gloomy, pinched face, expensive dark suit, heavy-rimmed glasses, a few wisps of black hair scraped back over his scalp, an air of coldness.

Keeping it casual, Wyatt turned and leaned his forearms on the canal wall. A couple of minutes later, he wandered back the way he'd come.

The sweaty man with the briefcase was arguing with Wilhemina at the reception desk. 'There,' she said, pointing at Wyatt.

The man turned. 'You are Mr Ross?' It was the voice on the telephone.

'Come with me,' Wyatt said. He returned Wilhemina's level, non-committal expression, took his key from her and led the way upstairs and into his room.

'You were told to stay here,' the fat man said. He wiped his face. 'Won't you open that window?'

'Windows have ears,' Wyatt said. 'What have you got for me?'

'This.' The man opened the briefcase and took out a blue folder fastened with pink ribbon. The words *Souvenir of the Rijksmuseum: Modern Drawings* were printed on it in Dutch, English, German, French, Spanish and Japanese.

'Something other than prints for tourists, I guess,' Wyatt said. He twisted his mouth in what might have been a grin.

'It is not necessary for you to know what it is,' the fat man said. He sniffed, holding his large body primly.

Wyatt walked to the door. 'Then it's no deal. Get out.'

The man gestured helplessly and wiped the perspiration from his face and neck. 'Original drawings, not reproductions.'

'From the Rijksmuseum?'

'Of course not.' The big man spoke in a rush: 'Stolen from private collections. We have a collector in Melbourne.'

'Show me.'

Wyatt leaned forward. A gust of perspiration hit him as the big man spread the drawings on the bed briefly before bundling them together again and returning them to the folder. The man seemed scared. Wyatt didn't touch the drawings but he recognised names and styles: Picasso, Grosz, Dali, Nash, Hockney. All were on stiff, heavy, expensive-looking paper.

He said, 'A customs officer wouldn't know an original from a print, is that how you figure it?'

The man smiled wetly.

Wyatt said, 'I deliver these to Milne?'

'Yes. He will pay you ten thousand dollars.'

'When do I leave?'

The man took a KLM ticket from his pocket and gave it to Wyatt. 'Tomorrow.'

'You're forgetting something.'

There was distaste on the big man's face. He took in Wyatt's slight, quick shape, worn jeans, T-shirt and sandals and said, taking out his wallet, 'You may have four hundred guilders.'

'It's not a handout,' Wyatt said. 'This is a job I'm doing for you people.'

It was an airport like any other in Europe, a glass, cement and aluminium structure hectic with streaming humanity, public announcements, duty-free shops, the cold, winking green of monitor screens. The airport police resembled soldiers. Some wore pimples and most had the look of men who'd prefer shooting people to watching them.

Wyatt did not check in but sat on a yellow vinyl bench under a plate-glass window, his suitcase next to his feet. The folder of drawings was packed beneath a layer of shirts. At no point had he let his fingers touch it. With the folder were some touristy gifts he'd bought that morning. Here was the traveller, returning to his family.

Wyatt waited, watching the staff at the KLM desk. If there had been a tip-off he hoped to recognise the signs: wary clerks and airport police; authority's anonymous dark suit and ardent expectation of the quarry in the trap.

As Wyatt watched, KLM opened its counters and queues began to form. He watched for thirty minutes, and saw nothing but unflappable clerks, weary travellers, efficiency. The two airport police nearby yawned and stretched the kinks in their backs.

Ninety minutes till flight time. Wyatt picked up his suitcase and approached the shortest queue—but then, like a man remembering something, he veered left and entered a duty-free shop. He was tense. His heart hammered.

He ignored the shop assistant. She spoke to him in Dutch, and then in English, but Wyatt didn't hear her. He peered between shelves of fountain pens, intent on the man he'd seen enter the terminal building and walk toward the KLM counters. Tall, receding black hair, a gloomy expression, prosperous-looking in a suit and heavy-rimmed glasses, wearing the same gloomy expression he'd seen in the side street outside the Duyfken less than twenty-four hours earlier.

Time enough later to work out what that might mean. Wyatt nodded absently at the assistant and went into the next shop. He bought a pair of close-fitting gloves and put them on. He went into another shop and bought a second suitcase, similar in size, shape and colour to his other one. In a women's-wear shop he bought bras, knickers, slips, blouses, a cotton pullover, slacks, a cotton skirt and a black dress, and perfume, tampons and make-up. The woman serving him smiled, a smile that grew tight and hot.

Wyatt didn't have much time. Still wearing his gloves, he took his purchases into the men's room, shut himself in a cubicle, and began stripping away the wrappings and price tags. He crumpled the new clothing a little, rubbed floor grime onto the neck and wrists of the blouse, and sprinkled small amounts of talc and perfume onto everything. He repacked the cases. It was cramped in the cubicle. Now and then someone used a washbasin outside. *Last call, KLM to Melbourne.*

When he had finished, Wyatt walked to the KLM desk and checked in both cases. He watched tensely as the clerk snapped a destination label to the handle of each suitcase and stapled the luggage tags to his ticket. She passed him the ticket and said, smiling tiredly, automatically, 'Enjoy your flight, sir.' Wyatt smiled back at her. She was startled by its intensity.

She had given him a middle seat, in the smoking section, but he had been late checking in and he could put up with it. The gloomy-faced man, he noticed, was sitting in the first-class section. It was a long flight. Wyatt dozed. At meal times he drank orange juice, not alcohol. On the last leg of the journey he washed and shaved and relieved his pockets of the airport bus ticket, boarding pass, one luggage tag from his KLM ticket, and other paper scraps related to his flight.

Low cloud in Melbourne, the captain announced. Some rain expected; maximum temperature, twelve degrees; estimated time of arrival, 5.30 a.m. local time.

When the plane landed, Wyatt shrugged himself into an old leather jacket and pulled on the gloves. By 6 a.m. three hundred passengers stood in a bottleneck at passport control. The air was chilly and Wyatt shifted his weight from one foot to the other and glanced around the huge hall. It looked normal enough, the usual range of airport staff working or idling at their jobs and no-one talking much at this hour on a Sunday morning. The man from Amsterdam was far back in the queue.

The officer who examined Wyatt's passport merely flipped through it and said, 'Next!', his manner bored.

Wyatt passed on to the luggage carousel. He felt more tense now, and forced himself to breathe evenly as he waited for the KLM luggage to begin tumbling out. Last on, first off, he thought, and within five minutes he had spotted both his cases. He let them go around twice, occasionally making a play of straightening other people's jumbled luggage. When he was certain, he selected one of the cases, turned with it, and began walking through the nothing-to-declare exit.

They must have been waiting for him. There was no discernible shift in the atmosphere but, almost immediately it seemed, two men were blocking his way and a customs officer was saying: 'Is this your case, sir?'

Wyatt said that it was.

The officer hauled it on to a bench. 'Open it please, sir,' she said.

It was a cheap black vinyl affair. Wyatt undid the buckled strap, pulled around the zip, and folded back the lid of the case. 'That's funny,' he said, peering in.

The customs officer ignored him. She burrowed into the clothing, found the blue Rijksmuseum folder immediately, opened it and examined the prints. She nodded to the two men. They clasped Wyatt's elbows and one man said, 'Will you come with us, please, sir?'

Wyatt said, 'That's not my case. You can see it's not my case.'

'Just come with us, please, sir.'

They took Wyatt to a small, stale-smelling room and told him to sit down. One man remained in the room, the other left with the black case. The room held an odour of years of fear and guilt; the dirty white walls seemed to shrill: *Someone must have planted it on me*. A polished steel lavatory bowl stood in one corner of the room. 'If they think you've swallowed anything,' an acquaintance told Wyatt once, 'they'll wait till you pass it naturally.'

The second man returned with a third man, who

carried Wyatt's suitcase. Cop, Wyatt thought, taking in the polyester shirt, loosened tie and stretched suit trousers. A pen had leaked in the man's shirt pocket.

'Mr Ross, is it? My name is Jansen, I'm a detective sergeant. Perhaps you wouldn't mind telling us how you came by this?'

He held up the Rijksmuseum folder and Wyatt said, 'Never seen it before.'

Jansen looked tiredly at him. 'Now I wonder where I've heard that before.'

The man at the door sniggered. Wyatt said, 'I picked up the wrong suitcase. Look at that stuff: bras, dresses.'

'Is a woman travelling with you?'

'Not that I've noticed.'

'Why are you wearing gloves?'

'The cold,' Wyatt said. 'I get arthritis, chilblains.'

Jansen nodded. Wyatt could not read the man's expression, but that was all part of the game, and he half-expected them to start using the tough cop/sympathetic cop routine.

'I'll show you,' Wyatt said, taking out his KLM ticket. By now it was creased and torn.

Jansen scowled at the other men. 'Did either of you check?'

One of them looked uncomfortable. 'We were told to watch for—'

'That will do,' Jansen said. He took the ticket from Wyatt, muttering, 'This looks as if it's been through a wringer.' He compared the label on the black suitcase with the stub stapled to Wyatt's ticket. Then he breathed out and it was a sound full of weariness and acceptance. 'Different number,' he said.

Wyatt nodded.

Jansen tried to rally. 'What I'm wondering is,' he said, 'was there a second luggage tag stapled to this?' He held the crumpled ticket to the light. 'Difficult to tell.' He looked at Wyatt. 'Take off your clothes.'

'Now come on,' Wyatt said.

'Quick about it,' Jansen said. 'You two, search pockets and linings. You're looking for a luggage claim tag.'

Wyatt stripped off all his clothes and waited, his arms around his chest. 'Nothing,' the men said.

'Get dressed,' Jansen said. 'Okay, Mr Ross, describe your luggage to me.'

'It's a case similar to this one,' Wyatt said, 'except the knickers fit.'

The man at the door stirred. 'Smartarse. Let me have him for a couple of minutes, boss.'

'Shut up,' Jansen told the man. 'Take this case downstairs and have it sent up on the luggage escalator again, then go back and see who picks it up. You,' he said to Wyatt, 'come with me.'

Jansen led Wyatt to the luggage carousel. Most of the cases had been claimed by now. The man from Amsterdam was not among those passengers who were still waiting. Wyatt leaned forward, picked up his case, and checked the number on the label. 'This is it,' he said.

'Come with me.'

Jansen took him back to the depressing white room. This time a sniffer dog was brought in. As Jansen stood by sourly, the dog ran its nose around the case, before sitting back on its haunches, its expression close to apologetic.

Jansen opened the case. Wyatt watched him sift

through the familiar jeans, T-shirts, gifts and shaving gear. Then Jansen jerked his head. It was a way of saying that Wyatt was free to go.

'Folders, sniffer dogs,' Wyatt said. 'What was all that about?'

'Don't push your luck,' Jansen said.

An hour later, Wyatt said: 'You owe me.' He said it several times as the day progressed, and by six o'clock that evening he had acquired a Smith & Wesson .38 Chief's Special revolver, two sets of handcuffs and fake ID to hire an old Datsun from Rent-a-Wreck.

Sunday evening. Milne would be at home, just starting to do business. Wyatt had spent most of the day in the exhausted streets of Footscray, and now he was passing among the screened, vigilant houses of Brighton, a region of beloved dogs, car phones and middle-aged men whose young wives seemed permanently dressed for aerobics or the Derby.

Milne's car was in his driveway and lights were on in the house. Wyatt parked the Datsun in the next street and walked back to Milne's house, slipping among a stand of ornamental trees and making for the garage at the back. He spent some time there, sniffing experimentally at gaps around the sealed door and windows.

Wyatt had never visited Milne here, and knew little about him, so he circled the house to get an impression of its layout. The curtains were open in only one room, the kitchen, where a light had been left on. It was a bare, gleaming room, showing no sign of a family's domestic clutter. Milne's got a housekeeper, Wyatt thought. He lives alone.

He made a second circuit of the house, testing locks on doors and windows. One window was unlocked; a small, narrow bathroom window. Familiar shapes showed on the shelf beyond the insect screen. Wyatt cut open a corner flap of the screen, lifted it, and tucked the .38 and the handcuffs behind a pack of toilet-paper rolls.

The man who answered his ring on the doorbell was one of Milne's hoons, Hempel, wearing a South Yarra disco suit, black silk shirt, tasselled shoes, designer stubble, earring, and his hair drawn back in a ponytail. It all made Wyatt bitter and weary.

'Milne in?' he said.

'Who wants to know?'

Hempel hadn't recognised his new face. Wyatt decided to keep it that way. He said, 'Tell him Mr Ross, just in from Amsterdam.'

Hempel's mouth hung open as he wrestled with this. 'Pardon?'

'Just do it,' Wyatt said.

There was a sulky flicker on the dull face. 'You can fucking well wait out here,' Hempel said. He shut the door behind him.

Wyatt waited. He heard a muttered curse and soon the door opened again and Hempel was pointing a gun at him, an automatic too heavy, too fancy, to be of much use to the little prick. 'Cowboy,' Wyatt said.

'Put your hands against the wall.'

'I'm not carrying.'

'Just do it,' Hempel said.

He patted Wyatt's legs and waist and under his arms inexpertly, then pushed him into the entrance hall. 'First room on your left.'

It was a large, oppressive sitting room. Milne stood before an open fire, a drink in one pudgy hand, the other draped carelessly along the mantelpiece. He was not alone. The man from Amsterdam, his face drawn and tired, sat on a sofa, next to an open briefcase and a stack of blue Rijksmuseum folders.

Milne smiled uncertainly. 'Wyatt? You look different, mate.'

Milne was a glossy, well-tended man at ease in his ugly room. There were three sofas, pink leather, arranged in a U-shape facing the fire; Ken Done prints hung on the walls; classy muzak played on the stereo; assorted liquor bottles sat on a silver tray on a chunky sideboard. The fittings were clearly expensive but they had the look of cheap vinyl and plastic wood veneer.

'Thought you must of missed your plane,' Milne said, keeping it light and cheerful.

'Didn't want to get here too early,' Wyatt said. 'Get you out of bed or something.'

Wyatt stayed near the door, staring at Milne. He saw the smile fade and turned his bleak face to the other man. He said nothing. Hempel hovered behind him with the gun.

'Come in,' Milne said. 'Have a drink. Hempel, put that bloody thing away. Wyatt, this is Walter Paulsen.'

Wyatt nodded briefly.

Milne moved to the drinks tray. 'How was the flight?'

Wyatt gestured suddenly in embarrassment. 'Actually,' he said, 'I ate something that didn't agree with me. Could I use your bathroom?'

Faint distaste showed on Milne's face. He looked past Wyatt to Hempel and said, 'Show the man where it is.'

Hempel grinned at Wyatt. 'Bit urgent, is it?'

They left the room and walked down to the bathroom. Hempel waited while Wyatt went inside. After several minutes, Wyatt flushed the toilet and stuck the .38 and the handcuffs into his waistband at the small of his back, under his jacket.

He came out, ignoring Hempel's mindless grin. Wyatt was not interested in Hempel, only in Hempel's gun. But not now, not here.

They returned to Milne and Paulsen, who were standing by the fire. The two men had been talking; Wyatt could sense their muttered recriminations and speculations.

'We have to talk,' he said.

'Of course,' Milne said. 'Walter is just leaving.'

'Walter too,' Wyatt said.

Then he stepped to one side, took out his .38 and waved it at Hempel. 'Drop your cannon on the floor and get over there with Milne and Paulsen.'

Milne's face went ugly. 'You useless prick, I thought you searched him.'

'I did,' Hempel said. His voice rose. 'Honest.'

Wyatt motioned with his gun again. 'Hempel, drop the gun and get over there with the others.'

Hempel hesitated. He took the gun from his pocket.

'Now drop it.'

The big automatic was loose in Hempel's hand. He was watching Wyatt's face.

'Don't even think about it,' Wyatt warned. 'Okay? Just drop it.'

Hempel began to raise the gun. He continued to stare at Wyatt.

'Oh for Christ's sake,' Wyatt said.

There was no point in trying for accuracy. He fired at Hempel's trunk. The bullet struck Hempel at the waistline like a punch, knocking him on to his back. His heels scraped along the carpet.

Milne said, 'Jesus, Wyatt.'

Wyatt stooped down and pocketed Hempel's pistol. 'If they carry a gun,' he said, 'I have to assume they're prepared to use it.'

'But Jesus,' Milne said. He cocked his head to listen. But these were oblivious streets, the houses set far apart from one another. No-one ever heard the miseries they contained.

'Put these on,' Wyatt said, tossing Paulsen the handcuffs. 'Your right wrist and ankle to Milne's.'

Milne and Paulsen, pale and shocked, awkwardly cuffed together, stood side-on as Wyatt began to speak.

'Six months ago, when I was forced to run, you set me up. You were moving out of the insurance racket into something you knew I'd never touch, so you had to get me off the scene.'

'Utter crap,' Milne said. His glossy head moved in irritation. 'Things got stuffed up, that's all.'

Wyatt ignored him. 'You set me up again this morning. You assumed the Feds wouldn't bother looking for a *second* courier'—he gestured at Paulsen—'especially one travelling in first-class and wearing a suit.' He shook his head at Milne. 'Trafficking in smack and LSD, I'd be put away for years.'

'The fuck are you talking about, smack?' Milne said. 'Drawings,' he said. 'Fucking *art*.'

'My guess is they're reproductions,' Wyatt said. 'What

matters is the paper itself.' He put on his gloves, crossed to the sofa and picked up a Rijksmuseum folder. He took out one of the drawings. It felt stiff, starchy. 'Soaked in heroin or LSD solution and allowed to dry, is that it? I heard all about the chemistry set in your garage today. Heard all kinds of things, Milne.'

'Look,' Milne said. 'We're talking goldmine here. We'll cut you in.' He craned his head, looking to Paulsen for confirmation.

But Wyatt said, 'All I want is the ten thousand you owe me.'

Paulsen's fee lay stacked in the briefcase next to the pile of folders. Wyatt counted out ten thousand dollars. There was at least another forty thousand there. He pocketed the money and began to wipe his prints off everything he'd touched.

'Mate,' Milne said, 'help yourself to as much as you like. Take the lot—there's more where that came from.'

He felt relieved. All this drama was just Wyatt's fucking sense of getting fair payment for the work he did. 'Just leave us the keys on your way out,' he called, lifting his cuffed wrist as Wyatt left the room.

Milne and Paulsen heard Wyatt walk along the hall to the bathroom. Soon after that they heard him leave the house. They soaped their wrists then, and fiddled with knife points and paper clips, but the cuffs stayed on, right through Jansen's arrival and the arrival of the reporters and the ride to the lockup in Russell Street.

The Two-Hundred-Dollar Picasso

'I want you to steal a painting,' Boyce said.

Wyatt nodded. This wouldn't be the first time; it wouldn't be the last. Stealing paintings was something he did when the big jobs fell through or got screwed up or failed to materialise in the first place. Like now.

'Insurance?'

That was the way it generally worked. Either he'd initiate the job himself and negotiate a reward from the insurance company or the owner would set it up and pay him a cut of the claim money. That was the way it worked, and that was why he assumed Boyce had something like that in mind.

'Not exactly,' Boyce said.

They were in Boyce Fine Art, the man's gallery on Greville Street in Prahran. The building had been a glove factory, a classically plain red-brick structure from the 1920s on the outside, all glass, marble and blackwood on the inside. There were vivid oils hanging on the walls, the work of a local artist who portrayed the streets and pubs and parks of Prahran as scenes from someone's headache.

Wyatt waited for Boyce to explain. The man was edgy and angular, clean-looking with fine hair cropped short, wire-rimmed glasses and ironed designer jeans and shirt. He plucked at his watchstrap. 'Boyce,' Wyatt said, 'I'm not getting any younger.'

Boyce stopped worrying his watchstrap and began to talk. 'I'd better start with the background,' he said, 'so you can put the whole thing into perspective—and believe me, you're going to have to put it into perspective. It might help if I tell you your cut is thirty-five thousand bucks.'

That made Wyatt sit up. He was broke. Also, when circumstances had forced him into this kind of work in the past, he'd never earned more than five or ten thousand dollars—five or ten thousand for Streetons and Dobells worth a quarter of a million. If Boyce was offering thirty-five, this painting had to be one hell of a valuable one.

But Wyatt didn't say any of that, preferring to hear it from Boyce. He waited, half-tuning the other man out. Boyce had a messy mind. He'd never say in one sentence what he could say in fifteen, hanging a load of conditions and asides on the central point. Wyatt let him ramble on, saying 'Sure' and 'Fine' and 'I see' from time to time. There was no point in hurrying Boyce: he'd only get hurt or flustered and more time would get wasted.

It took ten minutes, but at the end of it Wyatt knew all he needed to know. He condensed each layer as

Boyce ladled it on, and learned that there was a wealthy collector. Boyce was not prepared to give the man's name but did say that he was an Australian, a high-flier now living in hiding somewhere in Europe. The collector was living in hiding because he'd salted away twenty million dollars in various tax havens over the years, money that the Tax Office, Westpac and a host of friends and colleagues wanted back again. They also wanted the collector back again to stand trial.

The collector was a vulgarian, everyone knew it, but he'd tried to buy some respectability as an art lover over the years. Before fleeing overseas he'd built up a big private collection, set up a scholarship, and donated money to regional and state galleries.

He'd also loaned paintings to the National Gallery of Victoria in St Kilda Road. Now he'd never get those paintings back again and his name had been removed as a trustee and patron of the Gallery. He wanted revenge, according to Boyce. But stealing his own paintings back again wasn't going to do it: he wanted the Gallery's 1.6-million-dollar Picasso, *Weeping Woman*.

'You must be joking,' Wyatt said.

Boyce shrugged. 'That's what the man wants. Willing to pay top dollar to get it.'

'I don't mean what he wants and what he doesn't want,' Wyatt said. 'I mean you must be joking if you think I could walk out of the National Gallery of Victoria with a painting under my coat, let alone take it off the wall in the first place.'

There was an unnerving directness in Wyatt's voice and Boyce wilted in the face of it. He looked away, plucked at his watchstrap, his tidy lips now screwed into a pout. Then Wyatt heard a massive sigh and the words, 'I know. I told him the same thing.'

Wyatt waited. For the moment, he'd said all he needed to say. He knew Boyce hadn't. Finally Boyce looked directly at him and Wyatt saw desperation on the man's face.

'Mate, I'm in a bind. I won't bullshit you. The total fee is seventy-five grand, thirty-five to you, forty to me for finding the right man, getting the picture safely out of the country, etcetera, etcetera.' He paused. 'I need that money, Wyatt.' He waved a slender hand around at the walls, the fittings, the paintings. 'There's some people I owe money to, I can't move my stock, that little prick at the *Age* has ignored every exhibition I've held here. I've got some real talent on my books, but no-one's interested . . . .'

Wyatt let him talk. People were always trying to explain things to him, justify themselves. What did he care? Other peoples' problems were nothing to do with him.

'So I really need this one,' Boyce concluded, 'and you're the only bloke I can think of who's capable of pulling it off.'

'Boyce,' Wyatt said, looking around at the ceiling, the windows, 'you've got cameras here, alarms, security doors, and you're just a suburban gallery. Think what the security is like at St Kilda Road. I'd be jumped on before I even peered at the signature.'

'I wouldn't be too sure about that.'

Boyce grinned then and it transformed his face, taking away the tension. Wyatt stared at him. Evidently Boyce had a card up his sleeve, but it was more than that. Clearly Boyce was feeling encouraged—if Wyatt was still here and, more to the point, talking over the job, even if negatively, then he must be halfway interested in doing it.

Well, Wyatt was interested. He was interested in the thirty-five thousand dollars and he was interested in the challenge. There were times, like now, when he could admit to himself that he was addicted to risk and to the jobs that posed interesting problems.

But the cheesy grin on Boyce's face irritated him. He was about to wipe it off when the man tipped back his smooth throat and called, 'Janet, come here a minute.'

A door marked 'office' opened behind the sofa Boyce was sitting on and the woman who emerged was young, about twenty, wearing lycra tights under a tent-like T-shirt. Her hair was tousled, her face drowsy, heavy-lidded, as if she'd been sleeping. Wyatt watched as she walked around the end of the couch, climbed onto it next to Boyce, and curled her legs under her rump; then, apparently dissatisfied with that, she stretched out, putting her bare feet in Boyce's lap. She was like a cat. Boyce stroked her feet, reinforcing the notion.

'Wyatt, meet Janet.'

Wyatt didn't want to meet her. If she was involved in this she was a weak link. He had to force the words out: 'Hello, Janet.'

The woman said nothing, just nodded lazily at Wyatt, but underneath it all—the hair over her face, the slow warm bare limbs buried in the soft leather—she was watching him sharply, assessingly. There was paint on her fingers; paint flecked her thin forearms. He held her gaze for a time, revising his opinion a little. Something communicated itself between them, a recognition of ability and lawlessness in one another's natures.

Boyce reached along her leg, buried his hand between her knees. 'Janet helps out around the place,' he said. He patted her. 'She's also a painter, a good one, very good. Up and coming. I've got some of her stuff out the back.'

There was a point to this and Wyatt waited for it. The world was full of people who never did anything but talk, and for Wyatt that meant playing a waiting game. He inclined his head at the woman politely, as if to say he was prepared to accept Boyce's judgment.

'She's already been in four group shows,' Boyce said. 'Tasmania's got one of her canvases, a couple of oil companies, there's a buyer in Japan interested in her stuff.'

'You're waffling, Toby,' the woman said. She said it quietly, not bothering to look at him.

Boyce flushed. 'You're right. Sorry. The thing is, Wyatt, Janet knows the Gallery inside and out. She thinks it can be done.'

She was waiting for him in front of the water wall, wearing jeans this time, her hair pulled back from her face with a couple of plastic clips. She looked alert and young. Wyatt didn't know what she saw in Boyce, but he didn't think about it more than that. He was working and he was thinking about the work still to be done.

He stopped in front of her and nodded. A smile split her face. 'Some art student,' she said, looking him up and down.

Wyatt had done his best. He wore faded Levis, a

white T-shirt, a Levi jacket, the latter bought from the thousand dollars Boyce had given him for expenses. But Wyatt was forty years old, a long, narrow, hard man who pulled bank and payroll heists, an occupation that gave his hooked features a dark and wary cast. He didn't know what art students were supposed to look like. 'Dress casually, a bit scruffy,' she'd told him at Boyce's yesterday, and he'd done his best.

It was 8.30 in the morning and the peak-hour traffic on St Kilda Road was sluggish, fuming, inching uselessly toward the city's parking stations. There had been a gritty wind the night before. Leaves dotted the ponds; styrofoam containers and greasy paper had blown into the sheltered main entrance of the Gallery. Janet touched Wyatt's arm briefly and led him to a side door at the northern end of the water wall.

The attendant on duty looked inquiringly at them. 'Janet Vines and Robert Lake,' Janet said.

The man checked his book, ticked the names, gave them each a clip-on visitor's pass. 'Through here,' Janet said, and Wyatt felt her hand on his arm again.

She took him to the second floor, past costume, glassware and pottery displays, to the European Gallery. There were leather-topped benches at various parts of the vast room. She stopped at one of them, sat down, and he sat next to her. 'Give me your case,' she said.

It was a flat vinyl artist's folio case, zippered along three sides, the size of an open newspaper, and it belonged to Boyce. Janet carried one like it. She had loaded both with artist's paraphernalia the night before, and now she was taking out a charcoal stick and a sheet of cartridge paper. Apart from one other student and a cleaner, they were the only people in the European Gallery. That would all change at 10 o'clock, when tourists and busloads of school children would begin to pour through the place.

Wyatt asked quietly, 'Who else can get in before opening time?'

'Teachers, researchers, that's about it.'

She sketched as she answered him, bold, rapid strokes at first, then shading strokes with the flat of the charcoal stick. She smoothed an area with her thumb. 'Okay,' she said, handing him the sketch and the charcoal stick, 'this will cover you if anyone asks questions. As for the rest, that's your department.'

Meaning he was there to look and listen until he could see a way to walk out of a major gallery with a 1.6-million-dollar Picasso under his arm. She moved away to another part of the room, taking her folio with her. Wyatt looked at the sketch then and realised two things: that it captured the nervous intensity of a small, bright green oil painting on the opposite wall and that the painting itself was the Picasso, *Weeping Woman*.

Wyatt sat there until opening time. Now and then he added minute scratches to the sketch if someone drifted near, but otherwise he made mental notes about the room, the position and dimensions of the painting, the timing, manner and appearance of the cleaners, attendants and curators. Only twice did he get up: once to prowl the perimeter of the room, looking for cameras, sensors and alarms, the second time to note the location of the toilets, storerooms and exits. He also made a note for his shopping list, a special security screwdriver.

Janet collected him at 10.15, just as the first teacher

appeared with a crowd of surly fourteen-year-olds. 'Get what you wanted?'

Wyatt looked up at her. She was half-amused, as if they were involved in a harmless stunt or as if she couldn't take him seriously, this Wyatt that Boyce had been talking about. The other half of her expression he couldn't read.

'Yes,' he said.

It was time to establish a few things. Wyatt walked with her across Princes Bridge into the city centre. At Collins Street he stopped her from getting onto a Fitzroy tram and said, 'In here,' taking her into an arcade.

'I'm going to my studio,' she protested. 'I've got work to do.'

'Later,' he said, guiding her through the doorway of a coffee shop. It was a place made for talking, privacy guaranteed by the crockery din and a radio tuned to a talkback show.

Wyatt ordered black coffee, Janet mineral water. On the radio they were talking about capital punishment. After the waitress had placed their drinks on the table, Wyatt said, his voice remote and factual, 'What's your role in this? Besides whatever Boyce has offered you.'

Janet shrugged, put down her glass. She was young. Like every young person Wyatt had ever met she expressed herself as much with body gestures as with speech, especially when pushed, like now. 'To show you the Gallery.'

'I'm not talking about that. I'm also not talking about how you just thought you'd do your boyfriend a favour.'

'He's not my boyfriend. We just, you know.' She

paused, wriggling her shoulders. 'I feel I owe him something. He's a patron, kind of thing.'

Wyatt said, cold and hard now, 'I'm not interested in that. I'm only interested in the real reason you're involved.'

His words had the effect of shutting her down, clearing away the fog she'd created about herself. After a while she answered him, speaking clearly, firmly: 'The Gallery's supposed to support local painters, right? My father was a painter, in the fifties. He died when I was twelve. Sure, they bought some of his stuff, but did they ever show it? Then when I was at college I did a project on him. I asked to see the paintings.' She leaned across the table, putting her face close to his. '*They'd lost them.*' She leaned back again, looked down, played with the spoon from his saucer. 'Temporarily misplaced, they said. Permanently lost or sold, more like it.' She looked at him carefully. 'On top of that, I've been in three group shows where they've bought works by the other people involved. Didn't buy anything by me though, did they.'

The look she threw him challenged him not to see this as some kind of conspiracy. Wyatt gathered sympathy onto his face but underneath it he was wondering if Janet's wanting revenge would make her a liability on this job.

If he did it.

If what he had in mind would work.

Still, revenge was a good, clean, useful emotion, about the only one he would ever allow himself, so he put some warmth into his voice:

'Did you learn a range of techniques at college?'

Her face grew wary and suspicious. 'Like what?'

'Like doing copies of originals?'

Wyatt reasoned that if discovery of the theft could be delayed, he'd stand a better chance of getting the Picasso out of the Gallery in the first place and later of slipping away from the city with his fee intact. That's why there had to be a fake Picasso, a good one, to leave in its place. Working from sketches, memory and two further visits to the European collection, Janet spent the early part of the week painting a substitute *Weeping Woman*. By Thursday night the paint was dry, the canvas tight on its stretcher, ready to hang. Also by then Wyatt had acquired the security screwdriver and he knew exactly how the switch would go.

He played art student again the next morning. He had the fake in his folio case, together with a pine board of the same dimensions, and when the cleaners were finished for the day he slipped into a storeroom, pushed aside a ceiling batten, stowed the painting and the board, replaced the batten. Then he left the Gallery. His name was ticked off.

He returned, an ordinary tourist in dress and manner this time, an hour before closing time. He did not leave the Gallery, however; he stayed on, in hiding, as the building emptied of people and the atmosphere-controlled air grew dark and still.

At 11.00 on the night of Friday, 1 August 1986, Wyatt took *Weeping Woman* from its frame and substituted the fake. No cameras recorded him; there were no pressure alarms under the painting; his movements cut no sensor beams. There was no-one there to see him take the original back to the cleaners' storeroom, parcel it carefully with the pine board in brown paper and string, then again in the logoed paper used to wrap purchases in the Gallery's bookshop on the ground floor. When he was finished there might have been a book inside, a heavy coffee table volume on Rembrandt or the Impressionists. No-one saw him curl up on the floor and sleep through the long night.

In the morning he slipped from gallery to gallery and in and out of corridors and men's rooms, dodging cleaners and attendants until opening time. At 10.15 he met Janet in the Gallery's coffee shop. When she left him fifteen minutes later she was carrying the parcel that appeared to be a bookshop purchase. For verisimilitude's sake, she took the parcel to the cloakroom, showed the attendant a brass token for the shoulder bag she'd deposited there earlier, and asked him to stow the parcel with the bag, saying she still had a couple of exhibits to see. Wyatt himself could have done all this, but Wyatt's was a new face and it didn't quite belong and he didn't want to push his luck.

At 10.50 she collected both items and left the Gallery. Wyatt was where he said he'd be, leaning on a bridge pillar, watching for signs of agitation in her wake.

At the midpoint of the bridge, Flinders Street station ahead of them, Janet said, 'Now what?'

'We need somewhere to wait until this evening. You mentioned that Boyce has never been to your studio?'

'I don't like people to know where I live,' she said, defiant, as though she expected him to laugh or accuse her of creating a mystery identity for herself.

'I don't count as people,' Wyatt said. 'We're going to your studio.'

'Why not your place, wherever it is?'

Wyatt had no permanent base and he hadn't wanted to risk staying in a motel or a hotel for this job. If he'd been robbing a bank or snatching a payroll he would have risked one, for the hit would have been hard and fast and he'd have worn a mask and no-one would have seen his face. But on this job there was a chance his face had been seen, meaning sooner or later there'd be an identikit doing the rounds of registration desks. He was staying in a flat Boyce knew about. The owner was in Japan for the next month. Wyatt felt safe in the flat, but it was an expensive place, the kind that attracted burglars. Besides, it meant that Boyce knew where to find him. 'Your studio,' he repeated.

'Why don't we just take the picture to Boyce?'

'No.'

'Why not?'

'I want him to come to us.'

'Why?'

'Think about it. Maybe he can't pay for it. Maybe we've been set up. I don't know the people he's working for, do you? And what if he's being watched by the cops?'

'But no-one even knows the painting's been taken yet.'

'Your friend's not squeaky clean.'

'I feel like I'm being disloyal to him,' Janet said.

Wyatt stopped her, turned her around to face him. 'You've done your part in this. Now let me keep doing my part. It's what I do, it's what I'm good at.'

She flushed, looked out across the river to a stained, chunky dredger in midstream. 'I'm still involved, though. Keeping the painting at my place means I'm still involved.'

Wyatt nodded, a way of saying that he took her point. It was important that he keep her on-side in this. 'True. Just till this evening, when we'll meet him somewhere neutral.'

They continued across the river. On Collins Street they caught a tram to Fitzroy, alighting at the Brunswick Street, Johnston Street intersection. The Picasso was under Wyatt's arm and he held on firmly as Janet led him across the street and through a chipped, sun-faded wooden door next to a window display of moccasins and cobwebs. They climbed three flights of broad wooden stairs to the top level. Wyatt hadn't seen Janet's name on the door or letterboxes downstairs; nor was it on the door she now opened. He followed her inside.

It was a studio flat the width of the building, light pouring in from three massive windows that faced the street. Wyatt could smell oil paint, turpentine, linseed oil. There were spots and streaks of paint on the floor; canvases were stacked against the walls on all sides. The sparse furniture had been pushed into the corners: a sink, two divan beds, a bookcase, an electric cooking ring. The wardrobe was a chrome rail hung from the ceiling by chains. Wyatt couldn't tell anything from the jeans, shirts, coats and indefinable articles of clothing hanging from it. There seemed to be too much of it for one person, yet the room also didn't seem to be anyone's habitat.

Janet caught him looking. 'All I need is somewhere to work and somewhere to crash at night,' she said.

Wyatt continued his assessment of the room. There was nothing worth stealing here. No-one would even bother looking. If they had to spend time here, the Picasso would be safe. 'Where's your phone?'

She twisted the corner of her mouth at him. 'Take a wild guess.'

He was irritated. 'I'll be right back.'

He went down the stairs again, out onto Brunswick Street. He remembered seeing a post office and public telephones opposite the tram stop. Two of the cubicles were occupied; the other two were streaked with faeces, puddled with urine. He waited, and something about him, an air of coldness and judgment, reached the punk-styled teenager in the first cubicle, for he looked around at Wyatt, muttered into the mouthpiece, hung up.

Wyatt fed coins into the box. 'It's done.'

Relief seemed to bubble up in Boyce's voice. 'Fantastic. Bring it over.'

'I can't do that.'

'What do you mean? You haven't lost it?'

'It's fine, in a safe place.'

'Well, when can I have it?'

'We'll meet you in the Pride of Erin on Brunswick Street at six. Lounge bar. You'll come in, sit down, show us the colour of your money, and one of us will go and fetch the painting for you.'

Boyce had nothing to say to that. Wyatt, always at ease with silences, let this one lengthen. When the moment was right he said, 'Goodbye, Boyce,' and waited. Boyce spluttered, so Wyatt listened again.

'Don't hang up!'

'I'm listening.'

'I'll be there, six o'clock.'

Wyatt and Janet were there at 5.30. Janet complained of hunger, and while she ordered wine and steak for them, Wyatt checked the bar, lounge and corridors, noting exits and potential traps, then claimed a table in the back corner of the lounge bar. He could see the room and doorways from there. He wasn't worried about curious ears: a TV set was blaring above the bar and someone was playing Roy Orbison on the jukebox. When their meals arrived he ate slowly, fascinated by the girl with him. Janet seemed to shovel the food in, her head bent low over her plate. Colour seemed to come back into her pinched face. She had thin, angular arms, and Wyatt saw her jutting elbows, her sawing forearms. He wondered if a few meals like this one would put flesh on her bones. She finished, pushed her plate away. 'They've got apple pie,' Wyatt said.

She grinned. 'I know.'

Boyce when he came in looked hunted and afraid. He passed among the tables as if they housed predators, sat hunched over in the third chair, and seemed to say from the corner of his mouth, 'I'm here.'

'We can see that,' Janet said.

'You brought it?'

Wyatt said, 'You know the drill.'

Boyce looked at his hands, snapped his watchband, and at first Wyatt thought the man was going to dig in his heels, insist on seeing the painting first. He changed his mind when Boyce muttered, 'Haven't got it.'

Wyatt said nothing. Janet opened her mouth but he

stopped her with a look. Finally, Boyce pulled his shirt free of his belt and said, 'See this?'

They saw bruises and a raw welt on his stomach and rib cage, as if whoever had beaten him had switched from using fists to using a tyre iron. 'I had to pay up or he would've killed me,' Boyce said.

'Who?'

Everything about Boyce's manner said this was one of those things that happened every day, to everyone. 'I owe money to this SP bookmaker. He came around during the week and I had to pay up or he would've killed me. I still owe him.'

Janet leaned forward. 'You used *our* fee to pay off *your* debts?'

'Listen, this bloke is bad news.'

Wyatt stood up. 'So are we. Goodbye, Boyce.'

Janet joined him. Boyce said, expressing helplessness, 'What could I do? I can pay you when I get the other half.'

'When's that?'

'It gets paid into my account a few days after I deliver the painting.'

'I don't work that way,' Wyatt said. 'Look, beg, borrow or steal it, sell some of that crap on your walls, I don't care how you do it. If you can't pay me by lunchtime tomorrow, I'm gone.'

'But I sent a fax to Barcelona saying we had it. His contacts here are coming by tonight to collect it so it can be airfreighted out in the morning.'

'Explain the situation, see if they'll advance you the balance.'

All the bluster had gone out of Boyce. 'I'll see what I can do. Meet you here at midday?'

Wyatt shook his head. Now that others were involved he wasn't about to operate in a contained space where he might find all his exits blocked and something final slicing between his ribs. 'Whitlam Place. It's a little park next to the Fitzroy Town Hall.'

Whitlam Place was a sorry patch of lawn, trees and benches bisected by a path. Open on two sides, it offered all the exits Wyatt needed. 'Eleven in the morning,' he said. Eleven, an early hour in Fitzroy, too early for winos, kids or anyone else wanting a bit of wintry sun.

'I'll be there,' Boyce muttered, but Wyatt and Janet were already weaving their way between the tables and out the side door. On the footpath Janet stopped and folded her arms. 'I'm not liking this.'

'There's no other way.'

She ignored him. 'It's as if the picture itself doesn't matter to you people. All you care about is money and headthumping.'

'You knew the score,' Wyatt said. 'You were keen enough at the start.'

He was moving along the street as he said it and she hurried to keep up with him. In silence they passed the Black Cat cafe, an Indian restaurant, anonymous doorways. Once or twice Wyatt stopped abruptly and turned, but they were not being followed. At Janet's building he ducked in and began to climb the creaking wooden stairs.

'Where do you think you're going?'

'I'm staying here tonight.'

'You don't trust me, I suppose. You think I'm going to steal the painting.'

Wyatt stopped. Anger built in him, a cold slow rage. 'Janet, it's Boyce I don't trust.'

They were at her door. He waited for her to unlock it, then he pushed the door open and listened. The studio was dim and sleepy and undisturbed. They went in. Wyatt checked that the painting was still behind Janet's canvases, then stretched out on the spare divan bed, lacing his hands behind his head. He looked beyond the pattern on the pressed-tin ceiling to the complications the job now offered him. After a while he became aware that Janet was standing nearby, staring at him. He stared back at her and it was a while before either of them moved.

Wyatt slipped away before daybreak. He went to a house in Coburg and when he came back he had a Smith & Wesson .38 revolver in his pocket and was carrying a boxed pair of Motorola hand-held radios. He told Janet:

'I don't want you to show your face until I give the okay. When I see the money, I'll call you by radio, and you bring the painting.'

'Boys with their toys,' she said. 'Apart from last night, you and I might as well be living on different planets.'

That was true enough, but Wyatt was working and not interested in analysing anything. At 10 o'clock he left again and made his way to the park. He was early by one hour, thinking that if Boyce had a cross in mind, he might be early too.

The park was cheerless and deserted under a low, muttering sky. There had been a chemical fire in Yarraville the night before and the atmosphere over the city was still poisonous. Wyatt walked the perimeter a couple of times, looking into the rear seats of vehicles parked along the street. They were empty and there was no-one about who shouldn't have been there, so he sat on a bench to wait.

The car that cruised around the park at four minutes after eleven o'clock was a black Mercedes, waxy and long. Wyatt could see four men: the driver in front, three others in the rear compartment on facing seats.

Boyce wasn't among them but Wyatt wasn't interested in Boyce. He was more interested in the three passengers, now getting out of the car and crossing the park toward him, widely spaced, moving quickly, swaggering a little. One man, dressed in a costly double-breasted suit, had the solid, thrusting air of a private-school bully who has inherited the family business. The other men wore jeans and nylon sports jackets and were built like hired muscle. They moved in on Wyatt as though they intended to snap him in two. If this was the work of Boyce's collector in Spain, he had a long reach and plenty of clout.

The suit said, 'Boyce's description of you was spot-on.'

'Where is he?'

'Let's just say he won't be playing squash for a while. Where's the painting?'

'Where's the money?' Wyatt said.

'We've paid all we're going to pay at this stage. Your argument is with Boyce, not us. I'll say it again, where's the painting?'

The suit didn't wait for a response but nodded to the muscle, who moved in on either side of Wyatt. What

Wyatt did then was open and shocking and it knocked the fight out of them. He shot the man in the suit, a quick, careful shot to the fleshy part of the upper leg, then backed away, turned, and quickly left the park. Behind him he heard pain and confusion. Suit said, 'Help me!' and the hired muscle said, 'You never said nothing about no gun.' After that Wyatt heard car doors slam and the big car pulled away from the kerb. Later there would be sirens, but as Wyatt made his way through the back streets all he could hear was a tram rattling along Brunswick Street and the cries of children in a schoolyard. He checked the time: the confrontation and the shooting had taken less than a minute.

He put the radio to his mouth. 'Janet?'

'I'm here.'

'It's turned bad. I want you to stay where you are. I'll be there shortly. Don't answer the door to anyone but me.'

It took him ten minutes. He made a wide loop to put distance between himself and the park, and he took time out to watch outside Janet's building for anything that smelt wrong. When he was satisfied, he climbed the stairs. He went carefully. He believed, and he'd been taught, that stairs are risky places, hemming a man in by wall and banister, making him an easy target from above and below.

He saw no-one, heard nothing, but when he got to the top, and opened Janet's door, he saw that she was gone and the painting with her.

Wyatt didn't see her again. He supposed that they'd nabbed her, and the painting. He supposed it until the next day, Tuesday, 5 August 1986, when, at Sydney airport on his way to somewhere safer, he bought a copy of the *Age* and saw that he'd supposed wrong. There was a story splashed over the front page and it told him that she was alive and that she'd done something that would remove the threat to both their lives.

He worked it out. His warning on the radio must have spooked her into disappearing into the warren of converted stables and lofts and rented rooms of Fitzroy, where there were people like her to protect and shelter her. Then she'd gone into action.

First, she must have gone back to the Gallery, removed the fake, and left in its place a card bearing the words 'removed for cleaning'. Then, calling herself the Australian Cultural Terrorists, she sent a letter to the Minister for the Arts, Race Mathews, saying that the Picasso had been stolen 'as a protest against the niggardly funding of fine arts in this hick state and against the clumsy, unimaginative stupidity of the administration and distribution of that funding', and demanding a 10 per cent increase in arts funding and the establishment of an annual art prize to be called The Picasso Ransom. She called Mathews, also Police Minister, 'the Minister for Plod'.

It was a huge story. Wyatt felt that he understood her. She loved the painting for its own sake; she could not accept that its value could be measured in money or blood or the good names of governments or public figures. In one single, inspired gesture she had warned off the gunmen and saved the painting from men of greed.

Meanwhile, Wyatt went to work again (there was a

Labor minister rumoured to keep $100,000 in a satchel under his office desk) but he continued to follow the story in the national press. There were letters and demands. It all ended two weeks later, when Janet contacted the *Age* and directed them to locker 227 at Spencer Street station. *Weeping Woman* was there, undamaged, expertly wrapped in brown paper tied neatly with string. Later the Gallery's director was photographed next to the weeping woman: a cheesy grin on his face, calculated formal disquiet on hers.

Some papers valued the painting at 1.6 million dollars, others two million, maybe six million at auction in New York. The director said they would never have been able to afford another like it. Wyatt valued the painting at two hundred dollars. After expenses—the screwdriver, the radios, the gun, a plane ticket out of there—that's all he had left.

Enough for a set of lockpicks, though.

Threshold

'It's not that we're smart, Sunshine, the bad guys are dumb. Detective work, investigative procedures, it's all garbage. The reality is wrong addresses, phone numbers with the digits transposed, drinking shithouse tea in ugly sitting rooms so you don't offend potential witnesses—who invent things anyway, tell you what they think you want to hear.'

'Yes, sir,' I said.

'Yes sir. No sir. Turn right at the next set of lights.'

'Yes, sir.'

It was seven o'clock in the morning and we had a double homicide in Sandy Bay. It was my first homicide on Vestey's crew. Everything I'd been told about him was true. I sat tense and buttoned-up and didn't trust myself to speak.

'No, boyo,' he said, 'most cases are broken in the first twenty-four hours. More often than not your crim is caught in the act, or his wife dobs him in, or he forgets to clean the blood off his shoes, or he gives himself up. Feeling lucky?'

'Don't know, sir.'

'Don't know, sir,' Vestey muttered, and he settled into

the icy solitude that unnerved me more than anything else about him. He was burdened with perpetual anger and a hard searching mind, and for a week now I'd been feeling the force of it.

'Next left,' he said, closing the street directory, 'then two streets down.'

'Sir.'

He was respected at police headquarters but not liked at all. He was too secretive and private for that, and too straight, somehow. He viewed everything and everyone with frank disbelief. He loathed judges, magistrates, lawyers, criminals and time-serving cops. The day I joined his team he'd been on the front page, pictured in front of the latest gun-amnesty haul, throwing a challenge at the world.

'Rigby Street,' he said.

It was one of those broad leafy streets where the house prices reach half-a-million dollars. Vestey didn't have to tell me the number. An ambulance, divisional vans, and a huddle of neighbours were blocking the street a hundred metres down. I parked the Commodore and we got out.

Vestey seemed to know all about it. He led me along the side of the house to a vast garden at the rear. 'Numero uno,' he said.

The first body was lying half a metre inside the back door. The head rested on the outstretched left arm; a narrow watchband was visible below the cuff of a light-coloured coat. The right arm hugged the stomach. Dark hair curled to the nape of the neck. The legs were bent a little, the toe of one woven brown leather shoe appearing to chase the heel of the other.

In other words a configuration of sleep—except no-one would choose to sleep on a cold porch floor. The hand clasping the stomach had done a poor job of holding the blood in, and there was a small entry wound in the temple. A case of wrong time, wrong place, I thought, taking note of two items lying near the body: a small shoulder bag with an Ansett tag on it and a tiny rose cast in silver. The spiky metal had torn through classy black wrapping paper, probably when the woman fell.

Vestey made no move to go in so I stood there with him, looking at the body. After a while he grinned at me. On that face it was a brief, bleak spasm. 'Okay, Sunshine, first impressions.'

'Sir.'

I knelt next to the body. The entry wound displayed the classic stippling effect, pinpoint haemorrhaging caused when unburnt powder and tiny metal shavings are driven into the flesh. 'Shot at point-blank range, sir.'

'An effect of which,' Vestey said, 'is sound suppression. Let's see who she is.'

He crouched next to me, wrapped a handkerchief around his hand and removed a wallet from the woman's coat pocket. It was crammed with cards. 'Nina Galt, of this address.' He looked at me. 'Ansett ID. Check the case.'

I did what Vestey had done, wrapped my hand in a handkerchief, but he curled his lip as if I was overdoing it. I found a uniform in the suitcase. 'Some kind of flight attendant,' I said.

Vestey returned the wallet to the coat pocket. 'Not that it matters, poor bloody bitch.' Then I saw him reach out, clasp the dead woman's slender hand above the watchstrap as if to comfort her, and rotate her wrist. The watchface was cracked, the hands stuck at 7.03. 'Time of death. Just like in the movies, eh, Sunshine?' He stood, brushed at his knees. 'She's been here twelve hours, long enough for rigor mortis to come and go. Okay, give it your best shot.'

'Sir.' I pointed at the suitcase near the base of the steps. 'She arrives home from the airport yesterday evening, opens the back door, goes in, and he's waiting for her. Pops her one in the stomach, she falls, he pops her again in the head.'

'Don't give me *pops*, Mister. Why the back door?'

He was right. People generally let themselves in by the front door. I looked away, hunting for an explanation. A light had been left on above the back door. There was a small bluestone building in the garden behind us. One of the uniform boys was standing watch over it. A hundred years ago it had been a stable but now there were curtains in the windows, creepers on the walls and brass fittings on a Brunswick green door. 'Maybe she rents the stable. She's friends with the owner and was calling in to say hello.'

Vestey likes to drape his long frame in dark, expensive double-breasted suits. He brushed at invisible lint. He was elegant and dangerous-looking, as if he'd just stepped out of a cognac ad. 'The rose, Sunshine. The sexy black paper. Rushing in to say hello before she even unpacks her bags. That tell you anything?'

He didn't wait for an answer but stepped past the body and disappeared inside the house. I turned around in time to catch the uniformed constable disguising a grin. I ignored him and examined the garden, a sizeable area of fruit trees, wattles, wrought-iron chairs and a lawn that needed cutting. Instead of a fence there was a bluestone wall on three sides. A block of flats showed above the wall at the back. Apparently a woman who lived there had noticed the suitcase the previous evening, noticed it was still there this morning, and made a 'you'll-think-I'm-being-silly-but' call to the local station.

Vestey was back in the doorway. 'Communing, Sonny Jim? Think the answer's floating in the ether? Come and apply some lateral thinking in here.'

'Yes, sir.'

I followed the powerful, fluid shape into the kitchen. Now there were five of us there, counting an ambulance officer, Sally waiting with her fingerprint kit, Mack snapping pictures.

Six, counting the second victim.

She was dressed for a Sunday afternoon in Salamanca Place, designer tracksuit and Reeboks. She'd fallen onto her side in a foetal position. Masking tape bound her wrists and ankles and two strips of it had been pasted over her mouth. Her eyes were wide and alarmed, as if she'd seen what was coming. There were no marks on the body. There was no blood.

Without looking at anyone Vestey said, 'The coroner? Crime-scene unit?'

I happened to be looking at Sally when he said it. She was watching him covertly. I'd seen women do that, grow distracted and covetous around him, even if they wouldn't admit it. 'On their way, sir,' she said.

'Fine. So instead of contaminating the crime scene why don't you all bugger off outside until they arrive?'

He didn't mean me. The others began to troop out,

trying to look bored. 'Mack,' Vestey said, 'there's a crowd gathering in the street. I want you to take a few candids. Maybe our boy's hanging around, catching the action.'

'Sir,' Mack said, going out.

Vestey turned to me. 'Feel along the hairline.'

'Sir?'

'On the job training, Sunshine. Don't worry, you won't disturb anything.'

I knelt on the slate floor, steadying myself for a moment by holding the dead woman's shoulder, then edged my fingertips from her temple to the back of her head—almost as if I were working shampoo into a lather. The hair was fine and clean; I could hear the soft scratching of my fingers at the roots.

I found it where the skull meets the spine—a small patch of sticky dampness. I jerked my hand away, stood up and stared at my fingers.

Vestey may have thawed a few degrees, for he called me by my name. 'Well, Mr Niall?'

'He made her kneel on the floor, sir, then shot her in the back of the head.'

I stared at my fingers as I said it.

'Wipe them, for Christ's sake. What else can you tell me?'

I took out my handkerchief and rubbed hard at the blood. I had it on the tip of each finger. 'It's a pro hit, sir.'

'I know it's a pro hit. I expect our esteemed Commissioner could tell me it's a pro hit. I want to know what sort of forensic joy we can expect out of this, if you catch my drift.'

I felt my face grow hot—it was the lingering sensation of the sticky blood and Vestey bearing down on me regardless. I thought of other head shots I'd seen, the classic splash pattern of bone fragments and brain tissue. 'As with the first body,' I said, 'there's no exit wound, meaning a small-calibre weapon, probably a .22. If he used hollow-points—'

'All we'll get are fragments, meaning we can't match them to any gun, meaning the brain will be porridge. Well done.'

I peered around at the slate floor. 'Maybe he left a shell-casing behind.'

Vestey looked at me pityingly. 'Explain the tape.'

'To stop her from struggling?'

Vestey's handsome lean head swung down close to my face. His white shirt looked very white inside his dark suit coat. He smelt faintly of soap. He smelt clinically clean, like a surgeon, only no surgeon was ever this sharp and glittering. 'So why didn't he tie the Galt woman?'

'He wasn't expecting her, sir.'

Vestey nudged the taped ankles with his black shoe tip. 'Meaning this one's the intended victim, yes, yes, but *think*: why the tape, why the kneeling down, *why the formality?*'

I snapped the word, I couldn't help it: 'Execution.'

Vestey relaxed. He almost smiled. 'Give the lad a great big hand.' He looked bitterly at the dead woman. 'Execution. Know the rationale behind execution, Sonny Jim? You're a university boy, you've got letters after your name, enlighten me.'

'Punishment.' I was still bristling.

'Punishment. To teach a lesson. To restore honour. This isn't just a shooting, it has a signature on it, it's symbolically meaningful. It says this is what happens if you transgress the unwritten law.'

I thought I understood him. He hated criminal posturing. He hated the banality of the code behind this execution. I nodded. 'I see.'

'You still here, sport? We've got a dead dyke with connections—how else do you explain the execution—the little friend who walked in when she shouldn't have, and you're standing there with your mouth open?'

He said all this for the entertainment of the pathologist, who had just come into the room. Professor Quennell glanced at me sympathetically, nodded at Vestey, and opened his black bag. We watched him draw on latex gloves, hook a stethoscope to his ears and crouch next to the body.

'She's dead, Prof.'

Quennell ignored Vestey. He listened for a heartbeat then switched on a micro-cassette recorder and started talking: 'Preliminary indications. The deceased is a white female, aged approximately thirty years, bearing no visible wounds, but—' he bent over and sniffed at the woman's head—'the hair reveals traces of cordite, and'—he touched the back of her head without hesitation—'there is a possible entry wound concealed under the hair at the base of the skull . . . '

To look useful I got out my notebook and drew separate floor plans of the kitchen and the adjoining porch, showing each body in relation to furniture, doors and walls, and marking distances and angles. Then I looked around the kitchen. It was a copper, pine and skylight kind of place, with a vast refrigerator and farm-house-style stove. Potted ferns leaked over the edges of the pine benches.

At one end of a shelf of tattered cookbooks above the refrigerator was a shallow cane basket heaped with bills, receipts, postcards and letters. I lifted it down and began to sift through it using the tip of my pen, pausing at a postcard of a Gold Coast beach. It was a long-distance shot, the sand crowded with sunbathers. The word '*ME*' had been scrawled breezily in red ink in the top right corner above a red arrow angling into the anonymous mass of sunbathers. I flipped the card over. It was postmarked a week earlier and said simply, 'See you Monday.' Yesterday, I thought. It was signed 'Nina'. The rest of the message lay in the big red kiss and the tiny heart that dotted the *i* in 'Nina'.

I put the basket back on the shelf. I didn't want to hear the homophobia in Vestey's voice again, the note of ugly hate, so I didn't mention the postcard. 'Got a name, sir,' I said. 'Rosemary Joyce.'

'The silver rose,' Vestey said. 'The name Joyce do anything for you, Sunshine?'

'No, sir.'

'Let's just say it's known to the police. How does 7.03 p.m. yesterday grab you?'

Vestey was addressing the pathologist, who'd just withdrawn a thermometer from the dead woman's rectum. Quennell noted the temperature and went on recording, ignoring Vestey. 'Two factors affect this reading: the body is lying on a cold surface, slate, and the back door has apparently been open for several hours.' He bared the woman's waist where it met the slate. 'Skin coloration in the region of the trunk indicates that gravitational sinking is well advanced.'

'And we're not,' Vestey said. 'Come on, Mr Niall, we're twelve hours behind.'

By now the rest of Vestey's crew had arrived. While they searched outside, I took the sitting room and study, Vestey the bedrooms. I was glad of the solitude; I needed to shake off Vestey's voice. It had been living in my head all week, didactic, withering, full of hard judgments.

I glanced around the quiet, curtained rooms. I formed an impression of good taste and the money to support it. The floorboards gleamed, the rugs were muted and thick, a smell of polish clung to the simple, expensive chairs and cabinets. The ceilings were high and the entire wall space of the sitting room had been given over to turn-of-the-century oils and watercolours. In the study I found filing cabinets, bookshelves and a massive desk topped with scuffed, ink-stained leather. A computer crouched cold and mute on a portable stand. Neither room had been disturbed. They might have witnessed nothing more violent than a sneeze.

That's when I found the money. As I remember it, I noticed a gap at the top of the desk drawer and eased it further open with my pen. The money was fanned out over the surface of a writing pad as if it had been tossed in there carelessly. I looked, touched, gathered it up, I don't know why. A hundred and fifty dollars in twenties and fifties. Not enough to wonder at.

'No-one to see, Mr Niall. No-one to know.'

Vestey's voice was low and goading but somehow a chill came off it. I didn't move. He approached me silently, smiling a little. He stopped. We looked at the money. 'Neither of us earns much. The job is thankless. Come on, sport, what do you say?'

He reached out and took a fifty-dollar note. He folded it, never taking his eyes off my face, and slipped it into my top pocket. 'We could do ourselves a favour,' he said.

I tried to read him. Almost the first thing he'd ever said to me was, 'Give them the eye, Sunshine. Define them. Nail them.' He was doing it now. But it was more than that, somehow. He was making me his, I could feel it. A kind of aversion gripped me. 'Nup.' I took the note from my pocket, handed it to him and backed away. 'Nup.'

He half smiled. I watched him straighten the note, snap it with both hands, drop it in the drawer. 'Incident passed,' he said.

He continued my instruction back at his office.

'Always start with the victim, Mr Niall. Family. Known associates. Find me someone with motive, means and opportunity, the classic triumvirate. Don't look startled, Sunshine, I can read. Take motive.' He touched his forefinger. 'Revenge? Money? Sex? One of those. Means: the gun. If you can't find me a gun, find me someone with that signature, pow, in the back of the head. Opportunity. Find me someone who wasn't definitely somewhere else at the time.'

I began to drift. Vestey looked like a magazine cover, but he worked in a clutter of open drawers, overblown files and bent paperclips. His pinboard was famous. He never cleared it. Memos, cards and newspaper clippings were tacked on top of one another like dusty scales, all of it stirring like a forest whenever you walked past it.

'You with me so far?'

I straightened in my chair.

'Welcome back. Check parking infringement notices, cab companies, stolen car reports, the airlines. Talk to the neighbours. Take Mack with you to the funeral, get some snaps of the grieving mourners. Above all, concentrate on the Joyce woman. This smacks of a hired gun brought in to settle a grievance. If he's from the mainland, his real name might be on a passenger list somewhere. I want to see every bit of information the moment it comes in. When you turn up someone who can help us with our enquiries, we pounce immediately, no farting around. We need evidence, Sunshine, physical evidence tying culprit to victim, culprit to scene. Motive, means and opportunity mean fuck-all if you haven't got evidence.'

The voice wound through and around me. When the briefing was over I went upstairs, opened files on the victims, hassled the lab people, ground a phone into my ear, all the other things that Vestey had taught me to do. Every thirty minutes he asked me for an update. 'We're losing time, Mr Niall. Evidence. Find me evidence.' I felt that I was existing on a knife edge, that I'd miss something vital and let the culprit slip away.

Sally's report came in first: no fingerprints that shouldn't have been there. Later ballistics called to confirm Vestey's suspicions: no bullets, only unidentifiable fragments. The pathologist grumbled that he wasn't ready to file a report yet, but he was prepared to say that both women died at the same time and he had no reason to doubt the 7.03 time on Nina Galt's watch.

There was nothing in Nina Galt's background to excite attention. She'd been renting the converted stable for six months. Her job entailed regular lay-overs in various Ansett destinations, sometimes for days at a time. The last one had been Brisbane, hence the postcard.

So I concentrated on the Joyce woman, as Vestey advised, and by mid-afternoon had come up with an inheritance and an estranged husband. The inheritance was Joyce Constructions, a shadowy outfit named in two royal commissions. The husband was a nasty piece of work called Liam Flann, who'd worked his way up from union muscle to son-in-law. I pulled Flann's file and found convictions for demanding money with menaces, assault and resisting arrest. His photograph showed vacant eyes in a good-looking face. Rose had been twenty when she married him. Eight years later, when her father died, she'd dropped Flann's name, settled an allowance on him, and told him to get out. He lived in West Moonah now. I rang the local CIB, who told me that Flann moved in a world defined by the TAB, corner pubs and his mother's house in Glenorchy. He often got drunkenly sentimental about his marriage, and he gambled, got into brawls and was a general nuisance.

'I like it,' Vesty said. 'Dig a bit deeper and tomorrow we'll go and shake his tree.'

Eight o'clock the next morning found me accelerating past a dozy bus on Brooker Avenue.

'Steady on, Sunshine, set an example to the citizens. You were saying about the Melbourne casino?'

There was an unusual degree of tension in Vestey. It made me nervous, made me think I'd overlooked something. 'None of the Tasmanian casinos will let Flann play,' I said, 'so he's forced to go interstate. He spent the weekend at the Crown Casino in Melbourne. On Sunday evening he was barred from the gaming rooms for being drunk and abusive. According to the phone record for his room, he called Rose Joyce three times that night.'

Vestey grew more tense. 'Christ, I wish you'd told me this earlier. Did you check the airlines?'

'Listed on Ansett's 4.50 to Hobart on the day of the murder. The flight takes just over an hour, giving him plenty of time to pick up a gun and be in Sandy Bay by 7.03.'

'His first big case, and the lad's on a roll,' Vestey said, finally settling back in his seat. He didn't speak again but sat concentrated and still. I had no idea what he was thinking or what he expected. His rank meant that he didn't have to do this sort of hackwork, but he was a coalface cop, not a pen-pusher, and I also guessed that he didn't want me to stuff things up.

I slowed a block short of Flann's but Vestey told me to keep going. 'Right outside the front door, Sunshine, large as life.' He'd become hard and sharp again. 'It brings on the attitude. Have I explained the attitude? Defiance, the sulks, resentment, sometimes all three at once. You'll see what I mean. You take the front. Give me a minute, then knock. If he comes out shooting, you know what to do.'

Flann's house was the kind of cheap, two-storey glass and cement-brick structure that gets called a townhouse in the brochures. I contemplated the tasteless front door while Vestey went around to the back. I pushed the buzzer, waited, pushed it again. I pounded on the door with my fist.

I was stepping back to look up at the upstairs windows when I heard the first shot. It was the second shot that got me running.

I rounded the corner and paused, unholstering the .38 I'd signed out before we left the squad room. It was all sundeck and glass at the back of the house. The sliding glass door was open and I had a clear view across the kitchen to the bottom step of a staircase showing through an archway at the other end. Vestey stood a short distance from the archway. He was half-crouched with his back to me, tensely regarding a body sprawled at the base of the stairs. As I watched, he straightened, stepped past the body and darted a quick look up the stairs. Apparently satisfied, he began to climb them, his gun extended.

It hadn't occurred to me that Flann might have friends there. I went in fast and low, through the archway, and into each of the ground-floor rooms. Nothing.

I returned to the body. I could see that it was Flann. He wore underpants and needed a shave. I stood back, trying to work it out. There was a gouge in the wallpaper near my head. Vestey's first shot had missed. I wondered how he was going to justify this. I wondered what he'd want me to tell the board of inquiry. I could hear his voice winding through me.

That's when I spotted the gun. Flann had dropped it in a patch of dustballs and shadows at the base of the stairs. It was a little Colt, a .22 revolver, the kind of gun you'd use if you wanted a quiet, clean killing.

'As I told you,' Vestey said, coming down the stairs. 'The bad guys are dumb.'

In the days that followed, Vestey rode high at police headquarters, despite his aloofness. Even I earned a couple of friendly winks in the corridors.

But I was worried sick. There was an outcry in the civil liberties camp, Flann's mother and brothers cried 'set-up', and internal affairs kept going over my statement with me. There were TV cameras, abusive phone calls, my name in the paper for days at a time.

I needn't have worried, though. Vestey had commendations a mile long, the gun was real and loaded with hollow-points, and Liam Flann was the prime suspect in a double-murder inquiry. We came out of it with a pat on the back.

Typically, Vestey had no thanks for anyone. 'Police culture, my son. Take a group of unimaginative, undereducated men, give them a job that sets them apart from society, make them feel overworked and undervalued, and you can rely on them to stonewall and close ranks when the outside world gets too nosy.'

I couldn't work him out. I knew all about feeling different, undervalued, I felt it every time I walked down the street. I liked the idea of a police culture, even if bad cops did get protected sometimes. I concluded that Vestey had a kind of puritan's distaste for excess, deviance, manipulation and dishonesty of any kind. He must have been offended every minute of every day. It made me wonder if he had a threshold.

Life went on. We still had to prepare for the coronial inquiry. 'I don't want any "death at the hands of a person or persons unknown" about this one, Sunshine,' Vestey told me. 'This isn't going to be another unsolved mystery for a self-ordering society, a juicy story for the daily rags. We can lay this one on Flann. I want a solid, clear-cut submission, no fuck-ups.'

'Yes, sir.'

So I went back over the material step by step, extracting the relevant evidence from the mass of detail, constructing a character and motive profile of Liam Flann, building a logical case. It was meticulous, satisfying, calming work. I double-checked everything: the physical evidence; Flann's movements; his state of mind in the period prior to the murders.

I came unstuck with the airline. It was the fiftieth call of the day and I wasn't in the mood for mistakes. 'How could it touch down at 6.55 if it left Melbourne at 4.50 and it's only a one-hour flight? Check again.'

'I have checked, sir,' the Ansett clerk said. 'It's all to do with adjusting the clocks for summer time. Tasmania starts a month earlier and finishes a month later than Victoria. They're synchronised now, though.'

I went cold. 'He has to collect his luggage, get home, get a gun, get to her place. No way could he have shot her.'

'*Sir?*'

'Never mind.'

I hung up.

For some reason then I thought of the mother. After the shooting of her son, Bridie Flann went on every current affairs program. Everyone at headquarters mocked her, and Vestey had things to say about Irish clannishness, said because I was Irish I'd know what happens to the truth when mother love is involved, yet I'd been impressed by the woman. It wasn't only her singular and unapologetic grief, it was her absolute conviction that her son was innocent. 'Liam Michael,' she said, 'would do a lot of things but he wouldn't do this.'

The thing is, it took me a while to think clearly. My first instinct was for self-preservation. I didn't know how I was going to explain my carelessness to Vestey. I could hear his voice peeling layers off me until I was worse than nothing in his eyes, a slapdash cop who couldn't get his facts straight. It didn't make it any better when I thought more about it and realised an innocent man had been shot. The hassle was Vestey's but I was implicated in it.

That brought me by degrees to thinking about Liam Flann, his mother and her grief and vehemence, the way she spoke about him in the present tense: 'My boy doesn't use guns. He might punch someone, but he doesn't use guns. He's been set up.'

It's not that difficult for a policeman to come by an unlicensed gun. Vestey could've been holding onto it for years. But I needed evidence, and the most crucial, the gun amnesty inventory, was missing from the files. I kept digging, finding my answer in the proof-sheets at the *Mercury*'s photo library. The front-page photograph was no help—Vestey is obscuring the table on which the amnesty guns are displayed—but the photographer had shot two rolls of film that day. Several of the photographs clearly show four .22 pistols among the handguns. The guns were melted down several days later—Vestey's orders—but according to the firm that carried out the job, three .22 handguns were destroyed, not four.

For a while I wondered if Vestey had intended to replace the gun after shooting the two women, knowing that it would be melted down and there would be no ballistics evidence to link it to the murders. He'd have assumed the murders would remain unsolved—explained as someone settling an old grievance against the Joyce family, perhaps.

Then I wondered if he'd been opportunistic. He'd seen where my inquiries were leading me, and had retrieved the gun from the storeroom and conveniently implicated Flann by dropping it next to his dead body.

But the more I think about Vestey, the more convinced I am that he's not the sort to improvise like that. I remember the way he guided me through the investigation, pointing me where he wanted me to go. I think he had Flann marked for the murders all along. He simply waited until all the factors were right. The one thing he hadn't anticipated was Flann's trip to Melbourne. I remember Vestey's anxiety about it, and the flight times, and the way he relaxed when the timing seemed to fit.

I don't mind admitting that I feel spooked now. It's like I'm being watched, like footsteps are behind me only there's no-one there. I don't know whom to approach with all this. I don't know who'll listen.

And until a moment ago I couldn't even tie Vestey to the women. I couldn't see why he wanted Rose Joyce dead unless she was very bent and he'd turned vigilante, and that didn't seem likely.

Not Rose Joyce.

That's how he wanted us to read it.

Nina Galt.

The evidence has been here all the time—a dusty postcard, curling at the edges, all but obscured under the yellowing clippings and notices on Vestey's pinboard. Anyone would have forgotten they had it there. I wouldn't have looked twice at it myself if I hadn't noticed a red '*ME*' scrawled in the sky above the harbour, a red arrow isolating a tiny figure on the Opera House steps. She'd sent him the card two years ago. It doesn't take two years to fall out of love with one person and in love with another. It doesn't take two years to learn how to hate, either. Vestey has a lifetime of hate behind him.

BENT

My Brother Jack

It started at my new place, night-time noises that didn't sound right.

Ironically enough, noise is the reason I had moved there in the first place. Police helicopters, breaking glass, burglar alarms, the bass beat of stereos like repeated explosions underground, car alarms outside my bedroom window—some mornings in Fitzroy I'd wake feeling too wired to write. I was working on *Kickback* then, Jack's first story, and I'd find myself staring out the window, picturing the little place he had near the coast, the clean air, the birds, the silence, the peace of it all before everything went sour on him and he was forced to run. The double irony is, he left the coast, I moved to the coast—not far from where he'd been living, in fact—and before too long things were going bump in the night and robbing me of sleep and composure.

By then I'd written *Paydirt*, his second story, and *Deathdeal*, his third, and there were all those other yarns of his waiting to be shaped into novels, but my concentration was shot. The first wrong note, excuse the pun, was the wind chimes ringing out on a night when there was no wind. It was about 10.30 and I was in bed, reading. There was no wind but those chimes rang out with the kind of abrupt discordancy that made me think *prowler*, someone who didn't know the chimes were hanging there on the verandah. The love/sex interest in this story flung down her Sisters in Crime newsletter, revealing her small but high, low-slung but pointed, melony but round, sloping but curved, tanned but creamy breasts and said, 'What the fuck was that?' I yanked back the curtain and spotlit the verandah with a torch, but all I got was light coming back at me from the glass and by then it was too late. I didn't poke around outside; maybe I should have.

Then there were the other noises. You have to understand that although I grew up on the land I have lived nearly twenty-five years of my life away from it, so I was rediscovering the seasons, the animals, the birds. Especially the birds. They were nesting. I would look up from writing something—some stunt that Jack was pulling; some sentence where I was trying to convey the essence of stillness and dispassion in his face—and see sparrows and wrens angling up into the palm tree, trailing straw four times their length. The willy-wagtails intrigued me the most, their little grey mud egg-cup nests, their devotion to the eggs, the hatchlings, more than anything their fearlessness, the splatter of stuttering, scolding fury that said *back off* if you got too close. So who would they be sounding a warning to at one o'clock in the morning?

Then there were the messages on my answering machine. A couple of times the caller simply clicked off, so it could have been anybody, but twice there was no click, no voice, just a palpable sense of someone listening to the silence in the house, the silence that said the house was empty and open.

The voiced messages, they were something else. '*You got it wrong, Wyatt.*' Not that *I* had got it wrong, *Wyatt* had got it wrong. If I'd been told that I'd got it wrong, the author had got it wrong, I'd have been able to relate to it, and it wouldn't have been the first time. There had been the gun freak who left a message informing me that revolvers don't have safety catches; the purist who believed Wyatt did things that Richard Stark's Parker would never have done; the safe expert who pointed out that floor safes are bolted down, you don't just wheel them out.

(Where did these people get my number from, that's what I'd like to know.)

I can live with my fuck-ups being pointed out to me. It's my job to get it right (just as it's every crime writer's job, which is why I won't be lifting information about firearms and safes from other crime novels any more), but to say that Jack had got it wrong—Wyatt had got it wrong—is something else entirely. Of course he's fucked up sometimes. He's worked with people he couldn't trust, he's failed to see the wild balls coming in from left field, he's limited himself to old-style bank and payroll heists when he could have made a mint from dealing drugs (if you could call failing to deal drugs a fuck-up). So here was this guy on the machine telling me Wyatt had got it wrong and I didn't know what he meant. Four times he said it, four separate occasions, nothing more, just a low growl, cold and hard: 'You got it wrong, Wyatt.'

There were other things. My cat on a cushion, his

ears pricking up, every nerve ending along his spine registering something, someone, outside the house. A garden tap left running. *Two* flat tyres on the elderly Volvo, the twenty-five-year-old car I run because it's built like a tank and show me the writer who can afford a newish car anyway. A gate left open, allowing the old ewe that came with the place to get out, so now I have to plant fruit trees all over again.

I tried to tell myself it was the neighbour's kids, they're a wild bunch, the family has bred horses here for generations whereas I'm new, no better than a Collins Street farmer or a January holidaymaker in their eyes, but you don't see the neighbour's kids with books in their hands, which is why, when I found a page from *Paydirt* knifed to the back door one day, I knew the problem was very real and nasty, the sort of problem that had imagination and flair behind it, which ruled out the neighbour's kids.

The page? It was from Chapter 12, where Wyatt figures out how he's going to ambush and rob a security van on a lonely bush track. It was a good plan, only things went wrong. It's like that for Jack: he's smart but too often he fails to account for the stupidity and duplicity of others. He's preternaturally wary, he keeps his eyes open, his attitude says I'll-believe-it-when-I-see-it, but you can't cover all the bases all the time. Still, things-going-wrong is part of the appeal of his stories.

The knife? It was a kitchen knife. From the knife drawer. You could go into my kitchen and put your hand right on it.

So far I'm talking about gestures here, traces, signs, and all they added up to was a pissed-off character who wanted me to know that he was pissed off. Clearly he was pissed off with Jack, but I was easier to find than Jack and so he was taking it out on me.

Then a month later he stopped making gestures and tried to kill me.

It was a Wednesday evening and I'd driven up to Melbourne to take part in a crime-writing soirée organised by the National Book Council. It was held in Mietta's, a restaurant and bar with the dimpled leather armchair and open fireplace atmosphere of a gentleman's club. Anyway, the place was packed, but they were there to hear Kerry Greenwood, not me, so I got in a couple of gentle digs about the Phryne Fisher type of crime fiction and left to drive home.

I remember that I was somewhere around Abbotsford, stopped at the lights that would take me onto Hoddle Street, wondering how long it takes to establish a series character in the public's eye, when I felt a vehicle bump into the back of the Volvo. Now, the light was red, and this was the gentlest of taps, and my car is old, so I didn't bother to get out. I just waited for the light to change, idly thinking I was in Wyatt territory, things seem to happen to Wyatt in Abbotsford, when I felt another bump, much harder this time. I glanced up at the rear-view mirror and there were two implacable headlights there and an impression of bulk and muscle. It was a four-wheel drive, armoured with a massive bull-bar, and it was backing up, ramming me, backing up, ramming me.

It stopped. There must have been something wrong with the signal box, the traffic lights were still red, so I got out thinking, *Right, I'll have you, mate*. It did me no good. The guy had locked his doors, his windows were tinted, and he'd plastered mud over his plates. He was impregnable. I looked at the damage. There was a pulley on the front of the 4WD, not only a bull bar, and it had scored an expensive-looking dent in the Volvo's boot lid. I got back into the car, determined to U-turn out of there, but the moment I released the handbrake the 4WD rammed me again and this time he just kept going, pushing me metre by metre onto Hoddle Street, into the path of the ceaseless cross-town traffic.

Forget the U-turn. I spotted a gap and planted my foot, merging right, cutting in and out of lanes, heading north away from the freeway. At Langridge Street I turned right. My heart was hammering but by now I was calm enough to think I should do something about this guy. Besides, you're obliged to report accidents. I think. The Collingwood police station is behind the town hall. I pulled in there, went in, stated my case. The scene went something like this:

Cop: Can you describe the vehicle?

Me: It was a four-wheel-drive.

Cop: Toyota? Range Rover? What?

Me: I'm not sure.

Cop: You're not sure. How about the colour?

Me: Dark, possibly blue or black.

Cop: Well, blue or black?

Me: All colours look darker at night under street lights, so I can't be sure.

That earned me a sour look. Then the cop said: What about the driver?

Me: I couldn't see him.

Cop: Registration?

Me: The plates were covered in mud, I think deliberately.

A long look and the cop said: Why deliberately?

This was a tricky area I'd got myself into. I had no proof and there was a risk my explanation would drag Jack's name into it, Jack who has never been fingerprinted, photographed or arrested by the cops but who nevertheless is known to them, number one, so I changed my tune quickly: Sorry, I meant to say accidentally.

Cop: Let's take a look at your car.

Outside on the street the Volvo looked every one of its twenty-five years, and when the cop began doing a roadworthy on it, checking tyre tread depth, panel rust, windscreen chips, I began to wish I'd just gone on home with my tail between my legs. Then the cop said: Here's your motive.

He was staring at the back of the car. I joined him. He indicated the *Stop Uranium Mining* sticker in the rear window (that shows you how long I've had the car) and said: There, see?

Me: You think so?

He was a beefy character, puffy and beer-fed, wearing a Merv Hughes moustache. The moustache bristled, that's how I could tell he was grinning, and he said: Just asking for it, weren't you, pal?

Me: It's a free country.

Cop: And the other bloke was expressing his point of view. Look, I'll make out a report if you like, it's what I'm here for, but I'm telling you now, you're wasting your time. We won't be kicking ass on this one.

'Kicking ass.' Kicking *arse* sounds wrong, doesn't it?

It sounds weaker than 'kicking ass'. I mean, I have my down-market characters—Sugarfoot, for example—use expressions like 'kicking ass', reality for them being shaped by or filtered through American film and TV, but, really, more and more people are talking like that these days.

Then again, sometimes when I'm writing Wyatt I find myself listening for the beat, the cool, flip, wise-ass tone or style or personality that works best and that makes American crime fiction so appealing and distinctive.

Anyway, I drove home then, my tail between my legs. You can understand why I want to give cops a hard time in my crime fiction. I can't see myself writing police procedurals, somehow. Stephen Knight claims there's a national wariness of the police in Australia, so they don't figure very well in crime fiction. Maybe he's right. Maybe this would have been a different story if I'd met a few Morses or Wexfords along the line or had a few beers with Carella and the guys from the old Eight-Seven.

I pushed through the dark night across the Mornington Peninsula, much as I'd imagined Jack had done in *Kickback*:

> *The sky was black. When moonlight struggled briefly through the heaped clouds he saw fog wisps like people in the road ahead. Fog hung over dams and creeks. Otherwise he felt that only he was abroad, only he awake. (p.183)*

That made me think this was a ghost story, maybe a horror story, I was in. If there was a human agency at work, I hadn't seen the human. All I'd seen was the evidence of evil intent—signs and warnings—and that implacable throbbing 4WD like a living beast. Sure, the windows were tinted, but maybe there was no driver anyway.

It's what you think at night but not in the clear light of day. The next morning I unbolted the house, checked outside—morning sun, the dew like diamonds, a clop of horses along the sunken road—and went back in and phoned Frank Jardine. Frank works with Jack sometimes. He can be trusted. There has to be someone Jack can work with, he can't go a dozen books or even three or four without a reliable sidekick, someone like Grofield in the Parker novels. Jardine lives in Sydney, a hotel on Broadway, and I had to wait till he came on the line.

'Yep.'

I told him who I was.

He sounded pleased. 'Gaz, what can I do for you?'

I couldn't say Jack's name, maybe Jardine's line was tapped, so I said, 'I need to see Wyatt.'

'Trouble?'

'You could say that.'

I knew what Jardine was thinking, he was thinking cop trouble for Jack. Even with the elaborate artifice I've built around Jack—calling him Wyatt; the selection and shaping of the material; the invention; the tightrope walk between a story that is driven by character on the one hand and plot on the other—he still fears the cops might read the books, twig who Wyatt is, and use me to find him. In fact, in the early planning stages that's where I thought this story was headed, it was a cop getting at me, but the evidence didn't really fit that scenario and besides, I needed to bring Jack into it, and it's not likely he'd come in if cops were involved.

'I'll tell Wyatt you called,' Jardine said, and he broke the connection.

A note about the name. Jack wasn't always called Wyatt. He was called Cody at first, as in the story 'Cody's Art'. He was called Cody in the first draft of *Kickback*, the second draft, the third draft, a year's hard slog getting the story and the character to work, and every one of those drafts rejected. But by draft three I thought I'd got it right, so I tried a different publisher, Allen & Unwin, though I was also sufficiently demoralised to submit it under a nom-de-plume: I mean, what if the book *was* bad? I didn't want too many people to know that I'd written a bad book. Fortunately they snapped it up, the book got rave reviews, and the only thing they wanted changed was Jack's name. ' "Cody" is not hard enough,' they said. I thought about it and came up with Wyatt. It sounds right, a whip snap, and a friend told me she's reminded of Wyatt the meticulous architect, and Wyatt the poet: *They flee from me that sometime did me seek/ With naked foot stalking in my chamber*. (It can sometimes pay to drop quotes like this. To make it as a writer in Australia you have to become a darling of the English departments.) Jack didn't care either way about the name. 'Mate, you're the writer,' he said.

So I settled down and waited for Jack to contact me. I made notes for the next few Wyatts. It's possible that if Jack didn't exist I'd have been able to invent him, but not his capers. I mean, where can you pick up large amounts of cash these days? I wouldn't have a clue, it's all electronic transfer now. I'd have been able to invent obvious heists for him, banks and payrolls, but that would have been the extent of it. Fortunately Jack has always been able to sniff out other sources: a casino, an ALP frontbencher with $100,000 in his briefcase, a Medicare office in a large regional centre, the grand-final take from the MCG. If Jack can keep pulling these jobs I guess I can keep weaving stories around them. Once he stops, that's it, back to 'literary' fiction, 'blood from a stone' writing as Jean Bedford calls it.

Jack didn't call me, he just showed up the next day. I didn't hear a car, but I saw it later, a Hertz Falcon he probably rented with fake ID, screened from the road and the house by the leaves of the liquidamber. I didn't hear his footsteps on the gravel drive or on the verandah, but then, silence is his element, he would have used the lawn, his shoes are rubber-soled. I didn't hear the back door or any of the inner doors, I didn't hear the board-creak of his passage through the house, he simply materialised in my study doorway. I looked up and there he was, gazing at me.

'Christ almighty.'

He smiled, a brief twist at the edge of his mouth. 'Not quite.'

'You could've knocked.'

'Jardine said you were in trouble, so I came carefully, looking for the trouble.'

Jack is like that, flat and plain. I nodded. 'Fair enough.'

'You want to tell me about it?'

No small talk, he just gets right down to it. Anyway, he's no good at small talk. He'll engage in it for harmony's sake or to keep someone from losing his nerve, but generally he can't see the point of it.

So I explained what was wrong, all the details, leaving nothing out. Knowing Jack, I kept it clear and economical. 'I want you to find out who's doing it,' I concluded, 'and why.'

He looked at me, thinking it through. My brother is an enigma. I admire him, I always have, but I don't know him at all. No-one does. He left home when he turned sixteen and never came back. I was ten and I felt the absence like an ache. No-one knew the life he lead, the thoughts he had, what drove him. He was private, like a western loner. Once or twice a year there would be a phone call and something about it, the darkness of the hour, signals from the atmosphere sounding distantly on the line, made me think of my brother in a far off place, the flat planes of his face in the wintry moonlight, the dark and watchful cast of him. I was at school, Joan Baez's *Diamonds and Rust* was getting some airplay, and the line, 'a booth in the mid-west', ran in my head whenever my brother called home.

Years later he started to seek me out. Not often, just once in a while, sometimes hinting obliquely at what he'd been doing before he slipped away again. I know now, but our parents don't, that he spent time in the army. He picked up skills there. He came out knowing how to kill, how to look after himself, but he also came out with a wad of cash—a base payroll, a couple of fleeced poker schools, a few black-market scams involving guns, radios, jeeps. He came out and he went to work and in a good year he'd spend four weeks pulling a couple of big jobs and take it easy for the other forty-eight. That's how he acquired his place on the coast, his home before everything went sour on him. That part of it's in *Kickback*, if you're interested.

He looked at me and I looked back at him. Jack is

tallish, six-one, and, like a cowboy archetype, he's as long and hard and supple as a length of rope. He moves well, he thinks well, he perceives well. He doesn't paralyse himself with scruples and inhibitions like the rest of us. People say to me, always with a smartarse look, 'How much of you is in Wyatt?' and I can't tell them about my brother or alter egos or wish fulfilment.

'Find out who and why?' he said. 'So now I'm a private eye, is that it?'

He can make a joke. Hear him talk about yuppies, other crims, contemporary values, and you'll laugh; you'll also go a little cold, recognising an unimpressed and pitiless eye. He can make a joke, but the delivery is flat, the smile if it's there is brief and sharkish, so you have to learn to recognise it.

I smiled back at him. 'You're not so different from a PI,' I said.

'Okay, define the PI.'

I counted on my fingers. 'One, you're a loner, you're not interested in collective solutions. Two, you're sceptical about social redemption. Three, you do have some integrity, even if we can't quite approve of you. Four, you're the seeing eye, looking from below, but you're also a participant, not just an onlooker. Five, you allay middle-class anxieties. There are some nasty people out there and we feel better when you get the better of them.'

Jack cut in. 'Yeah, but I feed other anxieties, like if you happened to have a hundred grand sitting in the safe at home.'

I nodded, grinning. 'True. Six, you're street-wise, all those mental and physical skills we'd like to have.'

'I've learnt them, built on them.'

I knew what he meant. Too often I'm irritated by fictional heroes, all that unexplained know-how, all those abilities. 'Seven,' I said, 'you make sharp observations about contemporary life.'

Jack shook his head. 'That's *you*, Sunshine, intruding into the narrative.' He poked his chest with a strong forefinger. 'Me, I steal, simple as that. I don't give a stuff about values, politics, the way people dress.'

I shrugged. I didn't think he was right, but I said, 'Suit yourself. Eight, the rest of us, we let ourselves get pushed around, we're too polite, but you stand up for yourself. We'd like to be able to do that.'

The look on Jack's face said he couldn't see why that was so hard.

'Nine,' I said, 'our heroes don't let doubts and scruples and uncertainties hold them back.'

Jack's expression said I was generalising. I thought then about V. I. Warshawski, how she carries a bundle of ordinary traits and frailties around with her; how family and friends, affiliation and cooperation, mean a great deal to her. I guess her life is closer to the lives of her readers than is the life of the majority of male heroes, loners, punishing the Scotch, emotionally crippled. Not that you could say Jack's like that. He's not so much socially or sexually blunted or awkward as emotionally unreadable. Not for the first time did I wonder what hurt drove him, if any. Our poor parents, they were convinced it was something they'd done. Anyway, does it have to be explained? Can't he appear on the stage fully formed? This stopped me from listing number ten to him: an element of vulnerability. There's Matt Scudder's drink problem, Fred Carver's gammy leg, Kinsey Milhone's slapdash domestic life. Jack? I don't know. It's the not knowing that makes him appear isolated, unreachable, and I guess that can seem like some kind of ache, deep down inside him.

I don't think of Jack as a reader but he must have read the odd book or two, for he said, 'Private-eye stories are told in the first person. Are you going to have me narrate this story?'

I shook my head. 'I'll use an observer narrator.'

He looked right inside me then, and I blushed. It's as if he knew I'd tried to write about him in the first person but abandoned it: (a) because I didn't know what makes him tick, even though I'd argue that it's my job as a fiction writer to get inside the skin of someone who isn't me, and (b) because a chill comes off the page when Wyatt is around and that chill penetrated like ice when I tried the first person, I felt a bleakness and it scared me. I tried the third-person and that worked, distancing the reader, distancing me.

Even so, people ask me, 'How can a gentle-mannered bloke like you write books like that?' Well, a lot of the material is stuff Jack tells me, but don't these people read the daily papers? Don't they listen to the news? Do they go around with their eyes closed or something? Besides, I'm admitting to private demons. I couldn't write Wyatt if I didn't. I couldn't read Thomas Harris, James Ellroy. Maybe the people who ask me that question haven't got any private demons. Pig's arse they haven't.

Anyway, Jack and I were still there in my study, having this stupid conversation, my years in the classroom showing, and he was getting restless. 'How do you want to go about this?' he said.

I thought about it. Peter Corris says he learned about PI methods from Ross Macdonald and Raymond Chandler. 'Make a few house calls,' I said. 'Ask questions.' Corris also noticed that the trigger in Ross Macdonald is often something way back in the past, now playing out its effects in the present, but I didn't think that was relevant in this case. And Corris claims that 'crime is a sort of backdrop to the real action, which is a resolution of some sort of disorder in the lives of a set of people.' Well, that was true enough here, so I said to Jack: 'Find out who's hassling me, and why, and stop him.'

'Motive, means and opportunity,' Jack said.

'Hell, this isn't a murder story,' I said. 'Not yet, anyway. Just find me a mainspring that I can build, plot, structure and storyline around.'

So Jack went to work. When he's working, a film strip runs through my head, black and white, 1950s crime *noir*, something like Kubrick's *The Killing* (1956). One thing was different this time. The question driving Jack—driving Wyatt—was *Who is behind this?* rather than his customary *Can I pull off this robbery without getting caught?*

He returned two days later, mid-evening. There was no hole-and-corner approach this time, he drove openly up the drive to the back of the house, letting his headlights cut across the windows. I went out. The engine was running, the lights still on, and as I approached he opened the passenger door and said, 'Get in.'

'Just a moment,' I said. I went inside, told the love interest I was going out for a while, then returned to the car. 'Where are we going?' I asked, strapping on the seat belt.

'Frankston. His first mistake, lodging in the area he's actually operating in.'

That's one of Jack's cardinal rules: never find a bed near where you're pulling a job. 'Who is he?'

'I'll let him tell you that.'

'How did you find him?'

'I asked around until I came up with a name, someone who'd had his fingers burnt recently.'

I had to be satisfied with that. Jack taps into a network when he wants information or supplies—guns, explosives, getaway vehicles. I don't know who these people are or how it works and he'll never tell me, so I invent it.

Jack drove back across the peninsula to a hotel-motel near the seafront. It was a flash two-storey building with a drive-in bottle shop, restaurants, three bars, rooms. We got out. It was an ugly place, the air smelling of beer and scorched beef. Jack muttered darkly as he led the way across the poorly lit car park.

'See?' I said. 'You *do* comment on people and places and lifestyles.'

'Forget that. We've got work to do.'

I followed him across the foyer. The receptionist smiled automatically but something about Jack, some prohibition, wiped it off her face. We went upstairs. There was a fire alarm at the top. Jack broke the glass, pressed the button, and took me downstairs and out to the car park again. He stood facing the building expectantly.

'Well?' I said.

'You'll see.'

Sure enough, people started yelling *Fire!*, the restaurants, bars and rooms emptied, and everyone came storming out into the car park while sirens started up in the distance. Jack stiffened. 'That's him.'

I saw a guy of about thirty-five, wearing a moustache—not that that is unusual, these guys all watch 'Wide World of Sports'—jeans, Nike runners and one of those vast collarless patterned shirts that look as though they've been inflated with a bike pump. In the darkness Jack pressed his .38 into my hand and said, 'It's up to you, now. You can't be the observer any longer, finally you've got to be the active agent.'

I could see the sense of that, but still, I was shit-scared. I didn't know how I was going to get answers from this guy alone, Jack somewhere around but not about to show his face. I decided to play it as Jack, as Wyatt, would play it. Under the cover of the darkness and confusion I became Wyatt, grinding the barrel of the .38 against the hinge of the man's jaw and growling, 'Into the car.'

Fortunately the gun and the sirens subdued the man. He got into the back seat. Wyatt slid behind the wheel. Wyatt didn't do anything, just stared at the man over the seat, the cold mouth of the .38 trained at his gut.

'You know who I am,' Wyatt said, and there was no question mark at the end of it.

The guy nodded.

'You irritated me finally,' Wyatt said, 'so I went looking for you. You're stupid; it wasn't hard.'

'Don't shoot me.'

'That's up to you. What's your name?'

'What?'

Wyatt used psychology in situations like this. When he had the drop on someone it was important to give them back some dignity, some identity, or they'd panic or be otherwise useless to him. 'Your name: what is it?'

The man looked at him suspiciously. 'Steegmuller.'

Well, that was a relief. If it had been Wilson or Collins, for example, the editor would have red-pencilled *Two-syllable Anglo-Saxon names like this are too ordinary, too forgettable, they slide off the page.* 'What do people call you?'

'Steeg.'

'Okay, Steeg, why don't you tell me what's eating you?'

'What are you going to do to me?'

'That depends. You tried to kill me. To stop that happening again I should kill you now.'

'I was just trying to throw a scare into you!'

Wyatt said, flat and cold, 'It doesn't work like that. I have to assume you're serious. That means killing you. So start talking.'

There were red and blue lights in the car park by this stage—two fire trucks and a couple of divisional vans. Those lights were throwing the shapes from bad dreams around the interior of the car. There was enough light for me to see the man's face clearly. If I say his eyes ran over the seats and up the side windows and across the roof of the car the editor will red-pencil *Did they run on their little legs?* so I'll just say he looked around wildly for a way out. There wasn't one. He said:

'Twice you fucked me around. Like giving people

valet parking cards outside restaurants so they think you're parking their car for them only you're stealing it. I tried that and the fucking bouncer came and kicked my head in.'

'For Christ's sake,' I said, 'it was only a story.'

He looked at me suspiciously. 'So how did you know how to do it?'

'I didn't. I think I pinched it from an early Elmore Leonard novel.'

'You never tried it?'

'Not me, pal.'

He didn't seem satisfied but went on and said, 'Then when you climbed into the back seat of the car from the boot. I was going to rob this Seven-Eleven night manager on his way to the hole in the wall but I got trapped in the boot, I couldn't fucking get out.'

'I never actually tried it to see if it would work,' I admitted. 'I'd written Wyatt into a corner and I spent hours working out how to get him out of it.'

'You could've written something "With a mighty bound he was free . . ." '

I shook my head. 'Your reader's not going to buy that these days.'

'Or someone turns up in the nick of time.'

Again I shook my head. 'The reader won't buy that, either. The main character has to be the active agent. The answer had to be in Wyatt's hands. So I tried some lateral thinking and had him pushing through the window shelf into the back seat. I mean, I did do a bit of research. I went to car yards and looked in a few boots. It looked feasible. Maybe you chose the wrong sort of car.'

He was gloomy, full of doubt and regret. 'Maybe,' he said. Then some spirit came back into his face. 'So you just like fucking people around?'

'It's not real,' I said. 'I'm not writing about myself, or things that happened to me. I'm making it all up.'

'It seemed real. I went up north, thought I'd try hitting a security van.' He shivered. 'Nothing but saltbush and red dirt.'

Strangely enough the working title had been *Red Dirt Snatch* but the editor pointed out an unfortunate connotation with the word 'snatch', and they wanted uniform titles for the series anyway, so I accepted their suggestion, *Paydirt*. Who was I to quibble? It works for Sue Grafton, it worked for John D. MacDonald. I said to the guy, 'I write entertainments. No message, you're not meant to take it literally. When you put the book down there's the phone bill to pay, it's raining again, you forgot to buy milk.'

Here I was in an ending where the main players are brought together and there's plenty of dialogue and everything's explained and there are no loose ends. Just once in a while you'd like a shoot-out or something downbeat or morally ambiguous. I sighed. I was finished here. 'Stay away from me,' I said, pushing the guy out the door. 'Next time I'll kill first and talk later.' I could have shot him, but the imperative was gone now, it would have been gratuitous. When he was out of sight I wound down the window and called softly, 'Jack?' Nothing, no response, as if my brother wasn't there and had merely been some kind of device all along.

Time to go home. Lawrence Block, bemused by the Best This, That and the Other awards for crime writing every year, said that there were really only two categories, crime stories with cats and crime stories without. I went home to my cat.

And the love interest, of course.

Love and Grudges

It will be done this way.

We'll open with the city, layered and strife-laden. Above, the huge sky churns (time-elapse camera). Below, the dark waters are like an oily thing repelled. In the seeping dawn—smeared, yellowed, muttering—the city emerges, as low and sour as a resurfacing fact. This is a place of dreams and vows and love and grudges.

And this is what they can lead to.

We slip beneath the veiled water of the harbour, leaving no gulp, no eddying trace to betray us. It is dark down here, flecked with indissolubles.

Suddenly it begins to clear. Bars of cloudy sunlight strike through the water, revealing small blue shapes, dimpled and winking. Ceramic tiles. We are in a pool, an aquarium perhaps, free of sediment, and there is an underwater gate at the rear, the vast harbour pressing upon it.

Now pull back in one long take of the camera, retreating from the water, passing through to the safe side of the plate glass, emerging into air. Sounds begin to declare themselves: the distant commotion of the city; a hooting ferry. Closer to, some brat has spilt his ice-cream; witless thonged feet clip Coke cans; a mother screeches, her nerves calamitous; speech consists of grunts and upward inflections. You know the kind of thing. If this were America the men would be wearing John Deere caps and vast women in terylene knit pants would be reaching into crisps packets. We're among people who pay money to avoid solitude, who press shoulder to shoulder to peer through fences, glass, metal bars. (We don't see them directly, of course, only as reflections in the aquarium glass. We are still focused on the water.)

These people are the heartland, the source, passing down our lore: *If you see a shark . . .*

'You kick and yell. It scares them.'

'No way. It attracts them.'

'They reckon thump them on the nose.'

'I heard gouge their eyes out.'

'Yeah, sure, meanwhile you better start counting how many legs you got left.'

And so on and so forth.

Then the beast turns in the water, presenting that profile, that *fin*. Our unlearned fear. All breathe in. The beast approaches, yawns hugely across the glass, jaws open like a gash.

And it coughs, right in our faces, ejecting a hand and a hairy forearm, semen-coloured, a Rolex intact on the knobbly wrist.

One last, dreamy motion, almost like a wave goodbye.

That should grab the buggers, keep them watching.

Now for the story.

Bistro, a word neon-green and stylish in a night-dark window. Outside there's a rolling sea mist, but in here it's all clatter and chatter, every table taken. Smoky glass, leather-belted chrome, a chalked menu on each wall. *Prosciutto*, *tagliatelle*, *parmigiana*, always mispronounced.

The din is awful.

So are the diners. This much is clear from Julia's face, her fierce and solitary relish. She scribbles on her pad, articulates *parmigiana* for them, her mouth lovely, her tongue tip dipping sweet as a bird. This is no dummy.

Not that anyone notices, or cares. Flip, the pad is shut and in her pocket and Julia is riding high through the room, miserable tables falling away before her. She could run this place if she had to.

Then we see her wink and smile. It's significant: there is a girl sitting at a corner table and we sense that she never lets Julia out of her sight. Ten, maybe twelve years old, suddenly beaming—but not before we glimpse her undefended face, pale with uncommunicable doubts and agonies. This is Amy. Julia's daughter? Her sister? Both and neither, it seems.

Amy, overcome now, bends to the straw in her ice-cream soda, sending concealing black commas of hair down about her cheeks. An open book is on the table next to her elbow. Amy is able to read and watch Julia and nurse a soda for an hour or more.

Until Julia has finished work. Amy and Julia on the esplanade, one short, one tall, passing through the sea mist. They spin around, bound ahead, clasp and shout in the spark and spit of their crazy regard for one another.

Bringing gladness to the night. An old down-at-heels fellow shifts on a bench, gathers himself—'You'll do me, darlin'!'—and subsides again as they pass.

'Ame? Amy?'

Lucas has just come home. We follow him into the hall of the flat and peer as he peers into a kitchen, a sitting room, and finally with gloomy tenderness into a little bedroom, where James Dean dreams above a yellow-quilted bed. 'Amy? You home?'

Back to the sitting room, to the sprawling couch where Lucas cannot keep still. There is nothing on TV; he takes up and puts down a CD case; he fiddles with the ring in his ear; polishes his watch glass; probes a nostril. Lucas has moody, incautious good looks that can compel both desire and withheld trust. He stands and sits. There is no daily patience or sweetness in Lucas's life.

The telephone rings.

The man on the other end says: 'I seem to have heard that before.' He pinches his trousers' crease. 'Correct me if I'm wrong, Lucas old son.'

What we have here is A. J. Cruz in the back of a prowling Cadillac, taking care of business on his car phone. His driver sniggers, turns part way around at the heavy wit.

'*Watch where you're going!* Jesus. Now, where was I? Ah yes. We were expecting you, Lucas. We waited. It's bad manners to keep people waiting.'

Who wrote this shit?

Anyway, this is a restored 1957 Cadillac, pink, Fleetwood series, creeping along the esplanade. What the young bloods in their fuckwagons wouldn't give for this Caddy, for the accumulation and display and satisfaction and cruel luxury it implies. Those famous plates: CRUISE.

A. J. Cruz has black hair glinting tight across his scalp, and black sideburns like blades. 'You don't understand, Lucas. I don't intend to debate the matter,' A. J. Cruz says.

You can see that our man is taking a sly and natural satisfaction in all this. The car, the car phone, his leg extended along the back seat. The cold emphasis of his white shirt. The dreaming folds of his drape suit. Give the wardrobe girls a great big hand.

'You want another twenty-four hours. I see. Lucas, we seem to have a pattern here.'

Meanwhile Lucas has heard the key in the front door. He stands, turns around, hunches over the handset, muffling his tidal promises to A. J. Cruz, just as Amy and Julia enter the room, tumbling with laughter and scarves and flushed cheeks.

We switch to an aeroscan of the Cadillac at full throttle. It's on the main road now, approaching an underpass. A blaze of brake lights and it's swallowed by a tunnel.

A dreamy sweep of the car, from snout to burbling tail. What we have here is a thoughtful A. J. Cruz. He's made all his calls, he's going home.

When there is an eruption in the back seat. A. J. Cruz rubs his leg, curses, can't get comfortable. His face is in a pucker of misery.

'You okay?' The driver, eyes curtained by mirrored black lenses night and day.

'It's my sciatica,' says A. J. Cruz.

Okay, okay, it was just a thought. If you don't think a little humour is in order at this point, something that tags and humanises the character, then we'll bloody well take it from the top . . .

A. J. Cruz is gliding home in his celebrated car. He is in a thoughtful condition.

'I think,' A. J. Cruz says, 'that we should give our friend Lucas an opportunity of trading his way out of debt.'

The usual crap—cruel smiles, knowing looks exchanged in the rear-view mirror.

This is interesting: Julia is not proceeding beyond the doorway. She stops there, motionless, watching Lucas. She will never admit to hope and pain, it seems. And Lucas watches her. After a while they exchange wary nods.

But it is clear that Amy lives here. She tosses aside jacket and satchel and runs toward her brother.

Then wonders if she has done the wrong thing. She hovers at the midpoint between Julia and Lucas and we hear conspicuous, undisciplined longing in her voice:

'Look who I've got with me! Isn't that lucky? Oh Lucas, say a proper hello.'

Julia is watching Lucas. 'I won't stay.'

'Oh, please, a little while,' Amy says.

We are dismayed by her innocence.

Lucas's face.

Julia's face.

Amy's face.

Then a slow smile transforms Lucas's face. 'How have you been?'

Draw back from Amy, who is looking from one to the other with steady, helpless, unapologetic hope and love.

It's a morning to soar in. A little street, Amy blissful at her brother's side, approaching her school. Lucas—well, Lucas has plans, valorous plans, plans to lift them high and far away from all this.

'Julia? With Julia too?'

Yes!

Linger a while on Amy, treasuring and reciting, then notice that a whispering crush of car tyres is fading in on the soundtrack and A. J. Cruz is winding down his window to say:

'Bright and early this morning, Lucas?'

A terrible transformation of Lucas's face.

A. J. Cruz opens the car door. 'Heading for the school? Hop in, we'll give you a lift.'

'We can walk.'

A. J. Cruz says, 'Now that would be silly, since we've got unfinished business to discuss. Nice kid, Lucas.'

A. J. Cruz has turned to Amy with silky and absolute attention. Amy, quiet suddenly, steps closer to Lucas.

That's sufficient, surely. We get the message. Why do you people always want to spell things out? Cut the rest of this scene.

Taking us to:

A sweep of the marina: gulls, wheeling, crying out; beards scratched over the first coffee of the day; little boats crisscrossing the unhurried water; a smudge of freighters on the horizon; the tuning-fork ping of sail rigging slapping yacht masts.

Locking on A. J. Cruz's motor cruiser, low and fast and dangerous even at anchor. Boats like this slip out at night and return at dawn.

'You do this little thing for me, Lucas, and I'll forget about the money you owe me.'

When you're guzzling champagne at this hour of the morning, and the man's in a halfway decent mood, then you would have the nerve to raise doubts about the proposition he's putting to you. Lucas says: 'But what if he twigs we've ripped him off? He'll spread the word and no-one will buy from you again.'

A.J. Cruz leans forward.

'The bastard's trying to move in on my patch, Lucas. He buys from me, cuts the stuff with baking powder, then sells back to my clients. Now that's just not on.'

A.J. Cruz leans back. He smiles at Lucas. The smiles of A.J. Cruz do not bring comfort.

Well, not to most people. Lucas is impervious. His eyes gleam. He is full of schemes. He leans forward avidly. 'What you could do, A.J., the stuff I snatch off him you could sell back to him again.' He rocks back in his seat. 'Double your money.'

A clicking tongue and A.J. Cruz says, 'There's no doubting you, Lucas old son.'

It is evening. Julia has finished work. Amy will never feel unanchored again now that Julia is back in her life. Here she is, escorted by Julia under the lights on the esplanade, their voices joyous.

When Julia stops, suddenly hard and grim. 'What car?'

'Oh, sort of an old big one,' Amy says innocently. 'Sort of pink.'

Julia knows that car.

A repeat of that earlier tableau—Amy all flustered on the sitting room rug, Julia in the doorway, Lucas trying to look unconcerned.

'What are you up to, Lucas?'

'Me?' Lucas is dressed in black and we see him pull on a black jacket. 'Just off to help a mate move house. Legitimate. Look, make yourself at home. Won't be long.'

Okay, Julia, this is what we should be seeing in your face at this moment: *His life is messy and injurious, he is doomed to push and blunder, yet I go on offering him this self-deceiving, self-abasing, enslaving kind of love.*

And you'll say simply: 'No thanks.'

And you're gone.

Leaving Amy all desolate and a cold and hurtful need in Lucas.

One last run-through, people. I don't want any cock-ups like last night.

The Cadillac is parked in darkness, Mirrored-Lenses behind the wheel. We see Cruz's ill-advised business rival pass by once, twice, in a nondescript Datsun. He slows, stops, waits. The Caddy's headlights flare once and fade to blackness again. This is Datsun's signal and he gets out and approaches the Caddy. An exchange of airline bags. We see all this from a fixed point at some distance.

Now Datsun hurries back to his car and speeds away, twisting and turning through the back streets. He slaps his hand on the dashboard. He's done it.

And here is Lucas, newly in the employ of A.J. Cruz, ramming the Datsun with a stolen ambulance and hijacking a certain proscribed substance.

It's over in seconds.

We cut to a well-kept but edgy hand on a white linen tablecloth, one slender finger tapping *tock, tock, tock*.

It's A.J. Cruz and he says, 'We must be charitable. Friend Lucas might have run out of petrol, got lost, called in at home to tuck in the little one.'

Mirrored-Lenses is doubtful about that.

'Quite right,' Cruz says. 'He's ripped us off.'

He makes a brief and noteworthy telephone call.

Meanwhile, back at the ranch . . .

'All right, all right, I'm coming.' Then Julia pauses just inside her front door. 'Who is it?'

'Me. Quick, let us in.'

It's Lucas in a ferment and Amy all bewildered, a showy affliction on Julia's doorstep. They slip past her, and she locks the door and extinguishes the light.

'We need to bunk here tonight.' Then, elatedly, 'You won't believe.'

But Julia is not one for a summit conference in her hallway. She puts Amy to bed, secures the house, pours a couple of drinks.

Her lovely bum against the sideboard, her arms folded. 'Now, what won't I believe?'

Lucas opens the Qantas bag. 'This.'

'Oh Lucas.'

'Don't you see? This is our ticket out. This will set us up. The three of us.'

That's what he thinks.

Cut to a man at a plain wooden table, dismantling a stubby sub-machine gun. He oils and polishes each piece with lingering attention.

There is a grey-blanketed single bed, and a rickety wardrobe is open, displaying black uniforms and camouflage jackets. The walls are cold and white. Maps of the city. A wall rack of assault rifles, night scopes, pistols, mustard-gas canisters. *Creative Revenge* says a poster above the table. We also see that our man subscribes to *Soldier of Fortune*, and it's clear from his bookshelf that when the time comes he will draw upon certain survival skills. According to his white T-shirt, *happiness is a confirmed kill*. Somehow we are not surprised to see that he has a crew cut and a cricketer's moustache. And God knows what his wristwatch is capable of.

A squeaky yawn. Here we have Rex, a pit bull, what else, at his master's feet.

We are in the war room of Rhodric Reed.

Rhodric is glad to be in work again.

Meanwhile Lucas has tried apology and flattery and fear and stubbornness. Julia, sharp and self-respecting, has told him to give the stuff back before it's too late.

And now she can't sleep. Her fine, tormented cheeks in the blue moonlight. She reaches out her hand. She pats the empty space. She blinks awake.

Cliché. We don't need it. Why not simply start with Julia, standing resolute and sad in her kitchen doorway, witnessing Lucas hunched over her innocent pine table, applying nostril tubes to runnels of cocaine?

Says it all.

It is the next morning. We are at the marina again.

'This one has been opened,' A.J. Cruz says.

He looks up. Julia does not reply. She merely gazes at him. Just look at that face: what we have here, folks, is a contemporary condition, the female's massive and absolute distaste for the male.

Cruz, discomposed, looks down again at the packet of cocaine and answers his own question: 'Young Lucas.'

'Only a tiny amount,' says Julia wryly. 'He was in a bit of a state.'

Is she cracking a joke? At a time like this? Cruz stares at her. He expects flattery and fear, not this steadfastness.

'You're telling me Lucas knows he did a stupid thing, he apologises for it, and here is the full consignment—more or less—back again?'

Julia nods. 'That's what I'm saying. I'm also saying you're to consider his debt to you cancelled, despite this little hiccup.'

'Am I? Whatever happened to *please*, I wonder.'

'You're to leave him alone. He's getting out of all this. We're going away.'

'Awesome,' says A.J. Cruz, throwing up his hands. 'You have a deal, babe.'

Awesome? *Babe*? Have we strayed onto a Hollywood set? Who wrote this crap? Try *incredible*, maybe. *Amazing*. *Unreal*, if you absolutely must. For *babe* try *sweetheart*.

There is always a focal point in a good scene, illustrating the point of what is happening and making links backward and forward in time. Take an argument between lovers: we are engaged by words, gestures and heartache, but it is the claret, spilled on the carpet like a creeping dread, that fixes the scene in history.

And so it is that, when Rhodric Reed rackets out of the expressway underpass in his repellent 4WD, just car lengths behind Julia, he almost skittles a pedestrian, a doleful, daydreaming fat fellow, some old returned digger about to cross the road.

This scene says obvious things about Rhod baby, but mainly it tells us that Julia has been very unwise.

'You're not serious?'

This is Lucas, marked by panic and shock and greed and recent sleep, staring open-mouthed at Julia. 'I could've got a hundred grand for that stuff,' he continues, 'and you're telling me you gave it back? Jesus.'

But Julia is supple and hard-edged now. She has had enough.

'But it would have set us up,' Lucas persists.

'Lucas, look at me.'

We see Julia clasp his narrow, unruly head. Backlighting from the mid-morning sun in the window reveals her slender brown hands, her sun-bleached hair alight at the ends. She spells out urgent truths and love to Lucas for the last time.

Morning recess. The kids are playing hopscotch but Amy drifts and mopes, her white socks ringing her ankles like weights.

A.J. Cruz is reading a newspaper on his aft deck. He is utterly still. Gulls call. The sea slops and drains beneath the jetty.

Whap. Blink an eye and you'd miss A.J. Cruz snap-turn his newspaper to a new page.

Gulls floating and gliding above.

So what are we saying with these two brief scenes?

Something has been set in motion and it can't be stopped.

That moustache. The pale yellow aviator glasses (our man doesn't know that these are passé). The muted sun. A hand scribbling in a notebook with a ballpoint pen.

We are biding our time with Reed in his 4WD, looking not at his reflection in the tinted windscreen but beyond it, at Julia's little picket fence.

Reed turns his wrist. We read 10.30. He won't move before nightfall. Besides, he likes to rest before each job.

Nothing can be retrieved now. This man is patterned, limited, bad-hearted, serious about his work. His mother should never have spelt it 'Rhodric'.

I'm serious. I'm trying to help you think your way into the role. It all boils down to personality formation. Think what the poor bastard had to suffer at school. What if you'd been saddled with 'Geremie' instead of 'Jeremy'?

Anyway.

It's some hours later, mid-evening in the bistro. Julia's last night here, maybe? See her smiles span the room, embracing Lucas and Amy at their corner table.

Lucas raises his wine glass to her. He seems altered, his eyes less knowing and elusive.

And no more disappointed home for Amy. She might

reach out and touch the layers of harmony and trust in the air.

Julia slips among the clamouring tables.

When a voice growls, 'Coffee, please, miss,' and she turns with a smile, *and our hearts clench*.

Reed.

Not doing anything. Not a danger, not yet. Just sitting there.

But the end of that scene points to the beginning of this one:

Midnight. Julia's verandah, still and empty. A moment later a shadow materialises, crouching at the door, inserting a couple of lockpicks in the humble scratched Yale.

Reed holds the tension pick at an angle while he teases with the raking pick, turning the tumblers. He breathes out finally, stands, pushes the door inward with a latex-gloved hand.

A faint resistance, and then it's open.

For this hit he has chosen a 9 mm automatic. Once inside the house he fastens a silencer, his back to a wall, presenting the smallest possible target. Our Reed hates working in confined spaces.

We watch him glide through the house. He is quick. He has eaten little today; there is nothing to slow his blood. Every door is tolerantly ajar and as he locates each bedroom he fires, each shot like a sleepy cough in the night.

He leaves, tossing the gun aside. Reed uses a new gun for every job. Our man's a pro; he's not about to be caught in possession of a gun that may tie him to a killing.

Stylishly bleak.

Roll the credits.

The script says, the script says.

I *know* what the script says. But you can't blame me. Wouldn't you want to rework it? What's wrong with killing them all off? It's the sort of thing the French would do, someone like Chabrol.

My objections? One, I cannot accept your happy-ever-after with Lucas. He is tiresome, secretive, stupid, forever miserably tempted. He has to go. Two, Rhodric likes things tidy and conclusive.

But yes, I agree, there is that foreshadowing shark-arm. Whose arm? Whose wristwatch?

Okay, how about this, since you won't accept my massacre of the innocent and I can't accept that the script has Julia avenging Lucas, who, it turns out, is merely wounded . . .

Reed's contract is Lucas. Reed is a professional and never wastes shots. He has no argument with Julia, but awake she could be dangerous. So . . .

Reed materialises above Julia like a grinning demon. In a practised double motion he clamps a hand over her mouth and applies the cold gunsnout to her temple.

'Don't make a sound. Sit up.'

She does, and he hits the occipital bulge at the back of her head. She slumps.

Now for Lucas. Again the covered mouth, the cautionary gun: 'Cruz wants a word. If you wake the brat I'll kill her.'

They leave the house. Lucas feints once or twice and is smacked about the head for his pains. Reed handcuffs him to the window pillar of the 4WD and delivers him to Cruz.

We've seen it all before. They take the boat out, say oily things to Lucas, apply some extreme prejudice, then tumble his body into the watery depths. Where sharks lurk.

Christ, I'm bored saying it.

Let's try this.

Whom do we all love?

Julia.

So she can't die.

Start as before, Reed knocking her on the head and moving around to the other side of the bed.

Will he wake Lucas? Take him to see Cruz?

Ha. Clutch at that straw if you wish. Reed puts a bullet in Lucas's brain.

Lucas, perilous but appealing. Lucas, who had been on the edge of beginning a new life with Julia and Amy.

Loss, miscalculation, ringing pain. The room tosses with it.

Then silence and a kind of paralysis.

But we're not finished yet. Draw back, by degrees. *There*: Julia is stirring into consciousness.

She knows. See her sit, then stand, avoiding that side of the bed.

What's this? Something cold and hard beneath her slender foot. A gun, blue and lethal in the moonlight. She weighs it in her hand.

See concentration and dark judgments in her eyes.

See her say, later:

'I thought we might go for a little cruise.'

A.J. Cruz blinks awake on the pillow in his teak-lined cabin. He should never have given Mirrored Lenses the night off.

'Can't we talk about this?'

'Yes, but not here.'

The marina from above: mooring lights, jetty lights, a shadow crossing the dark water. Then closer, a motor muttering at the waterline.

The lights are far behind now.

'This is all I wanted to say,' Julia says.

And linger on Cruz's wristwatch.

A word about endings. Get in, get out, don't wait around. Don't restate anything. Don't state the obvious. Assuming that Amy doesn't wake up, find Lucas and lose her little mind, she will now make her life with Julia and together they will retrieve happiness. Our ending is the beginning of a new story. And it doesn't hurt to leave ripples and echoes: Reed has slipped back to his unknown room; it unsettles us to know that he lives on. Leave that detail to the imagination, however. Never introduce new material at this stage.

Break all of the above rather than direct something like this again.

Cockeyed at High Noon

Quinn? Sure, I knew Quinn.

A motion picture about his life and times? Hell, I was the man that shot him. You'd do better making a motion picture about me.

Besides, he was nothing but a punk.

I don't give a good goddam what the books say, son, I know what I know. I was there. Everyone else is dead.

'Memory skewed by time'? Why, for two bits I'd break that there recording machine over your head.

For two bucks and a fifth of bourbon I'll tell you my Quinn story . . .

It was in Lockjaw that I stopped my running. I rode out of the east with gold in my saddlebags and a heaviness in my heart and saw that Lockjaw was the place to hang up my guns. I remember resting a while at the head of the pass that day, watching the town go about its business in the noonday light, knowing from the sleepy main street, gleaming white houses and rich grazing land that a man with something to hide could settle in Lockjaw and never have to account for his past.

I touched my heels to Barrel's flank, cried 'Yeehaa,' and rode on down the incline and into the town. They were brewing coffee in the Cactus Arms saloon. A man in shirtsleeves swept the boards clear in front of the barbershop. A tumble of children crossed in front of me on their way back from the schoolhouse. At the Mills Boon stage depot passengers were boarding the 4.10 coach to Yuma. Outside the jailhouse the sheriff was nailing a wanted poster to the wall—but the face wasn't mine and the name wasn't Cody, so I rode on by. I saw all these things in my ride down Main Street, exchanged nods and howdies with a dozen folk, and lost any doubts I might have had that Lockjaw was the place.

I dismounted at the Silhouette Livery Stable, booked Barrel in for a service, and found a room in Ma Cartland's boarding house situated on the corner of Thataway and Main. Wyatt was the name I travelled under then. It had been a while since I'd used Cody.

Ma Cartland eyed me speculatively. 'You fixin' to stay long, Mr Wyatt?'

White-haired, old, haughty, spoilt, draped in a fluffy pink gown, cradling a puffed-up white dog in her arms, she had a smothering presence. 'Fixin' to settle down here,' I told her.

She eyed my Colt. She didn't need to say anything more, and the moment I was alone I unbuckled my gunbelt and packed it away. The good people of Lockjaw didn't wear guns. They weren't fussed that I was a stranger but they were fussed that I was a stranger wearing a Colt .44 Pacemaker low on the hip, so I took off that gun and I hoped I'd never have to wear it again.

I slept for the remainder of that first day and all of

the first night. I'd been four days on the road, pushing hard, putting distance between myself and the people who had put a price on my head. I awoke with a sense of purpose and relief the next day. After sampling Ma Cartland's coffee and grits, I bought myself a new set of clothes and crossed the street to the Titles Office. Twenty-four hours later, I was the owner of the Fourex, a small spread on the south side of town. A week later I bought a herd of longhorns. I had put the past behind me.

The first year passed peaceably enough. I kept my head down and nobody bothered me. I bought all my provisions in Lockjaw, occasionally stopping by the Cactus Arms for a shot of whiskey and a round of five-card stud with Doc Marten, the consumptive gambling man who was a permanent fixture in the place. Now and then I'd talk a while with Donna, the sharp, knowing owner of the saloon, or one of her girls. The temptation was there, but I didn't take it. Sheriff Marshall dropped by the Fourex a couple of times. I was wary around him, but not unduly concerned. Marshall was a weak man, bored, with little to do. Mostly I worked the ranch; it meant everything to me, it was all I wanted out of life.

Then in the spring of eighteen and seventy-eight I met two people who were to turn my life around. The wealthiest man in those parts was a rancher called Rochester. My place was a mere pimple on the northern boundary of the Bar B Q, Rochester's spread. A widower with two small children, Rochester was tall, brooding, vigorous, a man of natural-born authority and power. He owned the town; he owned the people in it.

One evening Rochester invited me to dine at the Bar B Q. His children showed me into the house, a boy and a girl aged six and eight. They were tireless, chattering charmers both of them, in the care of their governess, Miss Heyer.

Miss Georgette, as everyone called her, had green eyes in a smiling, spirited face. She was about twenty, a sweet, gentle, uncomplicated creature whom the children clearly adored. Her type was not unusual on the frontier. A young woman of good education and breeding, she had come west to do good works. She was alone in the world, her parents having died of the fever when she was twelve.

I bowed. 'Miss Georgette.'

Miss Georgette touched her hand to mine. 'Mr Wyatt,' she said gravely, her voice a soft, husky murmur.

She turned then to attend to the children hanging upon her skirts—but not before I witnessed a moment of appraisal in the green eyes that had roamed briefly across my face. Her loveliness was muted by simplicity, so I might easily have overlooked her if it had not been for that look. Now I could not get her out of my thoughts.

A short time later, other guests began arriving. Donna was there, in the company of a silver-haired man calling himself Robert James Lee Budgie, vice-president of the Indian Pacific Railroad Corporation. Now, that interested me. Lockjaw was served by the Mills Boon stage line. There was no railroad thereabouts. But I had no time to dwell on that, for soon we were called to the dining room.

The talk was civilised, the wine and brandy flowed freely, and Rochester's Chinee cook had fared well with the yearling calf. I held my own in the conversation, but it was a queer business. I was among robber barons, hard men who wore a veneer of respectability. What would they have made of me, had my past been revealed to them?

You listening to this, young fella? I'd been barely out of kneepants when I killed my first man, at the siege of Vicksburg. By the time I was fifteen I could ride and shoot and kill as well as any man. The rallying cry was the Confederacy, but the Confederacy meant nothing to me, just as the Union would have meant nothing had I been born north of the Mason-Dixon line. I was indifferent to collective solutions or creeds, hostile to being organised by any man or outfit.

The confusion and turmoil of the War Between the States gave me the cover I needed to operate alone. I spent those long years pillaging plantation houses, raiding banks, intercepting payrolls, looting the quartermaster's store. I carted boots and horses across the line and returned with wagonloads of sabres and carbines.

When things got hot for me I rode a while with Quantrell's Raiders, true scum, vicious, rapacious men. That's how I first met Quinn. I soon got out, but it was one of the disappointments of my life to see hoodlums from both sides spreading through the west after the war, bringing their ugliness with them. Men like Quinn. They would steal on a whim and kill without motive. If hired for a job they pulled a cross. If there had been any honour in my line of work, those men surely dirtied it.

I felt increasingly out of time and out of place. And note this: it was a final act of treachery by Harley Quinn that drove me to find a safe haven in Lockjaw and begin a new life.

Back to Rochester's dinner party. I remember hearing laughter at the head of the table, where Rochester sat with Miss Georgette on one side of him and Donna on the other. Something Rochester had said, some rough-edged aside, had discomposed Miss Georgette. Her breasts heaved and a slow flush spread to her throat and shoulders. Her eyes caught the sympathy in my gaze and she quickly looked away. Rochester paused a moment to sip from his glass, his fleshy lips coiling on the rim, and continued with what he was saying.

I looked to see what Donna was making of him. She was doing all the laughing. It was a loud, rich, free-wheeling laugh that issued from the pit of her belly. She was beautiful and sophisticated but there was a hard, experienced edge to it all the same, as if she were permanently disillusioned with whatever life had thrown into her path. She seemed to be paying a lot of attention to Rochester that evening, resting her hand on his fore-arm, leaning close to him. I couldn't help but notice her skin in the lamplight. It fairly glowed, dark and rich like a costly liquid. I guess a lot of men in Lockjaw knew that skin. A lot of men had heard her sing at the Cactus Arms, too, and seen the sinuous animal intensity that animated her. 'M'Donna,' they'd cry. 'M'Donna.'

It struck me then that Donna and Rochester were lovers. I mused on that. If she were to become the new Mrs Rochester, then some adjustments would have to be made in the household. I'd witnessed the surreptitious kick she'd landed on the hound that slumbered on

Rochester's hearth rug, and the unutterable looks of boredom she'd directed upon his children.

I glanced at Miss Georgette. It was clear to me that the lovely young governess was thinking along similar lines. She was watching Rochester intently. Pain crawled across her face. She loved his children, loved that dog, as though they were her own.

More of that rich laughter, Donna tipping back her long throat. It was infectious and I felt an elbow nudge me as R. J. L. Budgie hunched over to cackle in my ear: 'That's M'Donna.'

I stared at him. The leer left his face and his features settled into their familiar scowl. 'She's got a good head on her shoulders,' he said. 'She's investing in the railroad. What about you, Mr Wyatt?'

'What railroad?'

Ex-governor of an insignificant state and now a hack for a large corporation, Budgie relied on his man-of-the-people appeal to get him through the day. 'Why,' he said expansively, 'Indian Pacific is putting a line right through Lockjaw. It will mean jobs and prosperity for everyone.'

I asked for more details. 'Ask Rochester,' Budgie said vaguely, dismissing me.

I let the matter drop and talked guns for a while with Sheriff Marshall. We'd both heard about a revolver that never needed reloading, a useful thing in a shoot-out. Meanwhile I was acutely aware of the drama being played out at the head of the table. That young, innocent, yearning girl; her accomplished rival; the man seated between them, successful, well-bred, beautifully dressed. I can't deny that I felt a twist in my heart. But I could not let myself love Miss Georgette, and if she knew who I was, she would never love me.

After a while I grew tired of all the talk. A life on the edge had not prepared me for endless small talk and civility. Finding an appropriate moment, I bowed to the women and shook hands with the men and took my leave.

Rochester saw me out. We lingered on the stoop, talking idly in the light from the moon, watching the nigger saddle Barrel. Then Rochester looked at me keenly and said, 'Did Budgie mention the railroad?'

I nodded. Something was coming up and I waited, all my senses alert.

'You might want to invest,' Rochester said.

'Mebbe,' I said shortly.

Rochester watched me, his head tipped to one side. He was a powerful man, accustomed to getting his way in the world. 'We'll more than make it worth your while,' he said, 'on account of your losses.'

I stared at him flatly. 'What losses?'

'Didn't Budgie tell you? The line goes slap-bang through the centre of your spread. I'm prepared to offer you cash right now and a parcel of shares when the line goes through.'

'You must be joking,' I said harshly.

I swung into the saddle. 'No man touches my Fourex,' I said. Jerking Barrel's head around, I cried 'Yeehaa', touched my heels to his flank, and cantered away from the Bar B Q and into the biggest trouble of my life.

It started modestly enough—broken fences, missing stock, a dead steer fouling the waterhole. Unfortunately, incidents like these are the natural hazards of ranchers, scarcely evidence enough in my case to convince the world that Rochester was trying to force me to sell out—not that there was anyone I could go to, for they were all in Rochester's pocket.

But one night I woke to find the barn burning, the horses screaming in fear and pain. Later a low-down son of a bitch took a shot at me as I was examining mystery tracks in a dry gulch in back of the homestead. My stock began to fetch unaccountably depressed prices at the market. My provisions cost me more and arrived damaged. An Indian Pacific attorney wrote to say that he'd found irregularities in my deed to the Fourex. And a rancher whose spread also bordered on to Rochester's was bushwacked and left for dead.

Then for some reason the harassment stopped and I assumed that Rochester had given up on me. I didn't see him around, and someone mentioned that he had gone back east on business. From time to time I saw Miss Georgette in town or riding the prairie sidesaddle upon her Arab. She was polite enough but distracted, anxious, as if nursing some heartache.

I thought I had gone a long way to banishing her from my mind but one afternoon I encountered her in circumstances that burned her image permanently on my brain. I happened to be walking Barrel along the crick that divided the Fourex from Rochester's spread when I heard singing. The voice had the sweetness and clarity of a songbird and I dismounted to investigate. There, in a broad, still pool under the hanging willows, was Miss Georgette, singing a slow, sad ballad and gently splashing the river water over her long, gleaming flanks. She stretched her arms to the dimpling sunlight and stood to her full height. The breath caught in my throat. Taking in the boyishness of her thin hips, I felt an unbidden quickening in my loins. I was transfixed.

At that moment I noticed a movement on the opposite bank. A hand appeared from a tangle of tumbleweed and crept toward Miss Georgette's petticoats heaped neatly on a dry, flat river stone. There were black hairs on the back of that hand, and before I could act, it snatched up Miss Georgette's clothing with a triumphant cry and R. J. L. Budgie revealed himself. All his features were hooked toward the centre part of his face in a mocking leer.

Miss Georgette froze, doubled over, her poor thin hands darting this way and that to hide her charms. 'You dog, give them back.'

Budgie pursed his lips in consideration. 'What's it worth to you?'

'Why you, you . . . ' she said.

Budgie leered. 'The children's governess, cavorting bare-assed naked in broad daylight? What will Rochester think?'

Miss Georgette tossed her fine head, spraying jewels of water about her shoulders, and advanced on Budgie, naked and unashamed. Oh George, I thought, noting the taut buttocks dimpling and flexing. Budgie meanwhile was goggling at her, uttering snuffling giggles as she drew nearer, picking her way across the submerged stones. She reached the bank and he scrabbled back, still taunting her.

I chose that moment to reveal myself. Standing where Budgie could see me, I levelled the Axminster I

- Returns must be accompanied by the original receipt.
- Returns must be completed within 30 days.
- Merchandise must be in salable condition.
- Opened videos, discs and cassettes may be exchanged for replacement copies of the original items only.
- Periodicals and newspapers may not be returned.
- Items purchased by check may be returned for cash after 10 business days.
- All returned checks will incur a $15 service charge.
- All other refunds will be granted in the form of the original payment.

BORDERS®

- Returns must be accompanied by the original receipt.
- Returns must be completed within 30 days.
- Merchandise must be in salable condition.
- Opened videos, discs and cassettes may be exchanged for replacement copies of the original items only.
- Periodicals and newspapers may not be returned.
- Items purchased by check may be returned for cash after 10 business days.
- All returned checks will incur a $15 service charge.
- All other refunds will be granted in the form of the original payment.

BORDERS®

- Returns must be accompanied by the original receipt.
- Returns must be completed within 30 days.
- Merchandise must be in salable condition.
- Opened videos, discs and cassettes may be exchanged for replacement copies of the original items only.
- Periodicals and newspapers may not be returned.
- Items purchased by check may be returned for cash after 10 business days.
- returned checks will incur a $15 service charge.

BORDERS
BOOKS AND MUSIC
11301 ROCKVILLE PIKE
KENSINGTON MD
(301) 816-1067

STORE: 0010   REG: 15/15 TRAN#: 1292
SALE   05/12/2001 EMP: 00162

HOMICIDE
0758346   MM T   5.99
FLASHFIRE
6255341   CL T   22.95
BACKFLASH
5872375   QP T   12.00

Subtotal   40.94
MARYLAND 5%   2.05
3 Items   Total   42.99
VISA   42.99
ACCT # /5 4356024108232
AUTH: 093458
NAME: ENDICOTT/VIRGINIA

CUSTOMER COPY

05/12/2001 11:07AM

THANK YOU FOR SHOPPING AT BORDERS
PLEASE ASK ABOUT OUR SPECIAL EVENTS

Visit our website @ www.borders.com!

kept strapped to Barrel's saddle and called, 'The joke's gone far enough. Give the lady back her clothes.'

Miss Georgette swung around, spluttering, 'Joke? Hardly a joke, Mr Wyatt.'

She was right. She'd caught me in a thought-error. 'Harassment,' I said. 'Quit harassing the lady, Budgie. Give her back her clothes before I drill you where you stand.'

Budgie flushed. He flung down the skirts and petticoats. 'You'll regret this, Wyatt.'

'People have been telling me that all my life,' I told him. 'Now get lost.'

He blundered away among the trees. 'Miss Georgette,' I said, head averted, bundling the starchy, frothy, cotton garments into her arms. Then I turned my back while Miss Georgette patted herself dry and drew on her skirts. I could hear the soft rustle of fabric on her skin. I felt tense, alive, every nerve ending acutely receptive.

But I got a grip on myself and beat myself mercilessly: *What do you think you're doing? This is a sweet, chaste, innocent creature, and you are a man of the world*, I told myself firmly.

Gradually I recovered. A moment later I felt her soft touch on my quivering back. 'Mr Wyatt,' she said meekly.

I turned. Her chest heaved. So did mine. Abruptly we both looked away.

'Shall we walk a way, Mr Wyatt?'

I fell into step with her and we followed the path beside the water. Her long skirts brushed the ground. My spurs tinkled like temple bells. Insects buzzed in the breathless air. Above us a hawk wheeled in the sky.

Miss Georgette spoke first. She sighed. 'You must not

think ill of me, Mr Wyatt. The sun was so warm, the day so still, the water so inviting.'

'I understand.'

'I knew you would. You're a kind man. I have seen your way with pets and children.'

I felt choked up inside. How could I tell her that I was a man with a past? That I had the blood of a dozen men on my hands? That I'd purchased the Fourex with gold bound for the Bureau of Indian Affairs in Fort Garrison? That people had good reason to consider me cold, prohibitive, unimpressed?

Yet I was also a man driven by sadness and a deep hurt. Kindness and warmth had always existed in me. And here, for the first time, a young, sweet, boyish creature had recognised and drawn out those qualities. Miss Georgette understood me. I had not let myself love her before that moment, for she was temporarily unavailable, owing to her misguided attachment to Rochester, but now I felt hope.

Until she said suddenly, passionately: 'Oh, why is he so blind?'

I raised my eyebrow inquiringly. 'Miss Georgette?'

'Mr Rochester,' she explained sadly. 'I cannot let myself love him—not when he surrounds himself with men like Budgie, not when he gives his attention to that painted creature from the Cactus Arms. Can she seriously be considered as a wife and a mother to his children? She is fatally shopsoiled.' Turning to me beseechingly, Miss Georgette said, 'They will bleed him dry—can't he see that?'

What could I say? 'Well, I mean . . . '

But she was walking again, intense and passionate.

We came to a clearing and she put her hand on my arm. 'There's a mystery in Mr Rochester, some deep sadness in his past. I know that I can uncover it, if only he would let me.' She looked away sadly. 'But he is not yet available to me. I must hold myself in readiness until he is.'

To strangle the cry in my throat I took out my harmonica. Soon tones of longing, heartache and loneliness wailed and sobbed in the still air of the clearing. Miss Georgette watched me, head cocked, listening intently. When she had the rhythm she began to sing along with me, a hushed, bitter-sweet melody. It was a moment of astonishing gravity and beauty.

I saw Miss Georgette home, tipped my hat to her, cried 'Yeehaa,' and rode Barrel back across the sagebrush plain to the Fourex. I can say that I retired a little from life in the days that followed. I dreamed of Miss Georgette. I dreamed that she would recognise and appreciate my essential goodness. A chaste kiss. Her thin form trembling in my embrace. Her sweet submission on our wedding night. Only by punishing and rewarding her exactingly could I form her, tear off her chrysalis, make her mine forever.

Of course, what I should have been paying attention to in all that time was Rochester. It seems that he had grown impatient and decided to fix me once and for all.

My first inkling of trouble came the day I saw him handing a wad of cash to a stranger outside the First International on Thataway. I remember that I was hitching Barrel to the rail next to the telegraph office at the time, taking the time to tie a firm knot (too often would you see guys simply wrap the reins around the rail one turn, so you'd be distracted by thoughts of the horse wandering away).

Anyhow, they were watching me. The stranger was tall, with the slightly down-at-heel look of a decent man who makes an honest buck where and when he can find it. His hat was pushed casually to the back of his head, revealing a wry, bony, genial face. He was standing next to his horse, a weathered old hack you wouldn't look twice at. 'Falcon,' I think he called it, when he finally rode off.

I went into the telegraph office. 'Who's the stranger?'

Woody Grizzly looked up at me from under his green eyeshade. 'With Rochester? That's Cliff Hanger, the Pinkerton's man.'

I nodded thoughtfully. I had a pretty good idea what Rochester would be wanting with a private detective. Armed with my description and a few facts, this Cliff Hanger would start retracing my movements over the past couple of years and uncover secrets that were best kept buried. Rochester wanted a lever to use against me.

Sure enough, a week or so later, just on high noon, I rode in from the range, tied up outside the Cactus Arms, and came face to face with The Kid.

You know the type. You'd see his quick and glittering hunger and meanness in every saloon in every town in the west. He didn't make a move straightaway, just waited until I had propped myself at the bar and tossed down a shot of whisky and started on a beer chaser. I could sense his curled lip.

'Don't look like no gunfighter to me,' he said.

I swallowed my beer.

'Don't look like he killed no dozen men. Don't look like he robbed no banks.'

Over in the corner, Doc Marten fanned his cards and drawled, 'Drop it, Kid. Go on home to your Ma.'

The Kid sneered. 'Stay out of this, old man. Me and Cody here—sorry, me and *Wyatt* here—have got some unfinished business to attend to.'

I turned to look at him. A young, sulky face, under-nourished skinny frame, right hand itching over the Widowmaker riding low on his hip. I turned away again.

He came closer, jostling my drinking arm. Beer sloshed over the bar and dripped on my boots. 'Well, hell,' the Kid drawled. 'Cain't even drink without spilling his liquor.'

I signalled to the barman for another beer. He poured it, worry lines creasing his face. 'Kid,' he said, 'don't make trouble for yourself. You just ain't fast enough.'

It seemed the whole town had the lowdown on who I was. Clearly the Pinkerton's man had uncovered plenty and Rochester had wasted no time in spreading it around, hoping every quick-draw punk in the county would come running to Lockjaw to prove himself against me.

I turned. 'What's your name, Kid?'

'No name,' the Kid snarled. 'I come and I go. No name.'

I nodded, turned back to my beer.

'Your sister sleeps with nigras,' the Kid said. 'Your mother is so old and ugly now, even the horses over to the Silhouette livery stable wouldn't want her.'

Well, that did it. Quite apart from the thought-error and stereotyping, no low-down, yellow-bellied son of a bitch was going to insult my women and get away with it. 'Take it back, Kid.'

'Won't.'

'Will.'

As if by magic, the gun appeared in his hand. He was quick, make no mistake about that. If I'd been packing my Pacemaker, if I hadn't hung up my holster and turned my back on the past, the Kid might have got the drop on me. I gulped.

But at that moment, Donna materialised behind the Kid. She had a chair in both hands and she slugged him with it. The chair splintered as if it were a stage prop, the Kid's eyes rolled back in their sockets, and he dropped like a stone. A kind of relieved exhalation spread through the room.

'Damn, Donna,' I said.

I'd wanted a crack at him, for then the solution would have been in my hands. 'Damn.'

'Don't I get any thanks, big boy?'

She weaved toward me through the cowpokes and gamblers, her breasts riding high and proud, her eyes relishing me. 'Wouldn't want no holes in that pretty hide,' she said, placing her palm flat on my chest.

I winked, clicked my tongue. 'That's M'Donna.'

'My room, big boy.'

I sighed. 'Oh, Donna,' I said, my tone heavy with regret. I sighed again, and touched my fingers to her cheek. 'Donna, Donna, Donna.'

Did she understand? A long moment passed. I braced myself. No woman likes to be rejected.

But then she smiled. It was frank and generous.

Donna was a diamond under it all. We smiled together, shrugged, sighed philosophically. She understood.

I went out. The town was quiet as I walked down the sidewalk, climbed into the saddle, rode out, but in my wake there was an unmistakeable ripple of mingled apprehension and respect.

News travelled fast. The next day, fresh after riding the purple sage, I was consuming coffee and beans in my kitchen, lifting a cheek from the chair from time to time, when I heard a horse pull up in the yard outside. Rochester? Sheriff Marshall? I fanned the door on my way out and saw that it was Miss Georgette.

I watched her dismount. Her colour was high, her eyes flashing. Waves of alarming heat rushed through me as she drew near. Then, for the first time, I knew the crushing dominance of her lips, the bruising strength of her arms. My heart pounded, wild pulsations affecting every nerve in my body. Great shuddering sighs racked us and our energies surged together as though we were a bold eagle gliding over the vast prairie.

But then, the unimaginable. Miss Georgette pressed her—you know, her *toilet area*—hard against mine in a frank and knowing gesture and I heard her murmur eagerly through swollen lips: 'Oh, Mr Wyatt. Did you really kill all those men? Did you really rob those banks?'

Some temporary madness must have come over her. Humiliated at such a frank display from my darling, I tore myself away. We stood apart, panting, staring at one another. 'Miss Georgette,' I said, reaching out a puzzled, imploring hand.

There was a moment's bewilderment, then anger, and finally mortification. I saw the desire ebb in her eyes.

She swung wordlessly onto her Arab and cantered away, leaving me in a state of confusion and misery.

In the days that followed I dumbly went about my business. Were they alike under their skirts? Another possibility occurred to me, no less hurtful. Had Rochester rebuffed and so thoroughly ignored Miss Georgette that she had looked for cheap physical solace with me?

Was that all I was good for?

But no. When I had time to gather my tumultuous thoughts together I realised what had happened. The poor girl had finally acknowledged our mutual attraction and, momentarily derailed by the power of it, had given it an inappropriate expression. I knew that in her normal state she would gladly wait for me.

I observed her closely whenever our paths crossed after that. Sure enough, Miss Georgette flushed if she saw me, cast down her eyes, hurried to the other side of the street with a mortified little cry.

Meanwhile I knew that Rochester probably hadn't finished with me. With great reluctance I strapped on my Colt again, wearing it day and night, out on the range and in the town. Men crossed the street or avoided eye contact when they saw me coming. Sometimes there was a hush when I walked down Main Street—only the *clint, clint* of my spurs and the dry thud of my boots.

It was a still and brooding day, that final day in Lockjaw. All sounds were amplified under the great dome of the sky. I had parked Barrel, checked left and right, and was crossing Main when slow, slow and wailing, building to a lonely, iconographic note, came the cry of a jew's-harp. I knew that sound. I froze on the steps of

IBM Hardware opposite Ma Cartland's boarding house and slowly turned, shading my eyes.

A figure stepped out into the sunlight. Tall and expressionless, he wore the kind of ankle-length oilcloth coat that keeps you dry as a bone, a hat tipped low and black over his eyes, a cheroot in his bloodless lips.

He scratched his whiskery jaw. The cheroot scooted from one corner of his mouth to the other. 'Cody,' he said.

'Harley.'

When I'd last seen Harley Quinn there had been a smoking Colt in his fist. A child lay dead at his feet, and he had been daring the good citizens of Candy Mountain to take him. Froth flecked his lips, I recall. You want to make a motion picture about a man like that? Anyway, sickened, I had retreated into the bank with the saddle-bags of gold and slipped out the rear door.

'You ran out on me,' Quinn said now.

'I asked you to keep watch,' I said, 'not shoot an innocent child.'

Quinn shrugged. 'She was bugging me.'

We eyed each other. 'Rochester's detective found you.'

Quinn shrugged again, then hooked the edge of his long coat behind his holstered Colt. His movements were challenging, deliberate. He was trying to unnerve me, but any apprehension I might have been feeling simply vanished at that point. I mean, Quinn *looked* good, but show me a man who can draw effectively when his coat-tails are tangling his gun arm!

'How much is Rochester paying you?'

Quinn's eyes narrowed. 'You ran off with my share of the gold, Cody.'

We watched each other in silence. 'How are we going to do this?'

'We do it right here,' Quinn replied, 'in broad daylight. We stand back to back, count off ten paces, turn and draw.'

'No worries.'

I met him at the intersection of Main and Thataway, a broad, open arena in the baking sunlight. At the edges of my vision, people were scurrying for cover and there were faces in all the windows. Quinn and I got into position, back to back, his trim backside brushing fleetingly against mine. I wriggled to get comfortable, remembering a friendship lost forever.

Then he said *one* loudly and he was moving. I turned where I stood and watched him walk, counting his paces. I drew my gun. I cocked it. No, I did not shoot him in the back. At the count of eight Quinn whirled around, snatching for his gun, and I shot him where he stood. He dropped like a stone, his heels drumming the dust.

I stood over him. He was dying, the light fading from his eyes. 'You cheated,' he croaked.

'So did you. That wasn't ten paces.'

'Your cheat was bigger than my cheat,' Quinn said, and that was all he said, for the death rattle sounded then and the life ebbed from his body.

I'm telling you, son—that's the way it happened.

Anyhow, I straightened, looked around. Cautious heads were showing themselves around doorways and soon people were gathering to gaze upon Harley Quinn's prone hide. I turned and walked away, people falling back as I passed among them.

Barrel eyed me nervously, his nostrils flaring, one hoof striking the dust. I put my hand to his silky neck and whispered words of comfort. When he was still I swung onto his back and touched my spurs to his flank, called 'Yeehaa,' and cantered down the street and out of Lockjaw forever.

People watched me go. I heard their murmured awe.

'What did he say? Yaahee?'

'Sounded like Yeehaa.'

'Yeehaa?'

'Sort of means *Giddap* or *Forward ho*.'

'Couldn't be forward ho. That's for getting a wagon train on the move.'

And so on.

This was the final stage. I had unfinished business to attend to and I pushed Barrel hard out of town and along the trail that led to the Bar B Q. Rochester appeared as I dismounted, as grave, courteous and impeccably dressed as ever. 'Mr Wyatt,' he said.

'Rochester.'

'Coffee?'

'I didn't come here for small talk, Rochester.'

At that moment the screen door banged open and Miss Georgette appeared at Rochester's side. She was tousle-haired, an unhealthy flush on her skin, as if she had recently risen from her sickbed. 'Miss Georgette,' I said, lifting my hat.

Miss Georgette blinked. She yawned absently and scratched her thigh. She closed her eyes briefly, the lids heavy, the lashes resting on her plump cheeks. Then she opened them wide and looked up at Rochester's hawk-like face. 'I thought you said he—'

'You thought he said I was dead?' I interrupted.

She shrugged.

I had intended to shoot it out with Rochester, but here was an opportunity to reveal his crimes and true nature as well. Miss Georgette surely knew that he was fatally shopsoiled and could not be considered as husband material on that count alone, but it wouldn't hurt to reinforce the notion by revealing his vaunting ambition and greed.

Keeping one eye on Miss Georgette, I said: 'Rochester, you rustled my cattle, poisoned my waterhole, burnt my barn.'

Miss Georgette yawned.

'When that failed,' I went on, 'you hired a detective to look into my past. You knew that nameless youngsters would try to make a name for themselves by going up against me.'

Miss Georgette scratched her breast. I could hear the scrape of her fingernail; I saw the barely covered flesh move under it.

I cleared my throat. 'Finally you sent Quinn against me, knowing he wanted me dead and could beat me if anyone could.' I paused. 'He lost.'

Looking full at Miss Georgette I concluded, 'Your crimes and true nature stand revealed, Rochester.'

Rochester frowned, looked at the sky, tapped the toe of his boot in the dirt. Miss Georgette tugged at his sleeve. 'Honey,' she pleaded. 'Come back inside.'

I have to say that it didn't go quite as I'd imagined

it. 'Corruption,' I said. 'Greed. You're shallow and evil, Rochester. I call on you to draw.'

Rochester drew before I'd finished the sentence. He fired, missed. I fired and missed.

This went on for a while. We both felt exposed there in the open and headed for cover, me to the horse trough, Rochester into the barn. Miss Georgette remained on the stoop, wringing her hands, screaming, stuff like that.

A dry click in the stillness. The hammer of my Pacemaker had fallen on an empty chamber. Rochester heard it. 'You out, Wyatt?'

'Yep,' I said shortly.

'So am I.'

He edged into the open. I got to my feet. We eyed each other warily. Eventually I said, 'It's finished, Rochester. I'm leaving. Take the Fourex, it's yours.'

He laughed bitterly. 'Mine? Budgie's you mean. He bled me dry. He made a fool out of all of us. I've lost everything.'

Miss Georgette was staring at him open-mouthed. 'Lost everything?'

'The lot. I'm sorry, honey.'

She stamped her slender foot. 'Shit, shit, shit.'

He shrugged sheepishly. 'Like I said, I'm sorry.'

She was clearly confused. 'It's not supposed to go like this. You saw that I was the right woman for you after all. My reward for waiting was clearly laid out. Now you say it's all gone? I can't believe it.'

She turned her back on him contemptuously. 'Take me with you, Mr Wyatt.'

My heart swelled. The wool had finally been lifted

from her eyes. 'Why sure, Miss Georgette. Fetch your Arab.'

'He's not mine. He belongs to the children. We'll buy one.'

I scratched my head. 'I guess maybe I could rustle up a few dollars.'

She stared at me, puzzled, trying to take it in. 'But the gold,' she said finally.

'Hell, Miss Georgette, that gold is long gone,' I told her.

'Shit, shit, shit.'

'Honey,' Rochester said wearily, 'take the horse, he's yours.'

And there and then that fine young thing strapped a regular saddle to her mount and rode off into the sunset, leaving me to wonder, along with Rochester: *Who was that woman, under that mask?*

That's my Harley Quinn story, son. Take it or leave it.

BARBARA VINE

Stalking Moon

Funny how things turn out. Ever since the cradle I'd been burdened by a kind of restlessness. It had me circling the country in a clapped-out Kombi, taking the hippie trail overland to London, looking for the perfect wave in Honolulu, knocking about in South-East Asia, even studying medicine in a late shot at a productive career. It seemed important always to be moving on. Then, in the fifth decade of my existence, I found myself back where I'd started from, in the old house on the Peninsula, in retreat from life and love. What I didn't know was, there were others there more at risk than I had been.

On my first night home, Allie tuned the radio to the local community FM station in time for me to hear Neil announce: 'And this track is dedicated to my brother-in-law. Russ, glad to have you with us, old son.' The song was 'I've Been Everywhere'. I got a rueful laugh out of that. It was true that I'd been everywhere and true that my sister was glad to have me back again but you couldn't say that Neil was glad about it.

The song finished. Insects buzzed against the lamp in the corner of the room. It was late and I glanced at the man in the armchair next to Allie's. He was Mike Wedding, the local policeman. 'Our best friend', was how Allie had introduced him when he'd dropped by for dinner earlier in the evening. When Neil had left for work after a late dessert—he was DJ on the 11 p.m. to 3 a.m. slot—Wedding stayed on, saying he hoped the good citizens of the Peninsula weren't out killing, maiming or robbing one another. I liked him. He was a calm, reliable-looking man, someone who'd listened to lies and evasions for all of his life but hadn't let it harden him.

He yawned. 'Time I wasn't here.'

He shook my hand, kissed Allie tenderly goodbye and let himself out. We settled back in our armchairs again, too full and lazy to move. Neil's voice murmured over the airwaves, background noise.

'Ever listened right through?'

Allie laughed. 'I'd be a wreck the next day. I listen till I know Neil's safely at work and the show's under way, then I feel I can go to bed.' She added self-consciously, 'Otherwise I wouldn't be able to sleep.'

I was about to say something, but she stopped me. We heard Neil announce: 'And this one's for that special someone in my life. She knows who she is. Indulge me, folks, while I flog it yet again.'

Neil was a volunteer at the station. Apart from sponging off my sister, it was the only work he did. He liked to play Emmylou Harris, Paul Kelly, Hank Snow, Rita Coolidge, Dolly Parton, songs of loneliness, love and heartache for those people who were still awake when the rest of the world was asleep. He was a glossy charmer, a man who encouraged his listeners to call in for an on-air chat and who specialised in long, quirky meditations he called 'Life's Like That'. You wouldn't know that he was full of grievances and bitter envy under all that charm. You wouldn't know that he drank too much, you wouldn't know the cruelty of his tongue. I watched Allie now, the special someone in his life, as Willie Nelson's 'Moonlight Becomes You' drifted through the room.

A troubled expression passed fleetingly across her face. Eventually she closed her eyes and hummed along. I went to bed.

I slept for twelve hours and woke to find that I had the place to myself. Allie lectured at the naval college in the afternoons. Neil liked to haunt the art and craft barns and antique shops dotted about the Peninsula, searching for records to play on his show. I made a sandwich and settled under the fig tree with a book. I could hear the sea beyond the tea trees that fringed the lawn at the edge of the cliff. The book was heavy in my hands. I felt a little jumpy from the chemical residue still in my system. I wondered what I had made of my life and if I were in any position to judge my brother-in-law.

You may have noticed the house and wondered about its sprawling air of privilege and seclusion along a dead-end road above the beach, maybe even picked up a sense of the generations returning, summer after summer, for six weeks of quiet play—sundowners on the verandah, sprinklers flinging jewels of water across the lawn tennis court, classical music leaking through the open French windows, serious hardcovers face-down on the deckchairs under the fig tree—well removed from the smells of petrol, cheap sunblock and salt and vinegar, the roaring panel vans, caravan parks and takeaway joints on the busy side of the Peninsula.

You'd think *What a life!* but, back when I was seventeen, all I wanted to do was get away from all that rarefied air. I wanted the open road, some risk and chance in my life, far from the civilised, deadening notions of my family.

Allie stayed. She inherited the house when our parents died and married a man I loathed. Both things stopped me from visiting her as often as I should have. But when life went sour on me who else could I turn to? I lost money on a couple of ventures, kept hurting the people I loved, got caught sniffing halothane in the operating theatre, and was finally asked, more or less politely, to clean myself up or be struck off the medical register. I blinked awake one morning, gave a kind of shudder at what I'd become, and asked Allie if I could come home. I called it 'home'. 'Of course,' she said. I didn't ask what Neil said.

The side gate squeaked. I cranked my head around. The man approaching me across the lawn had the clenched-fist, raw-edged look of someone with a grievance.

'Get up,' he said.

I did, but only because I felt safer on my feet. I kept the deckchair between us.

'You know why I'm here. Stay away from her.'

I seemed to be playing a part in a farce. 'Who?'

'Cassie.'

'Don't know what you're talking about. Look—'

'You're Neil Monkhouse, right?'

'No.'

He wasn't listening. 'I looked in this book she's always writing in. It was there in black and white, Neil this, Neil that. Stay away from her or I'll fucking kill you.'

'You've got the wrong person,' I said.

'She told me last night she wants me to move out. She's keeping the boy. Arsehole, home-wrecker, leave us alone.'

'Neil's not here. Nor is his wife, who happens to be my sister. Clear off. You're trespassing.'

Underneath all the bluster, the man was distressed. His face suddenly crumpled, embarrassed, ashamed, grieving, and his shoulders slumped. 'She told me to get out.'

That had happened to me, too, more than once. 'Not my problem,' I said. 'You'll have to deal with it yourself.'

He stared at me miserably, forming words that wouldn't come. After a while he walked back across the grass. 'Can't. Can't get through to her.'

It was because I disliked my brother-in-law that I didn't take him aside and warn him about the man. Instead, I waited until I had Allie and Neil together, at the dinner table, before dropping my bombshell.

I didn't get the reaction I'd been expecting.

'Oh Neil,' Allie said, clasping his forearm. She has a lovely face, my sister, but right then it looked strained, the skin tight over her fine cheekbones.

Neil shook his well-tended head in bewilderment. 'All this stuff happening around me and I haven't done a thing to deserve it.'

He poured himself another Scotch. He was a good-looking man, with the kind of moody dark scowl that you might find soulful or attractive—until you noticed all the things that were missing from his make-up. Of course, his listeners heard only the honeyed voice, dispensing wisdom, offering a lifeline in the dark and lonely hours when their defences were down.

Allie knew. But people like Allie remain loyal to the grave. She turned to me. 'One of Neil's listeners is fixated on him. A woman called Cassandra Lyle. That must have been her husband you saw today.'

My face must have said something like *No smoke without fire*, for Neil shouted, 'Six months she's been hassling me.'

'Several letters a week,' Allie explained. 'Sometimes several letters a *day*.'

Neil seemed to like being at the heart of a drama. He leaned avidly across the table. 'It's even got to the stage where I've developed this phobia about emptying the letterbox.'

I trod carefully, with an apologetic glance at Allie. 'You haven't encouraged her in any way?'

'Never laid eyes on her. I encourage her by existing, full stop. I mean, she's got access to me, right, listening to the show?'

'How did it start?'

'She wrote telling me about a second-hand record shop over on the bay. I wrote to thank her, simple as that. How was I to know what she was like? Things escalated after that.'

'Rapidly,' Allie said.

I wondered what he'd written. I wondered if he'd read something between the lines of Cassandra Lyle's letter, a come-on that he in turn implied he might act upon one day. He had the freedom for it, after all, with Allie out every afternoon and his own days free. 'Well, the husband certainly thinks you're having an affair.'

'No way.'

'Does Mike know you're being harassed?'

'I've told him.'

'And?'

'He says there's nothing much the police can do.'

'Have you kept any of the woman's letters?'

'Have I?' Neil laughed, a short, harsh bark. 'Wait here.'

He went out and came back with a shoebox crammed with letters and postcards. 'There you are, *doc*. See what happens in the real world.'

I flushed at his tone. It seemed to please him that I'd come home with my tail between my legs, a man who'd enjoyed privileges he'd never had yet who'd still managed to come unstuck. It made him feel better about himself. I picked up the top letter. Cassandra Lyle's handwriting was round, unpractised:

> *I waited two hours for you. It's a long way for me by bus. There is only one coffee shop near the library, so you couldn't have gone to the wrong one. I could kill you. I could put Don's rifle to your head and pull the trigger. And your wife. She can't give you what I can. You must not treat me this way. I will give you a second chance. Here is a voucher for the Bay City Natural Healing Clinic. Meet me there on Wednesday morning at 10, tell the receptionist you've got an appointment with Cassandra. We can have a cubicle to ourselves. Don't be shy. You won't have to kiss me or anything. I know I'm not beautiful like the women who throw themselves at you but I think*

you could learn to love me. We could keep our clothes on or maybe just strip to our underclothes. I don't know all the pressure points yet but Jade says I have a good technique. Already I know some that help with my headaches. Please, please, please don't forsake me this time. I know from your voice when it's me you're talking to on the air. It is ordained, Neil, don't fight it. Remember, vengeance is mine. I don't want to punish you but I could, in the blink of an eye.

I looked up. 'Are they all like this?'

'Pretty much.'

'Sounds like erotomania,' I said, remembering a term from a med-school psych class.

'We tried marking her letters "return to sender",' Allie said, 'hoping it would put her off, but even that seemed to encourage her, a sign that she'd made contact.'

Neil laughed. 'It's a catch 22. We can't win.'

I shook the letter at my sister and her husband. They seemed to be so immersed in their own obsessive response to this woman's obsession that they couldn't see the danger they were in. 'She's threatening to kill you both. The police will have to act.'

But Neil had the confidence of his huge self-love and his adoring audience. 'She's out of her tree, that's all. Doesn't mean anything.'

Allie put in: 'And look how her handwriting changes. Look how she veers from anger to abject humility in the space of a few lines. Poor woman. A pain in the neck, but essentially harmless.'

'Has she ever been here?'

'No.'

'Any phone calls?'

Allie shook her head. 'That would make it too real. She's happy just fantasising.'

'Yeah, until the day she steps over the line and comes looking for some kind of reckoning.'

Neil curled his lip at me as if to say: *You'd know all about stepping over the line*. I ignored him and read the remainder of Cassandra Lyle's letters. In a couple of them she laid out elaborate plans by which Neil could test Allie's love for him. She promised to make him a millionaire, hinting at showbiz contacts and the songs they'd write together. He would adopt her teenage son and learn to love him. One letter was ten pages long, a coy yet fervent declaration of erotic love.

Mood swings, yearning, sadness, aggression—they were present in all of the letters. But the clincher was Lyle's conviction that she was the child of God and that Neil had been chosen to marry and mate with her. Time was running out. It had to be done by the year 2000. 'Think,' she wrote, 'of the power we'll have to lead the righteous and vanquish the damned.'

I glanced at Neil. At once he said, almost proudly: 'See what I have to put up with?'

If I'd had a mud pie in my possession then I might have shoved it into his face.

There was a knock on the back door and Mike Wedding walked in, dressed in his uniform this time. He gave Allie a shy kiss, acknowledged me with a nod, shook Neil's hand reservedly. 'Just thought I'd pop in.'

Neil launched into a jokey banter about the cushy life of the small-town cop. He seemed to think he was returning to an old joke between them—and missed entirely the flicker of outrage on Wedding's face.

I cut across my brother-in-law: 'Mike, we had an unwelcome visitor today.'

I went on to tell him about Cassandra Lyle's husband, his threats, his manner. 'But I don't think he's the problem. His wife is. She's going quietly mad and I doubt if he's aware of it.' I got out the letter. 'Here she's threatening to kill Allie and Neil.'

Wedding was sharp and attentive as I spoke, shooting worried glances at Allie from time to time, finally settling his gaze on Neil, who sniggered and shook his head and muttered, 'Mad bitch.'

'I'll call around and talk to the woman,' Mike said finally. 'Uniform, police car, it might be the shock she needs. And I'll have a quiet word with the husband, let him know what his wife's been up to.'

I walked Mike to his car. It was a fast, dramatic-looking pursuit car festooned with lights and the words 'police' in black and a thick black number on the roof. We shook hands. 'Maybe you could confiscate their gun?'

He pursed his lips. 'Not a bad idea.'

The days passed. It was Mike Wedding's custom to drop by once or twice a week for a meal or a chat. He'd been doing it for years. It occurred to me that he was keeping a watchful eye on things. He knew what Neil was like and he wanted Neil to know that he knew.

The first time he came around he had nothing to report. 'School holidays,' he explained. 'I've been flat out.'

The second time, three days later, he said, 'Well, it's done.'

We were eager for the details. He painted a sad picture. 'The husband wasn't there. Apparently he just packed his bags one morning and left. The son answered the door. He's about sixteen, super-protective, didn't want me to come inside.'

'Poor kid,' Neil said, 'living with a mad woman.'

'I don't think she is mad, not on a day-to-day level. She shops, cooks, cleans, takes care of him okay. He's protective because of the husband.'

At this point Mike glanced at a point above Neil's head. 'A pretty abusive type, apparently, jealous, a bit of a mean drunk.'

Neil flushed. I interrupted. 'The woman?'

'Scared, apologetic, fairly vague. Refused to admit anything. Just sat there stiffly, shaking her head. I warned her, that's all I could do. Difficult to say if she was firing on all cylinders or not.'

'*Mike*,' Allie said. 'She's a woman, not a car.'

'But still potentially dangerous,' I said, more sharply than I'd intended. How was I going to get through to her that something had to be done? Then it struck me that none of us had a clear notion of what could or should be done.

As if reading my thoughts, Wedding said, 'We'll see what result my visit has. If nothing changes, Neil will have to take out a restraining order through the courts.'

'You can't have her committed?'

He laughed without much humour. 'We'd have to call in all kinds of experts. It could take months to have her assessed, assuming we were able to convince anyone of the need for it in the first place.' He looked squarely at Neil. 'So don't chuck any of those letters away.'

Allie clutched his arm. 'The gun. She could be a danger to herself or her son.'

Wedding blinked, his business-like face altering at her touch. He said mildly, 'There is no gun. The boy seemed to think there used to be one, a .22 for shooting rabbits, but it's not there now.' He paused. 'Unless the husband took it with him.'

I was picking fruit the next day when a movement caught my eye. A figure walked past the house, then returned, a flickering shape through the box hedge. A woman. Each time she passed the side gate she hesitated, reached out a hand, thought better of it.

I thought I knew who she was. I crossed the grass toward her, calling, 'Mrs Lyle?'

Her face went sulky, as though I'd admonished her. She stepped back onto the dirt track. I slipped through the gate. Fifty metres down, at the corner, a taxi was waiting. The driver had his back to us, rump on the bonnet of his cab, smoking idly. I said it again: 'Mrs Lyle?'

'I, I . . . ,' she said, greatly agitated.

I wouldn't have glanced twice at her in the street. Ordinary pleasant face, skirt and blouse, flat shoes, leather bag on a shoulder strap. She was about thirty-five, small, tired-looking, a little fearful, her face etched with pain and exhaustion.

The words burst out of her. 'Sorry, sorry, sorry. I get so tired. It won't happen again. I won't write you any more letters. A policeman came. It was awful, a police car outside the door. Sorry, sorry, sorry. I just wanted you to know.'

Then, as I watched, an expression of alertness and

cunning replaced the shame. 'You're not him!' Her eyes glittered. 'Who are you?' Her hand went to her mouth: 'You're the wife's boyfriend!' She chuckled, a laugh full of bizarre vigour and glee. 'Wait till he hears about this!'

Another change. Coming close to me now, covert and complicitous, she said, 'You could run off with her. She doesn't love him, you know. Not like I do. Go on—it would be the best solution.'

'I'm his brother-in-law, Mrs Lyle. You're behaving inappropriately. You'd better go now. The police are already involved—do you want to appear in court as well? The shame of it? A restraining order, a psychiatric evaluation, welfare people taking your son away from you?'

I regretted the cruelty as soon as the words left my mouth. She was mad and she might even have been dangerous, but the cruelty was unnecessary. She gasped, went pale, opened and closed her mouth. I'd scared her. Finally she turned and ran, stumbling along the ridged, pot-holey track to the waiting taxi.

Mike Wedding arrived after the evening news, wearing jeans and a T-shirt this time. He ate pasta with us and we discussed Cassandra Lyle.

'Was she threatening?'

'Apologetic.'

Neil interrupted, saying what he'd been saying for the past few hours: '*She came to my house!*'

He was heavy-looking in the jowls that night, surly with all the Scotch he'd tossed down his gullet. Mike looked at him coldly. 'I made no promises. It's up to you now. A court order or at least a lawyer's letter warning her off.'

Neil scowled. 'That's going to cost.'

'Yep,' I said.

Allie said wearily, 'Neil, I'll pay for it.'

His face cleared. 'Guess it's worth a try.'

Mike left after a helping of the quinces I'd stewed from the ancient tree in the backyard. I used to climb that tree. There was even a length of rotting, greenish rope still tied around one of the lower branches. It had comforted me, seeing that rope again. And stewing the fruit had been a comfort, using my hands, giving my head a rest.

At 10.30 Neil loaded a stack of LPs, tapes and singles into a file box and drove to 3PEN-FM. At five to eleven Allie turned the radio on. I listened with her. The transformation in her face, from anxiety to edgy contentment, brought on an old feeling, a kind of sulkiness.

Neil was good at his job, I'll give him that much. He drew out the shy callers, joked with the jokers, cut smoothly across the garrulous. He didn't patronise, was engaging and patient. But he did assume that the average Australian was white, male, Anglo-Saxon and living in the bush, and that grated on me after a while.

At twelve o'clock he said, 'The witching hour. At this time every night we play a listener's request. Remember, all you have to do is write in. Tonight we have Sandy, from Seaford. Gedday, Sandy.'

Nothing, only a hiss in the atmosphere.

'You're on air, Sandy. Go ahead, I won't bite.'

Shyly, hesitatingly: 'Is that Neil?'

I froze. Cassandra Lyle.

'Sure is, love. I see you've requested 'Moonlight Becomes You', by Willie Nelson. And a beautiful moonlit night it is, too, let me tell you. Moonlight on the sea, moon shadows on the fields, the brushing wings of owls. Who's the lucky fella?'

Cassandra Lyle sounded confused. 'You're playing it for me, Neil.'

'I know that, love. What I meant was, who are you dedicating it to?'

Pause. Then—softly, admonishingly, as the song opened and began to swell behind her voice—Cassandra Lyle said: 'Neil, you always play it for *me*, the special someone in your life. I can always tell when you're talking directly to me and no-one else. I can tell from the signals you give out that I'm the one. It's ordained—'

Neil must have been sitting there thunderstruck, or he'd have activated the delay button much earlier. There was an unmistakeable '*Fuck*,' a too-late cough, as he cut her off.

Then there was an electronic whoop, as if he'd knocked the stylus in his attempts to snatch the record from the turntable. 'Sorry about that, folks. Technical hitch. Record's scratched. Moving right along . . . '

Allie was staring at me, the strain back in her face. 'That was her, wasn't it?'

'Yes.'

Her head collapsed back into a deep corner of the armchair. 'That was *our* song.'

They had a fight when he got home. There were heavy closed doors between us and plenty of high-ceilinged rooms and corridors to absorb the sounds, but I heard them nevertheless, enraged bellows and eruptive shrieks. *Couldn't you tell from the handwriting? Come home and you expect me to put up with this shit on top of everything else? Ruined. Tired of playing it anyway.* Once I thought I heard a slap, some kind of blow to the flesh. A form of self-disgust settled in me. I hadn't the moral authority, courage or indignation to intervene. Some people have it. Mike Wedding probably had it. I didn't.

On the surface they were arguing about a love song spoilt for them by a mad stranger, but really they were arguing about the slipperiness of that love to begin with, the void that lay there underneath. And they were paralysed and afraid.

The following evening Mike Wedding dropped in for a quick bowl of soup. 'Sorry guys,' he said, 'I guess I must've triggered something in her. Neil, you be careful.' He left soon afterwards, complaining, 'Pay day, always a bad night for us.' Neil left at 10.30. He held Allie tight for some time, murmuring endearments.

I sat up with Allie. She seemed to want it. I was deep in a book—I'd begun to read biographies and autobiographies, curious to learn how other people faced their wrong turns and doubts and fears—and wasn't aware that anything was wrong until Allie said agitatedly: 'It's after eleven. Where is he?'

I listened. Someone, probably the 8 to 11 announcer, had left a tape playing in the studio, some interminable, mind-numbing rainbow-and-waterfall music. No-one announced the time, no-one read the news, no-one read the community notices, no-one gave the station call sign.

'Phone them,' I suggested. 'There's sure to be a technician on duty.'

Allie complied. She tapped in the number, listened, held the handpiece away from her as though it were diseased. 'Engaged.'

She returned to her chair. She sat stiffly, knees together, hands clasped in her lap.

'Perhaps his car broke down,' I said.

She didn't reply.

At midnight there was a knock on the back door. Mike Wedding came through the house to us, calling Allie's name in a tone that seemed to carry dread and anxiety in it. He appeared at the door, moved urgently over to embrace her as she stood up. 'You'd better come. Russ, bring your medical kit. I think Neil's been shot.'

3PEN-FM was two minutes' drive away. Mike had called an ambulance but there'd been a spate of accidents on the Peninsula and the expected delay was twenty minutes. Neil's van was parked at the side of the building. Its headlights were still burning. As our lights swept over it, I saw a slumped shape in the driver's seat, a lolling head.

According to Mike, the station technician had noticed the headlights, heard the motor running, and come out to investigate. Thinking that Neil had had a heart attack, he felt for a pulse in his neck, and got fresh blood on his hands.

'Far as I can tell,' Mike said, 'Neil's been shot twice in the back of the head. Probably small calibre, like a .22, or he'd be dead by now.'

We got out. I established that Neil had a weak pulse,

checked his torso for other wounds, then dressed the head wounds. There were no exit wounds. I held him half-cradled in my arms. 'There's nothing more I can do,' I said. The air, I noticed, was chilly. We were losing summer fast.

Allie went with the ambulance. Mike wanted me to accompany him to the Lyle woman's house. 'She could need sedating. She could be suicidal.' He paused. 'If not before I question her, then certainly after.'

'You think she did it?'

'Don't you?'

I shrugged. *The husband, the son*, I thought. I strapped on my seatbelt. 'So long as you don't expect me to go up against a gun.'

Mike wasn't listening. He sped us through the night, through the darkened towns and past shadowy horse studs, deer farms and orchards. In all the vineyards, fine-mesh anti-bird netting caught the pale moon, an effect of long, lumpy worms side by side on the terraced slopes. The side window had been down in Neil's van. He must have pulled into the parking bay, reached for the ignition, then felt the cold nudge of the gun barrel behind his ear.

Cassandra Lyle and her son lived in a weatherboard house on an acre of dead grass and car bodies outside a small industrial bayside town. You'd go quietly—even noisily—mad in a place like that and no-one would ever know about it.

Lights were blazing inside. Mike warned me, 'Stay here,' and ran in a crouch to the porch and through the door. He had his police revolver out. He looked mean enough to use it. I hoped he wouldn't. If this were the city he'd have been able to call in back-up.

He was gone for about two minutes. He came out looking shaken. 'You'd better come and look at this.'

The interior smelt of damp carpets and damp foundations. There were cracks in the plasterboard walls. The ready-built furniture wore a cheap, fierce sheen and the shelves and tabletops were loaded down with glazed miniatures—dogs, cats, milkmaids in bonnets and skirts. Mike took me through to a cramped bedroom and another of the world's miserable tragedies. Someone had put a gun to the son's head and shot him as he slept in his narrow bed.

'Where is she?'

'Not in the house,' Wedding said. 'I'll check outside.'

There was no pulse. Rigor mortis was setting in. I looked around at the posters—Magic Johnson, swimwear pinups. There was a fat paperback on the floor, bookmarked with a letter. The return address was somewhere in New Zealand and the boy's father had written: 'My dear son. You can reach me at Auntie Kay's any time, night or day. I know things haven't been good. Maybe Mum needs a rest from me. Just remember, you old Dad loves you.'

What mother shoots her son?

'Their car's missing,' Mike said, coming back for me. 'I'll call this in, then I'd better run you home.'

Allie was waiting for us. 'He's gone,' she said simply. 'Died an hour ago. I came home. I couldn't stay there.'

All the tension seemed to leave Mike in a ragged sound close to a sob. He went to put his arms around my sister but she inclined herself toward me, leaving him to flounder a little. So he touched her shoulder and said softly, 'I'll drop by tomorrow.'

I heard about the killings and the roadblocks on the morning news. Mike and the other Peninsula coppers must have spent the whole night searching for the Lyle woman, but it did them no good at all. They would have been searching for a fugitive in full flight. They would have had no reason to search along the bracken-choked track that continues past the house where I had spent my childhood.

I was the only one who used that track. It was part of my self-imposed rehabilitation to walk through the long hours of the day, down the private steps that had been cut into the cliff by my grandfather, along the beach to the distant blowhole, and back along the clifftop.

Allie was still asleep, sedated from the night before, when I left the house. I found the car on my way back. It was a rusty yellow Datsun, and Cassandra Lyle had climbed into the rear of the car to shoot herself. She was upright, the .22 rifle between her knees, the muzzle under her jaw. I examined her. She was cold and dead. I supposed that it made sense for Cassandra Lyle to kill herself after what she'd done, and do it close to where the object of her twisted love had lived.

I set out again, toward the house. I felt keenly awake. I hadn't felt so awake in a long time. My system was clean, my head uncluttered finally. I began to muse on the things that didn't fit. One, Cassandra Lyle had come by taxi the day I saw her. Was it possible that she didn't know how to drive a car? I turned around, went back to the yellow Datsun. The driver's seat was positioned for a tallish person. Cassandra Lyle was short.

Two, the rifle was a long-barrelled .22. The distance from the muzzle to the trigger was greater than the reach of Cassandra Lyle's meagre arms.

Three, the blood in a dead body pools and settles after death. I'd have expected to see signs of lividity in the buttocks and thighs of a woman who'd died in a seated position. In Cassandra Lyle the signs of lividity were all along the back of her body. She'd been killed lying down, transported to the scene some time later, and propped upright with the murder weapon between her knees.

These were the doubts I'd be putting to Mike Wedding and the coroner when they came to examine the body. I rehearsed them as I walked back along the track to the house where I'd long ago lost a sense of purpose and only recently found it again.

I had an answer ready: *the husband*. New Zealand was only a few hours away by air. The fact that he'd posted a letter from there a couple of days ago didn't mean that he wasn't about to fly back to Australia.

I passed under the kitchen window. The ground slopes there, so that the rear half of the house is elevated. Mike Wedding had called in while I'd been out. He was talking to Allie, and at first I didn't hear the words, only the tone—low, concentrated and heartfelt—so that I thought this was a private moment between old friends and I ought to leave them alone for a while.

Until Allie said distinctly, 'Don't, please don't, it's not appropriate, you're mistaken.'

And Wedding replied, 'He wasn't right for you.'

I stopped to listen.

'I loved him. He loved me, in his way.'

'He used to hit you, Allie. You loved me, I know you did. I read the signals.'

'Please don't do this.'

'You told me so every time I saw you. The way you did your hair, the way you sat in your chair, the way you placed your knife and fork on the plate. I read the signals.'

'Mike—'

There was fear in Allie's voice. The fear got to me and I went in, went in against a killer, and I was thinking: we hurt the ones we love and we are legion.

Scrapings

Colby was drawn, one sodden morning in February, to a magazine kiosk by a canal bridge, to certain cold-hearted figures staring from the calendars on display for the tourists. *Febbraio. Carnevale.* Within a hatch, behind banked newspapers and wire racks, sat the vendor, an old woman almost in darkness. Chill and gloom clung to her. Colby stamped his feet on the wintry stone. In every calendar treacherous, two-faced figures were populating the parapets and squares of the city. They were whiter than ghosts and blacker than midnight, still and watchful in their black capes, and Colby felt unsettled by them, sensing blood on the flagstones. Until that moment he'd felt almost at home, able to move unencumbered through the city and his daily affairs, but here was a reminder of his provisional state. No-one had informed him that the city had a carnival. Nearby a butcher heaved open a metal shutter, disturbing the pigeons. They erupted, leaving a detritus of grime and fluff on the green iron canopy of the kiosk, and in the smaller canals the ice was splintering.

Colby turned away and climbed the approach steps of the stone bridge. He could feel the blank faces of the calendars behind him, withholding, utterly still, as if waiting for a death. He crossed the canal, entered the narrow corridor beyond the bridge, and turned side-on to avoid the wall-scraping umbrellas. People ducked and weaved around him, on their way to work, muttering *permesso*, *scusi*. The men wore cashmere overcoats, the women furs, and their gleaming shoes rang out in the hollows of the city.

The little street opened onto a deserted square. At the far end a woman entered a bread shop. A cafe proprietor swept his doorway with a twig broom. Colby began to cross, avoiding the erupted roots of the solitary tree and the water collecting in pools between the flagstones. He liked to take this route because of the well at the centre of the square. A ring of white stone, polished by shoe leather over the centuries, was set into the base of a low, circular wall. A black iron lid covered it, hinged and massive. It was Colby's daily habit to trail his fingers over the knobs on the lid. There were a number of them, smooth and cool, every one irresistible.

But at that moment school children ran into the square, met at the well, and ran on again, and Colby missed his chance. A boy more daring than the others called '*Ciao bella*,' to the girls. The girls swung their cases, pushed open their tartan umbrellas, and took one another by the hand, while the boys played up to them and again the pigeons rose and flapped away.

Colby trailed the children into an alley between the wall of a barracks and the side window of a framing shop, in which an empty gilded frame sat upon a velvet chair. Then the dusty window gave way to crumbling plastered stone and Colby found himself in a region of dampness and urgency again. Rain fell. People hurried by. Above him a man opened his shutters and hauled in a clothesline. Someone was brewing coffee in the apartments opposite the barracks. As Colby passed the studded doors, the sentry on duty turned negligently, the eye of his machine-gun sweeping across Colby's chest.

The street ended at a path that ran beside a small canal, and here Colby came upon the children again. They prowled along the tatty wall posters, jostling and declaiming: 'Miles Davis . . . *I Musici* . . . Jurassic Park . . . Madonna.' At once they all sang out: 'Who's that girl . . . ?' A black gate opened. The children disappeared into a courtyard. Colby glimpsed a cat twitching its tail, a small fat Pan, weather-stained terracotta urns, a palm tree set in chips of white gravel.

A hot country in the cold season.

'Signor Colby.'

Colby paused at the steps leading down to the crypt.

'Signor Colby,' said the caretaker again.

The man had been in the shadows behind the pitted column of the church, scraping up candle wax with a little trowel Colby had once given him. Colby waited. The caretaker reached him and gestured with the trowel.

'Yes?'

'Signor Nye was here. He asks you to join him in the Bar Rocca this morning at 10.'

Colby thanked the caretaker and descended into the crypt, a dim, low-ceilinged place that attracted the floodwaters. The electric fires were burning but still the stone walls and floor exhaled dampness.

Piera turned from her work, smiled, said good

morning. Her face was hawkish and dramatic in the spotlights, and her movements were reproduced in alarming black swoops across the fresco. The electric fires spat and popped. 'Good morning,' Colby said.

He called up to Allesandro: 'Good morning.'

Allesandro was crouched on a plank, preoccupied with the helpless white hands of the Virgin. His shoes shifted in answer. Colby left it at that. Allesandro was an uncomfortable man, full of insupportable burdens. He sought order at work, but he didn't always find it. Colby was the Australian. There had been one before him and when his year here was up, there would be another Australian. They were barely tolerated by Allesandro.

Colby hung his overcoat on a hook, stepped into a pair of overalls, and rummaged in his locker. He found his razor—an old bone-handled cutthroat—and began to scrape minutely at the shoulder of the Archangel. Colby's predecessor had reclaimed the robes. Colby was working on the wings. They were half furled, with beautifully articulated joints, and eyes that hunted one another down the plunging feathers.

Piera said companionably: 'They are very beautiful. The colours.'

Together they admired Gabriel's wings. Colby asked: 'How is your snail?'

'He is quite patient. He waits for me to finish the tiles.'

Piera had discovered a snail depicted in the bottom corner of the fresco. She called him 'he'. He had perfect, questing horns and he was gliding, unconcerned, across a tiled floor. He helped to establish perspective in the picture: snail in the foreground, Gabriel kneeling at the centre, the Virgin approaching through an archway at the top.

Piera touched her fingers to the whorled shell on his back, as if that would give her luck. 'On your way, snail,' she said.

At that moment her wrist, turning and flexing, seemed to be joined in beauty with the snail and the angel, and Colby felt an appalling need to touch her. But that wouldn't do. He returned to Gabriel, reason lapping and coiling inside him.

Colby went to the Bar Rocca knowing that Nye would be late. Coldness had reached deep into his bones and so he ordered a pastry cornet and coffee with hot milk. He slid them to the end of the marble bar and stood there, eating rapidly, before Nye could arrive. Colby didn't want Nye to see him eat. Nye never ate anything when the two men met like this, and he never drank coffee. It was Nye's habit to drain a tiny aperitif.

Colby saw Nye enter, shake the drops from his umbrella and edge through the room toward him. All the customers seemed noisier suddenly, the crystal lights and cut-glass cheerier, the smell of coffee much sharper, as if Nye had woken the place up. He reached Colby at the bar. As was his custom he half bowed gravely, toasted Colby with his aperitif, and said in a low, well-bred voice:

'Michael.'

'William,' Colby said.

And Nye drained his glass.

They scarcely knew each other, and this gesture of Nye's was apparently harmless, yet Colby always felt subtly insulted by it.

'Still scraping away?' Nye asked.

One could only say 'Oh, yes' to a question like that. 'And you?' Colby said.

'Busy.'

Colby had never been to Nye's studio. Few people claimed to know where it was. And Colby couldn't imagine Nye daubing paint onto a canvas. That day Nye resembled a fashionable actor in the successful middle years of his career, a talk-show professor or a minor count—a man easily deflected by pleasures but, still, a man you'd not want to cross. As Colby thought these things, people came and went in the Bar Rocca, catching Nye's eye.

Finally Nye turned his back on them and made an effort:

'Listen, Mike, are you going to be around for the next day or two?'

'Yes.'

'My niece is arriving tomorrow. Unfortunately I won't be here. Would you meet her for me?'

Nye was known to disappear for days at a time. People said that he delivered his canvases and had mistresses and attended exhibitions in other cities. It was said that he had houses here and there, all over Europe. 'Fine,' Colby said.

'She'll be on the four o'clock train from Rome. You should hold a sign up, Morag Nye. Settle her in at my apartment, maybe treat her to dinner.'

Nye took money and keys from his wallet and pushed them into Colby's coat pocket. 'I must go,' he said, looking at his watch.

'I'll walk with you.'

'Delighted.'

Again Colby was reminded of his provisional state. Nye took him on an inconceivable route to the water-taxi stop and they crossed squares Colby had never seen before, or only from a different aspect. At one point Nye indicated a restaurant and said, 'Bring Morag here tomorrow night; it's very good,' and at another he made Colby stop on a stone bridge and look along the canal.

'Marvellous, isn't it?'

The rain had stopped. Clouds merged and parted above the two men and the illusory sun lit the ochred walls and lay pale and greasy on the surface of the canal. A barge went by. It ploughed over the sun, leaving it stretched and ragged in the water.

Colby heard voices and looked up. Three small children had appeared on the bridge, full of tricks and secrets. Their faces were masked with white greasepaint, their eyes delineated with broad red and gold commas, and they wore black cloaks. Colby didn't think there was anything innocent about those children, but Nye beamed. 'The first sign,' he said.

The children came closer. Colby watched them warily, but he was too late. In an unprotected moment they threw confetti over him, gouts of it like blood, and rushed on by.

'Marvellous, isn't it?' Nye said.

Colby returned to the crypt. He peered into Gabriel's wings, agitating the filth with a brush this time, thinking of Nye's niece, a stranger, from Sydney, a strange place that had once been familiar to him. He could not recreate Sydney in his mind's eye except as a place with altered and unlikely contours. He found himself brushing and sluicing thoughtlessly, risking error. Nye had that effect on him.

At six o'clock Colby cleaned his razor, brushes and trowels, put on his overcoat, coughed uncertainly. 'Piera,' he said.

She looked up.

'There is a lecture, if you would care to come.'

But she smiled, shook her head, opened and closed the fingers of one hand in the local gesture of farewell. Colby managed a smile. 'Until tomorrow,' he said, returning her wave. As he climbed the steps, and drew level with the top of the fresco, Allesandro seemed to hunch, close and irritable, at the Virgin's wristbone.

The lectures were arranged by the British Institute and held in a church the Americans were restoring, in a precarious upstairs room lighted by candles and subject to air currents. The wooden floors, banisters and wall panels were heavily scored and worn and seemed close to collapse. There were tapestries decaying on the damp walls, grim depictions of martyrs, visions, entombments, the expulsion from the garden.

At the front of the room a slide projector cast a hot square of light onto a plastic screen. Colby was late. He'd first heard about the lectures from Nye, who had wanted to make him feel at home. He'd found himself being introduced to people who said, 'Ah, we knew your predecessor. Would you care to lecture to us too?'

Colby eased unnoticed into a metal chair at the back of the room. The white screen brightened and dulled as shapes passed across it. Last week it had been Scottish new-towns: cement-and-glass shops, banks, housing estates. This week it was carnivals, carnivals in hot countries where flesh was bared and blood was spilled. Soon the elderly Britons, Americans and Anglophile Italians in the room were muttering. A man at the front thumped his cane on the floor. Women turned to one another, their fur coats brushing at the shoulder. They clicked their tongues. 'Would you look at that?' one woman said. Colby imagined their lives: half the year in Venice, half in New York, Nye canvases on their walls.

The lecture finished and they clapped. Clapping, the British Consul's wife walked to the front of the room to thank the lecturer. 'May the spirit of our beloved *Carnevale* never be turned around,' she said.

On the way out, all those fur coats pushed Colby against the wall. He overheard laughter and planning. Seven o'clock: friends and lovers to meet, everyone pressing into the squares of the city.

There was a black mist in the alleys, rolled in again from the sea. Colby walked in darkness to his apartment, navigating the stone corridors from one community of laughter and floating light to the next, and as he passed his wishing well a figure leapt onto the iron lid. A man, gold-faced, wearing a three-cornered hat, a cape and breeches. Colby stood, paralysed. He opened his mouth to protest but the figure cut him off, drawing a gloved hand across his throat.

Four o'clock. Passengers from the Rome train streamed past Colby and on to the main platform. Above him a speaker crackled. He waited, a paper sign held at chest height, and saw a sudden shift in the composition of the pushing crowd as a young woman cut across to where he stood. She set down a heavy suitcase; there was a bulky pack strapped to her back. 'I think I'm the person you want.'

She briefly touched his palm with sunburnt fingers before snatching back her hand and plunging it into the deep pocket of her coat. The collar was up, trapping wings of sun-bleached hair. She looked bored, healthy. As though willing herself, she asked: 'Who are you?'

Colby told her. 'Your uncle had to go to Vienna.'

She laughed, a short laugh, no more than audibly cheerful. 'Or Nice or Milan or Heidelberg.'

'He does have that reputation.' Colby crumpled the paper sign and dropped it into a wire bin. 'Let me take your case.'

They boarded the canal ferry, where Morag Nye seemed to take up a mistrusting position at the brass rail. The sky was low, darkening, trapping sounds to the surface of the canal. The metal gate slid crashingly in the ferryman's hands. A barge passed and the ferry tossed in its bow swell, the diesel motor muttering at the waterline, and as they swept down the canal the gondolas rode at their mooring poles like alerted horses. Colby wanted to point things out to Nye's niece but all the while she faced outwards, staring at the palaces, a withdrawn figure amid the tourists winding their desirous cameras. Finally he moved out of the cold air, into the shelter of the wheelhouse.

A short time later she joined him, but said nothing. She hunched deeper into her coat. Colby said, uselessly, 'You must be feeling the cold.'

'Sydney was having a heatwave.'

The ferry slowed, bumped gently to a stop, and the

ferryman looped a rope around a stanchion. Passengers edged past, onto the quay, and Colby drew back with Nye's niece until they were shoulder to shoulder against the chilly wheelhouse wall. She said:

'Have there been any messages for me?'

'Messages?'

'Yes. Messages. Or letters.'

Embarking passengers began to fill the nearby spaces. Colby said, 'Your uncle didn't mention any.'

The gate clanged; the water surged again. They slid past the casino, galleries and damp, iron-hard buildings. Lighted chandeliers bellied behind flawed window glass in all the palaces along the canal.

'Next stop,' Colby said.

'I know.'

Colby stiffened. Her manner with him was curt, almost as if they were acquaintances who had last seen each other in some extreme—of love, or hatred, or disappointment. So Colby told himself: It's not my problem.

It's not my problem. He'd forgotten that expression. He hadn't used it in months. It was as if he'd forgotten a whole language, the careless, unconsidered, borrowing language of the country he'd left behind him. But now, in an instant, he was miserably at home again: a staff room, dim and populous, everyone wearing an odour of complaint and envy; petrol thick in the overheated air outside; endless tiled roofs baking above pinched and bitter plots of prickly lawn.

The ferry stopped. Colby took up Morag Nye's heavy suitcase and stepped onto the quay.

In the apartment above Nye's the opera singer was running through her scales. Colby unlocked the ground-floor door to the building and at once the singer stopped, as though listening for intruders, to climbing footsteps on the stairs at night. It wasn't Colby's problem, her fear.

There were two locks in Nye's door on the second level. The keys fitted and turned poorly and Morag pushed the timer switch for the stairwell light as Colby struggled. She knew there was a switch. She said nothing, merely waited, giving off a hint of exasperation.

When finally the lock tumblers fell into place, they did so secretively, precisely, reminding Colby of Nye himself. He pushed open the door and Morag entered the hallway ahead of him and hung her coat on a hook on the hallstand. She wore a dark pleated skirt which she smoothed briefly, looking down at her dark-stockinged legs and ankle boots. Then she looked about as if searching for changes. The hallway—small, elaborately tiled and well preserved—had not been redecorated for a hundred years. Candle globes illuminated it, dim behind fussy pink-tinted glass. She tried the first door. 'Bathroom,' she said. 'I remember now.'

Colby hooked his coat on the hallstand and indicated a door at the end of the hallway. 'The kitchen is through there.'

'I know.'

He followed her and they looked around at the modern benches, the glossy white cupboards, the slender white wall oven and refrigerator. 'It used to be old and cluttered,' she said.

Colby opened a door in the corner. 'Like the dining room.'

'Yes.'

By now she had softened a little. She wandered good-naturedly about her uncle's dining room, her expression amused and luxuriating. Nye had once held a small dinner party here for Colby, to introduce him around, his manner exaggeratedly, unseriously formal. The room was perversely old and polished and dark and heavy. Morag picked up and set down again the vases and the photographs in their silver frames. There was no dust, the carpets were not worn, but Colby had an impression of dustiness, of decay in the old, over-decorated fabrics. The curtains—clean—looked soiled, and they pulled down on their supports and brushed the tiles. Nye rarely used the room but he'd left flowers in Morag's honour, two tight red rosebuds in a vase and a camellia head floating in a shallow crystal bowl.

'It's just the same,' Morag said.

'How long has it been?'

'Since I was here? About three years. I had just finished my final exams.'

Colby smiled. 'The big trip to Europe.'

A mistake. Her face sharpened into lines of beauty and intolerance, as if Colby had been assuming common yet mortifying experiences between them. 'Not at all. I'd been several times before.'

'Right.'

Colby followed her back to the hallway, where she opened the door to Nye's living room, a long, well-lit, relaxing room. She began turning over papers and envelopes left on a small table next to the largest armchair.

Once or twice she stopped to examine both sides of a postcard or letter.

'Any messages?'

It took some time for her to notice Colby there in the room with her. He saw an alteration begin in her face, as if she were finally casting off the coldness in favour of joy and bright possibilities ahead. 'No messages. Let's break open the Scotch.'

She made her way directly to a glass-doored cabinet, took out two glasses and malt whisky, and poured two large measures. They sat and toasted each other. She appeared to Colby to be quite at home and she had the attractiveness of those who are knowing, greedy and unsentimental. 'Good old Uncle Will,' she said.

'You're close to him?'

Colby felt a searching scrutiny before her face shut down again. 'Yes.'

'Do you see much of him?'

'Several times here, plus he flies to Sydney twice a year.'

She seemed to want to get away from the subject. 'Has he done this to you before? Got you to meet people for him?'

'Never,' Colby replied. 'I'm not even sure why he asked me. I scarcely know him.'

'You don't have to look after me, by the way. I'm perfectly capable of entertaining myself until he gets back.'

'He mentioned my taking you to a restaurant tonight.'

'I don't think so, thanks.' She stood up. 'I don't remember those.'

Colby watched her cross the room and peer at the

paintings on the wall behind him. Her thighs filled the space before his eyes and then she was moving along the wall.

'Egotistical bugger,' she said, 'they're all his.'

Colby joined her. He had nothing to say about the paintings. When she strolled through a door in the corner, he followed her, and they were in Nye's study, then in his bedroom, a small, unappreciated room with a plain bed and a plain wardrobe and a glass of water on a chair next to the bed. There were no disregarded, familiar or comforting objects in the bedroom and Colby had a sudden and frightening intimation of deprivation in the artist's life.

The telephone rang in the study. Morag stiffened, luxury giving way to unease. 'Will you get that, please?'

'It will be your uncle.'

'Just answer it!'

Colby called down the line mockingly: 'Nye residence, may I help you?'

'I've been trying for hours. Is Morag there?'

It was not Nye. The voice was younger, and loud, competing with background noises, in a bar perhaps. Colby looked across at Nye's niece. She knew; she took the receiver from Colby and began to talk into it, her voice stodgy, telegraphic: 'Ivor, we've been through this before . . . You can't . . . There's no room . . . You can't . . . I wouldn't feel right . . . Ivor, I don't want you to . . . '

Colby returned to the living room and began a circuit of it. Morag came in. She stood, tired and adrift, by the door.

'He's coming here. He's around the corner in a bar.'

'Who is he?'

But she drew back the curtains and opened the balcony doors. A smell layered in dampness, commerce and wintry night rolled in and Colby realised how warm the room had been. They both shivered. Hastily, Morag shut the doors again.

The city's cheap hotels are near the station, down alleys or among souvenir shops in the streets behind the palaces on the canal. Colby stood in the rain outside Nye's apartment building, explaining this.

Ivor hoisted the straps of his duffle bag over one shoulder. 'Is it far?'

'Ten minutes by ferry.'

'I'll walk.'

The rain fell, stubborn and niggling. Ivor disregarded it. He was young, his face narrow and fine-boned as if reduced by coldness, rain and apparent poverty, but he seemed jubilant to Colby, buoyant, a little crazy.

'Have you been here before? It's easy to get lost.'

Ivor shrugged and smiled and made another hoisting movement with his bag. 'I'll manage.' He turned in the wrong direction.

'I'd better come with you,' Colby said.

Colby's life had become irregular, suddenly. He set off along alleys and over the tiny canals that fenced in Nye's segment of the city. Ivor kept pace with him, apparently unsurprised and ungrateful. Ivor was dressed in a long, oil-treated stockman's coat and a black airman's beret, absurd dress that attracted stares from the elegant men and women hurrying to restaurants and concerts. He was inept, and like most inept people he was literate and talkative, bumping Colby's elbow in the cramped streets, talking above the sounds of rain and harsh, crushing footsteps. Colby didn't know the young man's surname. Morag had simply said, 'This is Ivor,' then closed the street door on them.

At one point Colby said carefully, 'Morag didn't seem overjoyed to see you.'

Ivor laughed. He was a youth who laughed at setbacks and discomfort—which doesn't mean that he knows how to deal with them, Colby thought.

'I trailed her all the way from Sydney.'

'Have you known her long?'

And Ivor replied, pointing at the glistening flagstones, 'I could write "eternity" all over this city.'

He was young, young and unformed, his head full of strange, soft, sad notions. With relief, Colby delivered him to the Villanova, a hotel at the intersection of six stony streets behind the casino. Then, stricken at the sight of the young man's hollow cheeks, he said: 'Come on, I'm treating you to a hot meal.'

Ivor beamed. Colby found a tiny restaurant in a back street. Just as they were waiting for a table, Colby saw Piera step from one room to another in the cramped family quarters behind the servery door. So this was where and how she lived. He had time to notice a lilac tracksuit and a cigarette, and he heard her shout at her mother, her mother shout back. Then Piera saw him, put her slender fingers to her temple in an odd gesture of irritation, and disappeared. To Colby the encounter was almost like calling unexpectedly on a new lover in an unguarded moment, when she is faintly close and muggy, her mood scratchy. His face burned.

They ate. Colby didn't see Piera again. He took Ivor back to the Villanova and left him. Ivor was not his problem.

This time Harlequin and Columbine found him. He was passing the fish market when they materialised from the shadows, paced silently with him to the next corner, then veered away, fading into an alley that Colby was convinced went nowhere but simply stopped dead at the canal wall.

The next day was Sunday. On Sundays Colby liked to walk, roaming wherever the streets took him. He was like a zigzagging pinball, striking a glancing blow to churches, galleries, palaces, a wall of Moorish windows, a well with a black iron lid. He didn't need a map. He would walk for hours, startling the pigeons, watched by silent cats in barred windows.

Nye found him in the Campo Santa Maria Formosa. Colby had stopped to watch the tourists, who were in a buying mood. Stallholders had been allowed to set splintery trestle tables on the stones, and the tourist were buying masks, gowns, three-cornered hats. They were not buying from the Wannabuys on the perimeter, the thin north Africans who sold belts and cheap watches displayed on blankets and whispered, 'Wannabuy?' Colby watched, and heard Nye call his name above the whispers.

Then Nye emerged and clasped his shoulders. 'Michael!'

It was an uncharacteristic display of enthusiasm. Colby looked past Nye and understood. Morag was with him, and Ivor, and both were laughing, their teeth very white in their brown faces. They looked larger than life among the tidy Europeans, as healthy and prancing as young horses. As Colby watched, Morag held a gleaming white mask to her eyes, and it had the effect of shutting down her face before she reappeared, her eyes shining. Ivor meanwhile spun around on the spot, his cape flying around him.

Colby turned to Nye. 'When did you get back?'

'This morning.'

'Shopping for carnival costumes?'

Nye clasped Colby again. 'We must make a party of it one night.'

Colby said, 'Those two are getting on better. Last night I—'

Nye came close to him, lowering his voice. 'It's an act. He bores her. He's bored me in the few minutes I've known him. She's being kind to him.' He stood back. 'Thanks for meeting her. I'm most grateful. Needless to say I didn't know about the other business.'

By 'other business' Colby supposed that he meant Ivor. At that point Ivor kissed Morag and both men witnessed it. It was a simple act of affection but it was also a crashing mistake. Morag froze. Hatred glittered on Nye's tartar's face. Colby thought: *Forget it, Ivor. Go home.*

At six the next morning Colby was woken by a punt delivering crates to the bar across the canal from his apartment. He showered in his tiny bathroom, set coffee to brew, and slipped out, in the local manner, to buy bread and a pastry for breakfast. He arrived at the crypt at eight, before the others, and started work on Gabriel's wingtips. The floodwaters had softened them badly. It was like working with a soggy biscuit.

Piera came in, gravely beautiful, wearing soft wool and leather. She watched Colby for a while. 'What is your friend doing today?'

Colby explained that Ivor was not his friend, that he'd never met the young man before.

Piera pursed her lips and there was a hint of judgment in her dark eyes. 'He has somewhere to stay? The city is full for *Carnevale*.'

Colby named the hotel. He said again, 'I don't know him. What he does is his business.'

He felt a little hostile, sensing hostility. Piera said, 'I think he is lonely.'

That was the end of it and they worked through the morning in silence. Then at one o'clock Nye arrived with Morag. At once Allesandro and Piera grew animated. They liked Nye; they approved of him. Colby found himself stepping back as Nye and Morag were shown around the crypt. Morag's face was composed of high cheekbones and hollows, constantly shifting in the light of the lamps and the electric fires. She seemed to be in a state of suppressed excitement. So did Nye. They stopped to examine the box of tools, trowels, brushes and scrapers, and as Morag touched them she trembled a little.

They left a cold centre behind them when they departed. 'Michael,' Nye said, at the bottom of the steps, 'we'll see you later in the week. We're off to the Dolomites for a few days.'

He didn't mention Ivor.

Ivor appeared on Colby's doorstep the next morning,

huddled stiff as rope in his waterproof coat. His long face broke into a grin. 'Could I ask a favour?'

Colby felt his heart sink. Ivor had a daypack on one shoulder, the duffle bag on the other. 'Look, I'm sorry, my place simply isn't big enough, no spare bed, only two poky rooms.'

He was rattling on. Ivor cut him off, laughing. 'No need to panic. I just need to store this'—he dropped the duffle bag onto the doorstep—'for a few days. Some family from Munich has my room booked till after the carnival. Everywhere else is full.'

He looked at Colby. He was a youth brimming with goodwill. 'Sure,' Colby said. 'But where will you stay?'

Ivor gestured carelessly. 'Oh, I'll just hit the road for a few days, travelling light.' He rubbed his hands together. 'But Morag's taking me around the islands in the lagoon first. Great morning for it!'

Colby frowned. 'Are you sure? Isn't she going to the Dolomites with Nye?'

At once Ivor looked moody, hunted, all his youthfulness gone. 'It wouldn't be the first time,' he muttered.

Colby guessed that he meant *the first time she's stood me up*. 'Visit the islands anyway. You might find a hotel on one of them.'

'Michael,' Ivor said, looking directly at Colby, 'do you think there's anything going on between them?'

The moment Ivor said it, Colby knew it was true. Nothing else explained the languorous familiarity between Nye and the niece, the sense they gave of a secret history together.

He tried to formulate an answer, but Ivor saved him. 'Sorry, forget I said it, sorry,' he said.

The city seemed to tremble and hum now, marked by nervous energy and display. Colby could feel it when he walked in the evenings. A piazza that had been flat and stony damp one day might be hung with lights and flags the next. Bands played under the arches of the fish market on the Grand Canal. Young backpackers idled around fountains and monuments, and Colby recognised the songs they meekly sang, Joan Baez and Bob Dylan. He bought himself an eyemask on an elastic strap, and in the streets and on the humped bridges he was ceaselessly brushed by capes and gowns as soft and richly coloured as a monarch's.

He trembled. He joined the thronging crowds, got to bed late, worked an unimagined magic on the Archangel's wings by day. The razor was missing from his locker, lost or strayed or stolen, yet he scarcely grieved for it. Even the city's underside caused his blood to beat—the broken glass, unaccountable tears and cries and dejection in the hidden corridors deep in the night, the discarded syringes on the icy flagstones outside his front door.

Finally he said, late in the week: 'Piera, dance with me tonight.'

She uncoiled from the fresco. She had found the shadow cast by her snail, no more than a faint smudge of darkness on the tiled floor. Her teeth flashed at Colby. 'Dance with you!'

It was not a question or incredulity. Colby understood that Piera was considering him, an evening with him. 'Where?'

'Piazza San Marco. There is an orchestra. Everyone dances.'

Colby felt alive and he saw a warm light show in her face, getting warmer.

'We must be masked and costumed,' she told him.

'Of course.'

Allesandro was soundless on his plank high in the crypt but Allesandro didn't have to speak to communicate his disapproval. Colby could feel it crackling over the surface of the man's crouched spine. His problem, not mine, Colby told himself.

He discovered another side to Piera.

'The Bridge of Sighs, eight o'clock,' she'd said. He waited. At twenty-five minutes past the hour he felt an old blackness settle in him, compounded of the damp hour and old, remembered hurts. The people of the city were parading past him, pirates, courtesans and ermined counts, and Colby waited, exposed on the Bridge of Sighs. Those cruel, dead white faces: Colby imagined the cruelty and deceit behind the masks.

Until, for the fourth time, a figure passed so close to him that he was forced to press against the balustrade. She was dressed in black, eye-masked, a tiara flashing in her black hair. He said, 'Piera?' his fingers trailing over her departing cape.

She turned and grinned. 'This way, that way, this way, that way, for ten minutes now. Is my disguise so convincing?'

She didn't say *Or are you an anxious and thereby unperceiving man in love?* but her tone was faintly teasing, and Colby spun her away from there, toward St Mark's Square. He talked and laughed, to regain lost ground. He took her past a poulterer's, where scrawny plucked hens dressed as barmaids and musketeers swung against the plate glass. He gave her coins to toss to a clutch of Brazilian pan-pipers. He bought her a drink in Florian's, where she told him about Keats and Shelley. The noise: they had to shout, and her breath was warm against Colby's ear, her arm warm against his own. Colby felt a great affection for all the hooded figures now, after days of being spooked by them. He'd been mistaken. They weren't heartless or unreadable, white-faced and black-hearted: they simply loved life. He loved life.

Colby and Piera looked out onto the square. Dancers swirled, and Colby counted the beat: one two three, one two three. As he watched, a transfiguring sea mist rolled in and the dancers became dream dancers. It was an embracing mist this time. It wasn't the kind of mist that would hunt a friendless Colby through dripping stone corridors, licking and coiling at his heels as he made for home after some buttoned-down British Institute lecture. He dragged Piera onto the square and their capes flew out like fans, stirring the mist.

He saw Nye. Colby was sure it was Nye, exposed briefly in a pocket of clear light, bending to take Morag's earlobe in his perfect teeth. He saw Morag draw in her neck, raise her shoulders, wrap herself around her uncle.

Then the mist and other figures reclaimed them and Colby gave himself up to Piera's flexing waist and legs and her healthy delight.

There was no reason to suppose that it was uncle and niece. It had felt like them, that's all, some memory trace stimulated by just that conjunction of lips and chin, just that angle of the throat, just that hint of giddy laughter and greed.

In the crypt the next day Piera glanced warningly up at Allesandro and Colby knew that he should not embrace her or otherwise reveal his turbulent spirit. But she did touch his wrist, she did brush against him.

He worked on the Archangel. The floodwaters had smeared a wrack of industrial waste and detergents on the unfurling wings. Gabriel was as helpless as a gull caught in an oil spill—that's how Colby felt about him, and he crouched close with a brush and soapy water. He needed his razor for this, some gentle scraping to rid the wings of the mass binding them, then finish with the soapy water.

'You haven't seen my razor, by any chance?'

Piera had been in a trance at the glistening track of her snail. Colby had to say it again. She focused on him. 'When did you lose it?'

He shrugged. 'I noticed it missing a couple of days ago. I last used it when Nye was here with his niece. I don't recall using it after that.'

She knew nothing and had nothing to say. Colby tipped back his head. 'Allesandro? Have you seen my razor?'

Nothing. Allesandro had cleared a space around the dove in its descent on the Virgin. The dove represented the Holy Ghost, and Allesandro wore a hallowed silence as he recovered the true white of the lily borne by the dove. Colby sighed and returned to Gabriel's wings. Anyhow, Allesandro disapproved of Colby's scraping techniques, disapproved of his razor. He would know nothing about the razor and nor would he care.

Unless he had hidden it out of spite or disapproval.

Piera lived in a tiny apartment in her parents' apartment, three tiny rooms separated from their quarters by a door at the head of the stairs above the restaurant. 'Sit,' she said, pushing Colby into an armchair. She poured him a glass of wine and found the evening news for him on her television set. 'Wait,' she said, and disappeared down the stairs.

They were showing footage of Torcello when she came back carrying heaped plates on a tray. There had been a murder. Piera stared, aghast, at the screen. Everything about her fascinated Colby. He had seen her poised and unreadable, he had seen her carefree, and now he saw dismay and fear. She had no appetite for her father's cooking. 'That poor boy,' she said.

The body had been discovered in the drainage channel that ran between the isolated ferry stop and the ancient distant church. The camera made a half circle sweep and all you could see was emptiness, flat empty spaces with only a hint of the lagoon, the rushes and the flat island. A perfect place for a killing. The only time Colby had visited the place he had been the only tourist. He remembered thinking at the time that he'd made a mistake, no-one lived there. The land itself was scarcely above the waterline, the water swelling and sucking through the reeds. A perfect place to ambush a young man and slice open his throat.

Piera watched, appalled. No belongings, no identification, no witnesses, no apparent motive. Eels had stripped the flesh from his hands and face, rendering him unrecognisable. So young. So many dangerous places and dangerous men in the world. She said suddenly, 'How is your friend?'

'My friend?'

'The young man you brought to my father's restaurant.'

Colby explained.

'Oh,' Piera said, when he was finished. She did not sound convinced. She seemed to Colby to be chiding him, telling him that a young man adrift in the world was owed charity, that he was everyone's responsibility, no matter who he was or where he came from.

'I'm minding his bag for him,' Colby said.

The appointed day came and Ivor did not collect the bag.

Colby left a note and a map on his door, but Ivor didn't come to the crypt to find him. He waited in his apartment after work, but there was no knock, no phone call. Later he went out to meet Piera, leaving a note. The note was there when he got back.

Ivor did not appear the next day or the next. Colby reasoned: If I tell Piera, she will urge me to inform the police. But I have delayed too long, further proof of my lack of charity. So I will not tell her. Colby knew that this was not enough, but he hoped Ivor would simply show up and sweep all his doubts away.

Then one morning Piera failed to appear at the crypt. A migraine, according to Allesandro. She gets them from time to time, crippling ones. Colby worked badly through the hours, and after work he went to the restaurant. They would not let him go up. The signora shushed him, frowning furiously, turning him around in the corridor and urging him out onto the street. 'Maybe tomorrow, maybe the day after,' she told him.

The city was winding down. The tourists had gone and Colby saw only locals as he made his way to the square. The days and nights seemed icier; he heard ice cracking on the surface of the smaller canals. Colby didn't know why he was returning to the square. There were no dancers, no flags or bunting. There might never have been orchestras playing there.

'Colby,' Nye said.

Nye was approaching arm in arm with his niece along the cloistered walk near the famous bars. Colby stopped. He said immediately: 'Have you seen Ivor?'

'Rather too much of him,' Nye said. 'But I expect you mean: Have we seen Ivor recently? The answer is no.'

Morag said, 'He could be anywhere. Rome, Vienna, Crete. He would like to be regarded as a vagabond, a freewheeling spirit. He's a little out of date, is our Ivor.'

'And out of his depth,' Nye muttered.

Why were they having this conversation, standing face to face like this on the chilly stones? A simple 'no' would have done. 'But I've still got his bag,' Colby said. 'He hasn't been back for it.'

A kind of wary stillness came over Nye and his niece. Then Nye beamed expansively. 'Let's have a drink.'

Colby felt a costly overcoated arm slide around his shoulders. Morag was close on his other side. He turned willingly, almost in relief, almost as if Nye and Morag were draining off all his troubles, and let himself be walked by them across the hard square to the muted yellow lights on the other side. He found himself babbling:

'Incredible to think that I was waltzing right on this spot just a few nights ago.'

'Marvellous,' Nye said.

'I saw you,' Colby said.

Fingers tightened on his elbow. 'What shall we have? *Amari* to burn away the cold?'

They settled into velvety chairs around a gilt table. For a moment in the dimness Colby saw scratchmarks on Nye's forearm. 'Your costumes were the equal of any that I saw during the festival,' he said. He wanted obscurely to flatter them.

Morag said, 'I don't think so.'

She was unsmiling and level with him. 'We were in the Dolomites.'

'We got back yesterday,' Nye said.

We. A simple word but it was a loaded word in the mouths of Morag and Nye. It was loaded with more than simply *We are uncle and niece*. Colby watched for tiny shifts of the body, tiny signals, the *lack* of signals. 'They're banging like a shithouse door,' he told himself, an expression from his old language, a satisfying antidote right now to all this good breeding, polish and high art, all the secrets of the ancient city.

'Ivor wouldn't be dead, would he? They fished a body out of the water while you were away.'

Morag threw back her head. 'Ivor? Ivor has nine lives.'

Nye was calmer and steadier. 'Our young friend will show up, you'll see. Or he's latched on to someone and he'll send for his bag.'

'Exactly,' Morag said.

'You didn't take him to Torcello?'

'Michael,' she said, 'you are beginning to annoy me.'

Half-awake in the half-light of morning, Colby sees his razor move, scraping the waterlogged flesh from Ivor's face, scraping him featureless. Then, turnabout, Ivor's nails rake deeply down Nye's forearm, catching traces of skin. But, before the forensic pathologist can act, the sluicing waters shift in the lagoon, washing the evidence away, leaving Nye to walk a free man upon the earth. Leaving Colby the one with questions to answer. Gloved fists pound upon Colby's door.

Colby sat bolt upright, thinking: *Get rid of the bag*.

He listened. If that had been a knock, it was not repeated. Boots clumping on the bridge, a punt delivering crates of vegetables, the neighbour flinging her shutters open against the wall—all these could account for the sound of a gloved fist pounding upon his door.

Colby sank into his pillows. The last days of the young man called Ivor may have gone like this:

Nye and his niece are lovers. It would not do for the family to learn of this. Perhaps it would not do for the dowagers of Venice to learn of it. Ivor learns of it. He becomes a threat to Nye. Perhaps Nye, sixty and getting older, has additional reasons for fearing the young man.

Ivor becomes a pest. He will not leave the pair alone. Nye is not a man to be crossed, he is not a man to wait. He lets the world understand that he and Morag are in another part of the country, lures Ivor to the lonely towpath, slices open the young throat.

Nye being interviewed by the *carabinieri*:

'We had nothing to do with that young man. However, I understand that Mr Colby spent some time with him. Mr Colby found him a hotel, I believe, and took him to a restaurant. I also understand that some of the young man's possessions are with Mr Colby. In fact, it is entirely possible that Mr Colby was the last person to see him alive.'

Colby put all that together with Nye's visit to the crypt, the missing razor, and saw how neatly he'd been framed, a tidy configuration of circumstantial facts.

Get rid of the bag.

Colby in the interview room this time:

'No, *comandare*, I threw the letter away. It simply said: "Please forward my bag to . . ." '

Where? Colby tried to think of a likely destination.

The razor. Should he buy another one? Scratch and age it convincingly, say that he'd found it again? But wouldn't that announce his guilt? Surely the police had the original razor, left by Nye at the scene, all part of fitting Colby up? Colby pictured Piera and Allesandro in the office of the *comandare*, presented with the two razors. *Are you able to identify which of these is Mr Colby's original razor?*

But the police don't know the identity of the corpse laid out on the slab. Who will point them in the right direction?

Nye.

Colby sat bolt upright again and the light in his eyes was very bright. *Not Nye.* Not now that he knows I saw him here in Venice when he was supposed to be visiting the Dolomites. He won't say anything.

Colby sank back.

Unless Piera voices her doubts. Piera full of scruples, grieving for all the youngsters sliced open by madmen.

Get rid of the bag.

Colby drew on gloves, just as a killer might. He wiped the bag. The first ferry left before sunrise. Colby stashed the bag by a sea wall on the island of the lacemakers and was crouched at the Archangel's wings well before Allesandro arrived for work.

When he got back from siesta there was a note from Nye. Nye had been called away unexpectedly. Would Colby escort Morag to the station on Sunday? Back next week.

The postcard dropped through the flap on Saturday. It was a postcard of Florence, postmarked Florence, exactly the kind of card a backpacker might send. The handwriting was round, vowelly, unformed, exactly the mark of a young man. The tone: full of hesitations, apologies and exclamations. Colby listened for Ivor's voice in it. 'Would you please forward my backpack please, care of the British Institute? Sorry to be such a drag! Uni starts next week! Ciao!'

I don't know your handwriting, Colby thought, but I do know it was a dufflebag you had, not a backpack. Unless you're sloppy with your terminology.

Or Nye heard me say *bag* and interpreted it as *backpack*.

When he called for Morag the next day, Colby said, 'You should travel light, as Ivor does.'

He was feeling marginally safer now that he'd got rid of the bag. He didn't fear Nye or the niece. The niece might still lure him to some dark place but, still, he felt secure enough to needle her a little. Hauling her heavy suitcase to the top of the stairs he said, 'What have you got in here? A body?'

Morag turned, her backpack scraping plaster flakes from the wall. 'Just shove off, Colby. I didn't ask you to help me. I can make my own way to the station.'

'Nope. Your uncle asked me to help you, and here I am. Where's he gone this time? Florence?'

Morag plunged down the steps ahead of him. 'That's right.'

She stopped suddenly, curiously embarrassed. 'No. Paris. He went to Paris.'

'Sorry, sorry. *Ivor* is in Florence, that's right. I just heard from him.'

Carefully: 'Did you?'

Nodding: 'I sent his bag on.'

'Good.'

'What's Nye doing in Paris. A wealthy client?'

'If you must know,' Morag said, 'a gallery wants to stage a retrospective of his work.'

Colby got her to the station. He helped her on to the train. There was no doubt that she was on it when it left the station, meaning she wouldn't be luring him to where Nye could kill him, supposing Nye were still in the city, supposing Nye wanted him dead to begin with.

Colby walked back through the stony passageways, feeling the rain in his shoes, muttering *permesso, scusi*.

Paris, or Florence. Morag had been uncertain, just for a moment, about Nye's destination. It was as if she'd been coached by Nye to tell everyone that he'd gone to Paris, but knew full well he'd gone to Florence in order to fake a postcard from Ivor, and in a momentary lapse of concentration had named the wrong place. You might make a lapse like that if you were under pressure. If you thought you'd been found out, for example.

Piera returned to work on Monday, white, hollow-eyed and closed-down from her days of pain, and when she saw what Colby had done, any dreaming they might have shared together evaporated around them. 'My snail,' she wailed. 'What have you done to my snail?'

She poked at the grey sludge accumulating on the stones at the base of the fresco, the pollutants and the mud left by the floodwaters, the plaster too ancient and friable to cling any longer to the wall. 'Where is he?'

'I'm sorry, Piera,' Colby said.

He'd completed his restoration of the Archangel, and Allesandro on the plank near the ceiling had been cold and repelling, so he'd turned to Piera's snail glistening across the coloured tiles in the foreground. She had been working on his little shadow. Colby had gently washed and brushed, washed and brushed, then watched, helpless, as a plaster flake the size of a child's hand had fallen to the floor and turned instantly black. He'd fished for it. It had crumpled and dissolved like a wafer on the tongue. 'I'm sorry,' he repeated.

She shook her head. She had no energy. Above them, Allesandro's spine seemed to say, 'I told you so.'

But they were experts. This was their craft. Piera touched the tiny, shallow crater in the wall, a smudge of darkness that took in half of the snail and a few centimetres of his shadow beneath him, and murmured, 'I shall fill in the hole, then match the colours and give him back his soul with my paintbrushes.'

She turned and looked up at Colby. 'But it won't be the same!'

'I'll help.'

She hardened. 'No.'

Colby looked around the crypt. Behind the spotlights and the electric fires were the other walls. He had photographs from the archives to guide him. He would be careful, extra careful.

After lunch—bread and soup with a straggle of tourists along a glass wall above the Grand Canal—Colby prowled the margins of the city, conversing uselessly with ghosts. I'm sorry, I'm sorry.

Nye was emerging from the crypt when he got back. 'Just wanted to thank you,' the artist said.

He looked relaxed, a man with no unfinished business hanging over him. To wipe that off his face, Colby said, 'How was Florence?'

Nye knew. It seemed to tickle him as he walked away. 'Paris, old son. Gay Paree.'

'Of course.'

Colby stepped down into the crypt. He worked through the long day, his back to the stiff and reproving backs of Piera and Allesandro. St Sebastian roped to a stake, riddled with arrows, surrounded by the bowmen—no, the *killers*—bending their elbows for another volley. Colby couldn't bear it. He searched the fresco for a place where blood had not stained the soil. According to the archival photographs there were olive groves behind Sebastian, cypressy hillsides.

At one point he was obliged to hunt in the communal box of tricks for a certain brush. That's how he discovered his razor. He picked it up and rolled it from palm to palm, touching every familiar scratch in the blade, every nick on the ebony handle. There was no blood.

He stood for a while, staring through a window of regret, down the decades to his grandfather who stood lathered before a shaving mirror. Even the smell of the soap was in his nostrils. He could have done more for the old man, could have visited him on his deathbed, for example.

That razor. Nye finishing unfinished business? Allesandro making a point? Or had Colby himself misplaced it? Colby could elect any one of these, but he was still a stranger in a strange land, he still couldn't come in from the cold, he didn't think.

Airship

You try to ignore disturbances of sound and light beyond your window glass because you could easily take a gun to the people from the Flamingo Gate townhouses across the street and whenever Liz from next door catches your eye she cavorts on the footpath. But a car alarm has sounded. The woman from two doors down is getting into her red Saab. She likes to wear summery cottons; pale blue today, a full, 1950s style with a broad black belt. According to Liz she is very quiet. Her name is Marion. She paid two hundred and five thousand. You watch her rummage in her lap, straighten, put on sunglasses with both hands, and push her hair behind her ears. She has been in the sun. With her hands up like that, a thin gold chain has dropped to her elbow. She reaches out for the door handle and the chain slips to her wrist again. With those looks, Liz once said, the rest of us might as well give up now. She closes the door and drives away. The street is quiet. Something about her walk and the set of her head these past few mornings tells you she has an apprehension of eyes at her back.

You return to the Apple and edit a media release for a client and fax it through to him. A shadow falls on your desk. Liz is making a maniacal face. Her nose is flattened to the window.

You open the front door and she walks in, saying, 'Can you lend us five dollars?'

You follow her into your room. 'Just till tonight,' she says. 'I need it for the tram, and my lunch.'

She sits on the ergonomic chair and regards the blinking cursor on the screen. She types: *Memories are made of this*. She pushes herself away from the desk and turns the chair around on its castors. She is tall, hectic, tensely boned at the neck and shoulders, but her face is always drowsy and quiescent. In hot weather like this she wears sandals, harem pants and short-sleeved shirts open over singlet tops.

Your wallet is in the bedroom. When you get back to the front room, you see that Liz has keyed in another message. She is standing at the window, looking across at the Flamingo Gate townhouses, her palms on either side of the frame.

She turns around to face you. 'Thanks. I tried Marion, but she wasn't home.'

'She left about half an hour ago.'

'What was it this time, a little silk number?'

You hesitate. 'A little blue number.'

'Blue. Have you talked to her yet?'

'I'm working up to it.'

Liz sighs. She puts her hand to her chest. 'Love blossoming. Right here in my street.'

When she's gone you look at the screen. It reads: *Catch me if you can*.

When the two teenage boys pass across the space where

Marion's car had been you focus on them and not the other things and understand that you should call D24. You press B and listen to the ringing tone. A is programmed with your sister's number. You have not programmed the other keys. A man answers and you tell him you suspect that the flats opposite you are being burgled. 'When I say flats, they're more townhouses.'

'Yes, sir. Your name and address?'

You say, 'They went down the side where the pool is and over the wall.'

'We need your name and address first, sir.'

From the names on the spines in the bookcase you give him Ross Macdonald. He asks you to speak more clearly. He asks it again when you give him Allen Street and a model number from a software disc.

'Now, sir. Describe what you saw.'

You tell him that two youths carrying green and gold nylon sports equipment bags and dressed in multi-coloured board shorts, white T-shirts and, you think, gym boots, had emerged from the shrubs in the garden of the front townhouse and climbed over the bluestone wall at the side of the whole complex, tossing their bags over first.

'You said a pool,' the man says.

'Where they climbed over there's some sort of recreation area with an indoor heated pool and a spa and a sundeck, then a couple more townhouses. They're still in there.'

'Someone will be along soon.'

'The place is a warren,' you tell him.

By soon they do not mean within ten minutes, so you find yourself taking an idle stroll in the sunshine, down Allen to Frome, right, and right again, a generous circuit that takes in three sides of the townhouses. At the far corner you hear whispers in the shrubbery and a bag being zipped. You stroll on; you're just some guy on his way to the milk bar.

But you've raised the temperature for them. And now the muttering sky conspires. The HELM Lager airship is prowling the air currents above the Carlton Gardens. Its white flank passes across the sun. The shadow is on you then gone again like an eye blink. Inside the Flamingo Gate they will be pulling back, retreating for cover among the courtyard trees. You sense this in a tingle of solicitude.

On the way back you pause at the entrance to Allen Street. They have sent a Falcon van with twin blue lights clamped to its roof. A policeman is facing the Flamingo Gate, his hat tipped back, his hands on his hips. You mutter: 'You can't afford it, pal.'

Behind him a second policeman has knocked on Marion's door and is turning away to knock on Liz's. Yours will be next. He catches your eye. You walk on.

They have not blocked any of the exits. They have not bothered to go in. In the milk bar the proprietor's daughter, who is rarely at school, gives you change for the Red Phone and you tell D24 that you happened to be passing some flats and saw kids breaking in.

'Your name and address please, sir.'

You look up. The daughter is near the Coke machine, picking at the split ends in her hair. The old woman, the grandmother, is watching you from her chair in the corner behind the wire bread racks. You turn away and say: 'There's a police car there, in Allen Street, but it's a big place, lots of exits, goes through to the next street.'

'Hold the line.' The voice returns and says, 'The officers attending have been notified again. Thanks for your cooperation.'

Before leaving the milk bar you stand in front of the old woman and ask for a Dutch wholemeal. You have never known her to speak or to move. The daughter hurries around from the cash register, her smile asking you to understand about the old woman. You part the plastic beads in the doorway with the bread and step outside. You are a block away from Allen Street but you can hear the squealing tyres.

You give them half an hour and then go in. Nothing. No broken glass, no scuff marks.

The only thing is a notice taped to the outside of the steamed-up glass doors leading to the spa and the swimming pool: *Flat 12 reserves the rec. room for a party starting 8.00 p.m. on the 24th, thank you for any inconvenience*. You write on it: 'Don't you mean *sorry*?'

Just as you are emerging onto Allen Street from the courtyard, Marion pulls up in her Saab. She gets out and locks her door. It is too late for you to slip back into the courtyard. You begin to pat your pockets for your keys. 'Short cut,' you tell her, jerking your head at the Flamingo Gate.

She pauses to regard you. In one hand she holds the hooked end of a wire coathanger on which hangs a narrow black dress sheathed in plastic wrap. She has been to a hairdresser. She has a fringe now, springing free as though charged. Streaks of white have been pulled through the straw colours. The air around her is scented. You distinguish dry-cleaning fluids and shampoo above the day's toxins. She is half-smiling, waiting for you to go on.

You gesture with your arm, expressing the geography of the area. 'I hate having to go all the way around.'

She says, 'At least you walk. I'm too lazy.'

Her voice is a low, mild growl. She folds the black dress over her forearm. You notice how well shaped her hands are. The fingers are long, the joints narrow and supple. On one finger she wears the kind of old ring passed down by mothers and grandmothers.

'You missed the drama,' you say. 'Police cars, the whole works.'

She inclines her head, telling you to go on.

'Break-ins,' you explain, pointing to the Flamingo Gate.

'Did they catch them?'

You tell her you don't know, you only heard about it.

Suddenly she stiffens. 'Twice where I used to live,' she says. 'Hold this.'

She thrusts the black dress at you, unlocks her front door and disappears inside. You wait. The door has been varnished, not painted. Two frosted panels are set in it. Your own front door is painted the period red and Liz's the period blackish-green popular when the houses were built. You support the black dress by the coathanger, letting it follow the shape of your body. You don't want to drop it. You don't want it to wrinkle. You look down the length of it.

Marion appears in the doorway. 'I didn't mean you had to wait out here. My kitchen could be crawling with hoons.'

It is cool and dim at the back of her house. You stand with her on the slate floor, looking through the glass door at her garden. Her face is close to the glass. 'There,' she says, pointing.

A terracotta pot lies on its side under her Japanese maple. It is broken. Black loam and geraniums have spilt onto the red-brick paving. She turns away. She wrinkles her nose, as though suppressing mirth. 'Liz's cat? Here, I'd better hang that up.'

She takes the dress away and when she returns you see that she has taken off her shoes. This gives her a challenging, flat-footed, skirt-swishing way of walking. 'I see you in the mornings,' she says, 'out of the corner of my eye.'

Your voice catching, you tell her you work from home; the front room is your office.

'How inspiring for you,' she says. 'All our sleepy faces in the mornings, plus the lovely Flamingo Gate.'

You say, 'There's going to be yet another spa party over there tonight.'

Marion mimes suffering in the heat. She pulls at the front of her dress. 'We'll have to get ourselves invited sometime.'

The day is on the turn. The air is laden, the city waiting for a healing wind. At home you close your windows and curtains, tugging at the heavy insulation backing wherever you see a chink of light. You stand for a while in each room. In the bathroom you open the mirror door on the medicine cabinet. One full and one half Valium remain in the foil-and-plastic strip.

Later, when Marion leaves again in her car, you cut through the townhouses to the Safeway on Drummond. Frozen pizza, a spray can of touch-up paint, Earl Grey teabags, laundry powder, other things.

Liz crosses into your backyard from hers during 'The 7.30 Report' and lets herself in the open French window. She has your five dollars but now she wants to borrow your dress shirt, dinner jacket and bow tie. She has been invited to the Women's Ball. She is dressed in scarlet tights and a neon-green tank top. She has very long legs. She expands in your house. She says, 'Crossing to Paul Lyneham in our Canberra studio.'

You turn the sound down. When you come back from the bedroom, she is on one foot, her hands on her hips, pointing and coiling a shimmering leg. She relaxes immediately, fishes a bow tie from the clothing bundled in your arms, and holds it up. 'A clip-on? Is there style anymore?'

'And these.' You spill the shirt studs, in an expensive glitter of ebony and gold, into her palm. A bruised, lazy smile grows on her face. She sways. She draws down her eyelids.

'The police were here this morning,' you tell her.

'I know, Marion told me. I found jemmy marks on my back door.' She places the black tie at her throat. 'Our Marion thinks you're—what was it?—very serious.' She pirouettes. On her way out she points and winks at the television set and says, 'Good point, Paul.'

Their sound system is apparently inside the pool room, for you cannot hear the music, only bass notes that reach you like repeated explosions underground. Guests come and go in the starlight on the sundeck. You took the Valium with a Scotch boost at eleven, when you got home from visiting your sister. At two, when a Silver Top rapped its horn, voices came through the darkness, inviting the driver onto the sundeck. There have been other taxis and cars.

Liz comes home at three. She prowls about in her Volkswagen, searching for a space. When you realise she has begun a set of manoeuvres outside your window you snap out the lamp. You continue to hold *Paris Trout* open, as though reading it in the dark. You began it at half past one. Its air of dread has leaked into the room.

Liz locks her car. 'You awake in there?' she whispers, close to the window box.

You lie still, waiting for the double click her front door makes, and then put down the book. You stretch out on your back, your head on the pillow. Paris Trout believed that he would be shot from below. He clamped a lead plate to his bed base. Over at the Flamingo Gate they are winding down, for you cannot hear the bass percussions any more. Cars start. People call goodnight and one or another of them cries 'Born in the USA'. It is a caste mark, a password, a trace of the night.

At four you peer through the curtain. They have switched off the sundeck spotlights. There are no cars that you do not recognise.

You dress in black: jeans, T-shirt and black Chinese slippers. You push your thumb against the pouring flap on the box of laundry powder and when that doesn't work you cut the perforations with a knife. You shake-stir the spray can of paint. It rattles like a defective clock.

You partly open the front door. A distant siren, a cat in the alley, the police helicopter probing the alleys of Fitzroy with a searchlight. You open the door fully and retract the tongue on the deadlock. With the laundry powder and spray can in one arm, you step out and pull the door to behind you. It looks securely shut now. You can feel the day's heat still locked in the brick wall.

Liz says: 'Let me guess. Indiana Jones?'

'Shit.' The ball-bearing clatters in the spray can.

'Balmy night,' Liz says, 'you know, thought I'd sit out here for a while, and look what turns up.'

She is sitting on her front step, drinking from a champagne glass. Her face is mask-like, white with exaggerated black eye sockets. Her forearms rest on her knees. You realise that she is wearing the dress shirt and underpants. Her long feet are bare. She is sniffing.

'Have you got a cold?'

She rubs her nose. 'I did a line of coke.' She looks at you, at the laundry powder, spray can and concealing black clothes. 'You do this often?'

You crouch on the footpath next to her gleaming legs. The streetlight outside Marion's house is flickering a little. It has attracted a mist of summer insects.

'All right. Be mysterious.'

'How was the ball?' you ask.

'The ball. Your tux was a great hit. Everyone loved the studs. I outdid myself in outrageous behaviour.'

'Good.'

She throws a pebble. It pings on the wheel trim of someone's car. 'But I blew my chances, didn't I? She storms off home, and now it's welcome to avoidance city.' She knocks you with her knees. 'Come on, tell us. Are you the graffiti phantom?'

You gesture at the townhouses. 'It's about the sixth time they've partyed on all night. No consideration. We're supposed to grin and bear it.'

Liz leans back, assessing you, then sways against you again. 'You little bugger. Let me do the paint.'

She takes the can from you and uncoils from the ground. You follow the long white shape, the erratic tick-tock of her. Outside Marion's she begins to skip and swoop, her arms outstretched. You have an intimation of something. But then she beckons. 'Come on,' she calls, leading you by the hand into the grounds of the Flamingo Gate.

She enters the wrong path. 'This way,' you say, pulling free your hand and leading her to the left, between small ornamental trees and across beds of bark chips bordered with volcanic rock. She says, 'How come you know all this?'

The wooden steps leading to the pool room are sodden. One door is ajar and condensation streaks the glass. The air is heavy with odours: chlorine and alcohol and heated water. There is a gentle splashing inside, as if a row-boat is pushing against tiny waves. The lights are off but the pool is illuminated by the laneway streetlight, suspended beyond the streaky glass like a faint new planet, and you can see that Marion is preparing to dive again. She is naked. She is as wet as a seal, her hair water-darkened. Her limbs close like a fisher-bird's as she strikes the water. Liz has seen her too. She steps by you into the pool-room and waits at the pool's edge until Marion has surfaced and returned. They watch each other. Liz is the first to move. When she extends her foot and smooths away the strap of hair adhering to Marion's cheek, it is as if she is erasing a brush stroke.

Early Warning

I didn't go to my normal GP but to the twenty-four-hour clinic opposite the Housing Commission flats, and when the doctor there informed me the results were clear I said lightly: 'So I'm HIV-negative.' It was the lightness of nervous relief, but still, he didn't like it. He wore one of those Tissot rock-watches and shot a white cuff over it and straightened the papers in my file and closed it as if to say he had me pegged as someone who'd now go out and get HIV-positive.

In fact, the whole business had been demoralising and there was some unattractive posturing I wanted to atone for. I left the clinic and walked back along Brunswick Street. In the traffic bunched behind a tram was a badly-tuned Falcon with a holed muffler, and at once my eyes and throat began to burn. I jotted time, date, location, vehicle registration and the nature of the hazard in my notebook. When I say unattractive posturing I mean I'd had trouble getting my mind around Anna's stipulation that we have tests before we embarked on this thing. *Bit extreme. What are you implying? So much for romantic love*. I went into Quill's to get her something on Tuscany or goddess worship.

Rick was changing the window display. His teeth gleamed briefly at me. I checked his ponytail. I liked its neatness. I liked its bravado. My own was still a stub. Meg was applying bar-codes to a carton of new Picadors. Her teeth gleamed at me. In Quill's it's Radio National, customers in armchairs around a hearth, Mapplethorpe nudes on the wall like unhinging images in a dream. There's an upstairs room for readings and launches, and someone puts a little magazine together in the back room. New releases are chalked on the board outside. Rick and Meg stock everything from *Rolling Stone* to Irigaray and brew a pot of Earl Grey whenever reviewers for the Sunday papers come into the shop.

I liked *A Tuscan Table* as soon as I saw it. I picked it up. I rubbed my fingers experimentally over the coarse-grained dust jacket, then opened the book, listening for that satisfying creak and not being disappointed. The pages were thick, uncut, the colour of unbleached straw. They'd used a crisp typeface and sepia-coloured ink. The illustrations—imagined tables in imagined villages—were luminous watercolours. *A Tuscan Table* was also no bigger than a paperback and four times the price.

I reshelved it. I idled along the walls, thinking how I would do this. In Crime I found paperback titles on my permanent list, but their size was wrong for my needs, they were small pulp American imports, so I kept looking. On the bottom shelf were oversized paperbacks. It was a toss up between Barbara Vine and the latest Andrew Vachss. In the end I picked out a big Bodley Head edition of the latest Vachss and took it to the cash register.

Rick climbed out of the window, dusting his hands on his stone-washed jeans.

I said, 'Plastic okay?'

'Sure.'

I handed him Visa and watched him process it. He checked the date and the price and ticked where it said Visa. I indicated the Vachss. 'This selling okay?'

He held his hand flat and waggled it. 'Reasonable.'

'You read it?'

He looked at me. 'The first one was enough. I mean, God. A psycho hero with a super-dog and a secret loft and sicko friends? Give me a break. He writes fairy tales.'

He waited. I said, 'Never read him.'

'Yeah, well. Want a bag?'

I said yes and he gave me the Visa and the receipt and I was relieved when he slid the Vachss into a large plain paper bag. I walked out of the shop. He returned to the display window.

He'd sealed the flap with a strip of Scotch tape which I prised away, and a few seconds later I was stepping hurriedly back into the shop, frowning a little, rolling my eyes, saying I had a mind like a sieve.

I was poised there. I was ready to retreat if I had to.

But nothing happened. No-one looked up. Rick's ponytail swung offhandedly, a tram rumbled by outside, that's all, while across the room Meg applied her bar-codes, walled in by Picadors, and a solitary customer browsed at the Lifestyle shelves.

I crossed the room. I slipped *A Tuscan Table* into the bag with the Vachss. I went out again. 'Thanks!' I said. 'Changed my mind!'

At home I wrapped the book in sleek grey paper patterned with miniature yellow ducks and tied it with straw string I'd saved from a Market Imports parcel. For background I played Tom Waits: I had a Sony system two days old and I was still reassuring myself I had an improved sound.

When I called Anna at work, she knew the reason why, and it made us both tentative, like a couple of kids. We hedged for a while, and I was wondering how to kick-start the issue when she beat me to it. 'You don't sound,' she said, 'like someone with a death sentence hanging over him.'

'Clean as a whistle,' I said.

We pulled back again from the edge and talked about the things we'd been doing. I told her about the new Sony. 'Thirty per cent off,' I said.

'What about your old system?'

'The ad's in. No replies as yet.'

Her tone changed. 'I hate this. It's like making an appointment to screw. Why don't you get us a nice red and I'll see you at my place after work.'

She broke the connection. I stared at the wall, then unfolded my handkerchief and stretched it over the mouthpiece of the telephone. When Lisa answered in Communication Studies I told her I'd just come from the doctor's. 'It's only a twenty-four-hour thing but he said I shouldn't teach tonight.'

'You sound terrible. Want me to ring everyone?'

'Tell them go on with the next story.'

'The next story.'

'They'll know what you mean. Also, they should watch the Barbara Vine mystery this week.'

'I'll put a note on the board as well.'

'Thanks,' I said.

She told me to take care of myself. I slotted a Roy Orbison tape into the Sony and fetched last week's stories and settled in the recliner with a pencil and began to correct them. When the phone rang it wasn't about my old sound system.

'I don't know what you mean by genre story.'

'Hang on a tick, John,' I said.

I turned down the volume and went back to the recliner. 'Genre story.'

'I don't know what you mean by it.'

'It means a category,' I said. 'Crime, romance, horror, science fiction . . . '

When he didn't respond, I said, 'The sort of thing people read on holidays. You know, airport fiction.'

'If I read on a plane I feel nauseated. Never fails.'

I switched the receiver to the other ear. 'You know the kind of thing I mean, though.'

His voice took on a side-of-the-mouth quality, as though he'd just lit a cigarette. 'I thought this was suppose to be a riding course.'

'It is.'

'Well how come we have to learn bad riding?'

'You're not. After your genre story and your post-modern story, you're free to write what you like.'

I waited. 'Tell me again about genre,' he said.

'Have you read any of the examples I gave?'

'Mate, some of us have to work.'

I'd taped the Roy Orbison from an old pressing. The sound lacked definition. 'Just one of each to get an idea,' I said. 'Say a Cliff Hardy and a *Women's Weekly* and a

Stephen King. Just so you get a feel for the rules governing them.'

'You said there weren't any.'

'Weren't any what?'

'Rules. You said if it works, do it.'

I placed the pencil on the top manuscript and watched it roll down into my lap. I did it again. 'It's a bit different with popular fiction,' I said. 'There you've got conventions. Take the private eye—he's a loner. Take Mills and Boon—girl meets boy, girl seems to lose boy, girl gets boy in the end.'

He said nothing. He was breathing and possibly making notes.

'When you say girl and boy you mean teenagers, not little kids.'

'I tell you what, John, try a crime story. Got a pen?'

'Hang on.'

He may have bashed his receiver with a brick and then he came on the line again and said, 'Okay.'

'These are the elements of the detective story, for example: a criminal, a crime, a milieu—that's sort of like the world of the story—a victim, suspects and a detective. Okay?'

'Wait. Okay.'

'Under "suspects" put motive, means and opportunity.'

'Hang on—you told us this Monday.'

I rubbed my face hard with my free hand and said, 'Well, see how you go. But plan it first. This sort of fiction has to be plotted closely.'

'I was away when you did plot.'

There was a clack as the Sony went into reverse

mode. I waited for the recording-level lights to flicker again. I wasn't convinced that I'd balanced the left channel with the right. It seemed to stray too often into the red. I said:

'Would an extension help? I could give you till the end of the month.'

'How serious is the three thousand words?'

'It's flexible.'

'The end of the month.'

'Read a few examples first, John,' I said.

I continued to mark last week's stories and I was sharpening the pencil for the second time, bawling out 'In Dreams', when Hoke smacked through the cat-flap, his fur on end, his tail lashing, his eyes alight. 'You stay here where it's safe, Hoke,' I said.

He saw that his bowl was empty. He turned bitterly away, jumped onto the stack of unmarked stories, cleaned his paws and went to sleep. 'Thanks,' I said. Someone pounded on the front door.

I went down the hall and opened it. Magda was standing there, so I said, 'Sorry about the noise.'

'That cat,' she said, looking fierce.

She was bare-skinned under her painting overalls, speckled and striped with acrylic paint. 'What's he done now?' I said.

'Same as yesterday. Same as last week. Same as last year.'

'He gets plenty to eat,' I said, frowning and shaking my head.

'Just now he go like this—*scratch!*—at Mr Wig.'

'I'll get you a water pistol,' I said. 'He hates getting wet.'

Magda opened her eyes wide. 'No. Poor Hoke.'

So I said, 'How's your work going?'

She came closer and lowered her voice. 'I have been using him, you know. I call him Tiger. Tiger burning bright.' She waved a paint-flecked hand at the terraces of Frome Street, the townhouse complex, the old chimney stack. 'A yellow tiger creeping like a yellow mist in the night.'

I looked doubtfully at Hoke. 'Him?' I said. 'What about Mr Wig?'

'Mr Wig. Mr Wig is a gentleman. So, it's okay? You don't copyright your tiger?'

'Invite me to the exhibition,' I said.

'Okay.'

'Be firm with Hoke. Don't let him in.'

Magda fixed her face and limbs in a demonic rictus. '*Yah!* Like that.'

'It worked just now,' I said.

She turned to go. I said, 'I thought you'd come about the noise.'

She stopped and put her head on one side. 'First when I hear it I think it's coming from over there, like always,' she said, meaning the Flamingo Gate townhouses.

'Sorry. I'll keep it down.'

'Like you were angry,' she said.

'Well, you know,' I said, and I lifted my hand and stepped back inside.

Magda crossed the road to her house. They'd been tossing UDL cans into her front garden again. I saw her pick up a can and throw it hard. It cleared the wall around the townhouses and clattered onto a sundeck.

I went back to work and at five o'clock I drew the curtains and locked the windows and the back door. The settings on the timer were okay. I plugged it into the wall socket and connected the reading light and the radio. After a few minutes, I touched the timer. It seemed to be warmer than normal. I unplugged it and switched on the reading light and the radio and left them on. Then I scattered the Green Guide on the recliner and placed a coffee mug on the floor nearby and rumpled the cushions. I went outside and sized up the house from the back garden and the side windows. I connected the timer again before I left the house but this time I moved the bottom edge of the curtain away from it, and thirty minutes later I was in King and Godfree choosing a red with the chianti cockerel on the neck.

By six o'clock I was caught in a peak-hour jam outside the MCG. A top of thirty tomorrow. More war news on 'PM'. What bothered me was the van in the adjacent lane, rocking on its springs, releasing short snarls of unignited exhaust. I wrote down the details and was launching Scuds at it when the guy behind me leaned on his horn and I became aware of the widening gap ahead. I shifted into first and closed it.

We edged like that onto Hoddle Street and under the railway bridge and eventually onto the south-eastern freeway. By the time I exited at Glen Iris I had details of three more pollution infringements.

Anna lives in a white-trimmed Federation house on a tree-choked street. She had just got home, and answered my knock wearing her tapered jacket, white silk top, short binding skirt and stilettos. I kissed her and stepped back and looked her up and down. 'Sort of dart shaped,' I said.

She touched the padded shoulders. 'We call this power steering.'

I followed her through to the kitchen. When she turned around I said, 'A little something for you.'

She examined both sides of the parcel, one eyebrow hooked, then shook it next to her ear. 'Nice and solid, no moving parts, classy wrapping.'

'Actually it's my licence from the clinic,' I said.

'Very funny.'

I watched her undo the straw bow, my heart turning over at the configuration of her long fingers drawing on the knotty cord. '*Ducks!*' she said, peering at the paper. 'You remembered.' Then I watched her face, and when she squeezed the breath from my lungs, my own smile was wide as a house.

'It's sort of a combination cookbook and cultural history,' I said.

'It's wonderful. Pour yourself a drink and I'll be back in a minute.'

She was in the doorway by then, but she didn't go through. 'Aren't you supposed to be teaching tonight?'

'I called in sick.'

She didn't say anything. 'Only this once,' I said. 'I had to see you. I'll make it up to them.'

We were at that stage where you learn the major things by putting a foot wrong. Eventually she shrugged, said, 'I suppose I should feel flattered,' and went through to her room.

After a while I called the EPA using the wall phone mounted next to her fridge. I waited for the beep, then stated clearly each vehicle number, location, time and environmental offence. Thirty seconds isn't long; I had to call twice to get everything down.

Anna came back fifteen minutes later wearing shorts and an Ethnic top. I ran *Something more comfortable?* through my head, rejecting it. 'Cheers,' I said, handing her a glass of the chianti.

'Come through.'

Our place was the sofa in her sitting room, and she leaned against me there, rotating the crown of her head under my jaw. I looked out over the seat back. Lemons were rotting under the lemon tree. 'You haven't changed your mind about dropping out?' I said.

Her head moved more sharply. 'No.'

'Choir before literature, huh?'

'We've been through this. *I* didn't change the times.'

'You could go into my Thursday class.'

'I'm already doing too much. I want some evenings free.'

'But you'll keep writing.'

'Oh, I'll keep writing.'

Then her scalp knocked my bottom jaw against the top and she heaved around to face me. 'Listen. Define women's story.'

'Women's story?'

'It's what you wrote on Clare's assignment. Plus "I've read this a million times before," stuff like that.'

'Well it's true.'

'But what do you mean by it?'

'Oh,' I said, keeping it light, 'the female characters

are all unhappily married, their husbands are shits, the house is a mess, they can't cope with the kids, and either they take an overdose or some woman friend comes along and it turns into a sisterhood story. I get it all the time.'

'My first story was like that.'

'But yours was well written.'

'So was Clare's. I liked her story. She said she doesn't know what your comments mean and she doesn't think she'll be returning to class again.'

'I'll talk to her.'

'I don't like your chances,' Anna said.

Hoke knows the Honda, and he appeared in the moonlight, stepping high and fast through the jasmine growing along the top rail of Magda's fence. I locked the driver's door, watching as he quivered on the corner post, stretched down it, and leapt to the ground. 'Bad boy,' I said, reaching for him.

They were partying under the spotlights on the sundeck again but I heard the phone. I dropped Hoke and ran inside and kept my voice flat and low as I said: 'Peace offering.'

There was only line hiss like signals centuries old. Then a woman said, 'You the one selling the Akai?'

I said, 'Sorry about that. Thought it was a friend.'

'Oh well, maybe next time. The Akai?'

'Good sound,' I said. 'Everything works okay.'

'How come you're selling it?'

'I've upgraded the whole system.'

'Oh. Right. I could come now.'

'Now?'

'To see it. I could come now,' she said.

It was a deep, good-humoured young voice, driven to high notes by dismay and laughter, when it would break in a way that made me think of plump arms and lazy eyelids. 'My boyfriend's having his twenty-first,' she said. 'I have to get him something. But if this is too late, if everyone's going to bed?'

It was ten o'clock. I said now is fine, there's only me, and gave her the address.

There were four of them, and my first notion was to ask where the girl was. My guess now is that she was in the van Magda saw when she went out to yell at the sundeck. The only useful thing I had to report was: there were four of them, and they came in hard and fast and cleaned me out. 'Pros,' the cops said.

Trusthouse

There's a book about the case, and it mentions me, mentions the Parr children, but treats us as if our importance was marginal. In fact, I was infected with a drowsy kind of badness, that final summer at The Trusthouse, and the Parr children were so heavy, uninventive and susceptible that I baited their hooks for them. You could say I was innocent, but lost it, bored by their greater innocence, and our parents, diverted by the sun, the abductions, the claims of the clairvoyants, had no idea of what was happening to us.

This story is posed in oppositions. One, above all, accounts for what happened: we were rich and the Parrs were not. In those days of inland families coming south to make The Trusthouse their home for six weeks of the summer, the Parrs could only afford ten days. Where we made the hotel crackle with life, the Parrs were like shadows on the walls. Even the manner of our advance on The Trusthouse revealed the disparity between us.

It was a Saturday just before New Year. We sealed the house at 5 a.m. and set out through the station country, pushing south in our dusty car, a barrelling Customline expressly washed but dusty before we reached the first cattle grid. My father drove. He'd say, every December, 'Just point her south and plant your foot.' He was a big, vigorous man. The world to him was ordained, agreeable, completely understood, and when he powdered us across the saltbush flats, breaking the backs of black snakes, our place in it seemed secure. We had the confidence of our isolation, our landing strip and radio call-sign, our fifty miles in from the highway. While we swayed against each other, still half-asleep, the dawn kangaroos stiffened in the cropped grass or slipped away into the scrub. My father cursed them, but it was affectionate cursing, background noise, no more than a ritual marking of our boundary before we ventured beyond it.

At the turn-off he braked, did not look, and then we were emerging from the chasing dust, nose-up on the bitumen for Adelaide. Twelve hours—that was our record. There are no towns out there, only nude stone chimneys, mirages, birds stupefied on the wires. We might have been the last, ransacking inhabitants: a mother, a father, a boy and his sisters. I leaned into my open window and watched our shadow on the road's edge. It ran with and nudged us, yet it was a distortion, the tarpaulin wind-plumped on the roofrack, lumpish on our potent lines. The big engine rumbled. Then the sun climbed and I was lost to dreams.

It was very hot. My mother reached around often and touched Jess's knee. 'All right, sweetie?' Jess was five, our afterthought, a receptacle of love. She sat low between Diana and me, her small face sulky and fatigued. 'Take off her frock, one of you,' my mother said, 'and lay her along the seat. Cool her down with this.' She passed us a damp washcloth.

Diana put her hand behind Jess's back and pushed her forward. Jess protested, jerking her shoulders and mumbling, inarticulate but persistent in her misery. 'Lean forward,' we said. I undid the four buttons down her spine, loosened the bow around her waist, lifted off the dress. For a moment her tiny back was revealed to me, hot and damp, the bones close to the surface, her shoulder-blades like wing buds. I saw that Diana was watching me. Then Jess flopped back against Diana and kicked out at my legs. 'Shh,' Diana said, applying the washcloth to the cross cheeks. Jess relaxed and lay back along the seat, her head in Diana's lap, her feet in mine. Once or twice I drew my hands along her instep, as you might stroke the forefoot of a sleeping cat, but she tossed and fretted. 'Don't,' Diana warned me. The day passed. Jess slept on her stomach, her back, her side. Once I caught her staring at me in mild, hypnotic languor; I winked, but she grew alert immediately, stiffening her legs ready to strike out.

At the border we reset our watches, which refreshed us in unnameable ways. We rode high, down into a region of silos, sidings and sharefarms, the country of small towns, where the railway children would stare after us. Otherwise there was only the wheat, in populations of leaning bags ranged along the stubble lines or spilled in crescents at the paddock gates where the galahs scratched. Jess, reviving, stood upright, her chin on the seat in front of us. My mother smiled around at her. 'Better, sweetie?'

We began to sing scraps of songs from Jess's school-of-the-air broadcasts. Diana and I had grown up with these songs, over countless mornings in a shaded room, supervised by our mother. She was an unlikely advisor and tutor. She would listen with relish to the crackling voices, alert for the agonies, bewilderment and wispiness of the children, the sweetness of the teachers, then nail them to the wall. She wanted us to be sharp and self-respecting, sly and durable. She was preparing us for leaving home, I think. Diana was sixteen that year: she would soon be gone. I was only twelve.

My father swore suddenly. We had swept over a crest and come upon a small, overloaded sedan advancing with threadbare decency along the Adelaide road. He throttled back; we seemed to crawl along. Then the road was clear and he accelerated. We all looked—the Parrs! A man, a woman, and two children of about my age, staring forward, intact, patterned and cautious. We passed, in all our swagger and glory, and it seemed to me that their little sedan faltered and there was estrangement on their faces.

Eleven hours. There were more cars now and bigger towns. Our first traffic light. A paperboy cried out: *Second child missing!* We subsided, a hard, angular, sun-bleached family in a long, low, muttering American car.

The Gawler bypass, Gepps Cross, Henley Beach Road. 'Who will be the first to see the sea?' my mother said, her voice sweet, a sing-song, a sign that she was dangerously bored. 'Not far now,' my father said. His hand left the wheel and I heard it on her thigh, a reassurance, maybe a warning.

I saw a seagull on a bus shelter, the summer shops where proprietors took brooms to the tracked-in beach sand, then the clock tower, palm trees, the sea at the end of the tunnelling street. We left it to Jess. She pointed suddenly, darting her arm between my parents. 'There!' my mother agreed.

We angled like a feeding beast into the kerb outside The Trusthouse, inches from a blistered, salt-scummed verandah post. An airliner banked above the sea. The wind gusted, throwing grit into our eyes. We stripped the car and swept into The Trusthouse foyer. There were gleeful shouts; we had that effect.

I remember that I idled in the doorway. Men and women were streaming up from the beach, sour and exhausted, holding tight to children who couldn't see the need for it. This was the fag-end of a Saturday afternoon, when inlanders would arrive in triumph and strange men begin to prowl. A small car crept into the square. I watched it nose fearfully at a space next to the Customline, back away again, try elsewhere.

Satisfied, I went upstairs to my room.

The Parr children waited for me. They waited every year. I'd descend the broad staircase, sandals upon my feet, comb tracks in my water-darkened hair, and find them in the evening gloom, prepared to smile or flee. They never did anything, just sat mute and diminished on a massive dimpled sofa, waiting for me to appear. Trevor's tidy teeth rested on his bottom lip. Lorraine was round-faced, her knees forever opening and closing like bellows, denying the pressure in her bladder. The Parr children wore socks and shiny shoes and an air of longing and helplessness.

Then Lorraine said brightly, 'Hello, Nick.'

I turned away. 'Come into the lounge.'

Their shoes clomped behind me across the foyer. As I paused in the cavernous doorway, the Parrs huddled at my heels, stricken by the vast room. They stayed with me, past the armchairs clustered like islands on the limitless floorboards, over the Persian rugs, to the seaward windows. There was a tossing buoy out there, the lights of a liner.

We perched on the windowseat. Before long the country families began to drift into the room. The men and the women stretched their legs and sighed, marking time until the dinner gong sounded. Their voices never quite reached the chandeliers but seemed to hover above the armchairs: Girton, PLC, fifty thousand for the wool clip, what sort of monster would do that? Some children gathered at the baby grand, where Jess and Diana pounded out 'Chopsticks' so vigorously the roses trembled in the vases and petals fell, seeking their likenesses in the polished lid.

I said, 'I'll order drinks.'

Waitresses were emerging from the wall panels. I liked to watch them lean into the rich air, slapping silver trays against their thighs. 'Something to drink?' they'd ask. I liked the way their uniforms frothed black and starchy white about their knees.

Meanwhile Trevor and Lorraine struggled with my suggestion. They looked to their parents, but their parents, smiling tormentedly at mine on the far side of the room, were no help. I could hear my father's shouting laugh. It seemed to ring the hotel, and it affected my mother, for I saw her tip back her throat and blow a narrow stream of smoke into the air above their heads.

I said to the Parr children: 'One with all the colours.'

Greed seeped into their faces. They remembered the tall, frost-beaded glasses, layered red, yellow and green, topped with crushed ice, a straw buried deep in the oily fluids.

'I'll pay,' I said.

I had a pound note in my pocket. There always was money when I needed it, in those days, in that place. Money released me, it released my parents. 'Don't wander, and mind who you talk to,' they'd say absently, poking cash into my pocket, and for six weeks I'd roam the stairs, the endless corridors, the beach, discovering unexpected corners, bathrooms, servants' quarters, court-yards, hollows in the dunes. It was a world inhabited by children. No-one bothered us. No-one noticed us. No-one wanted us.

I signalled to a waitress, endured *My, haven't you grown!* and gave our order.

Then I began to spin stories for the Parr children. That was the beginning of everything. I did it for their greed, their avid faces, their squirming, slack-jawed torment. I could see their awful need. They had been good all year, dreaming of badness, and now I was making it real and possible for them.

'Flip it,' I said.

Lorraine was breathing audibly. Heat rose from her body. Her eyes were fevered, her face provoked and insatiate, drawn to the aching stalk between her brother's legs.

I crouched with her. 'Flip it.'

As though testing for a current, she reached out her plump arm, touched, snatched her arm back into the comfort of her bare stomach again. But she'd scarcely made contact. In Trevor there was only the pump pump of the blood in him. Frustrated, he tapped down hard on himself. 'Like this.' He seemed to snap back in the space of an eye blink. 'See?'

Then in a puddle of clothing in a forgotten room on the third floor, Lorraine would pose for us. She bowed her knees, bent her head forward to look, as we squatted shoulder to shoulder at her feet. She was rounded, creased. In the skin around her waist and thighs I could see the cruel red impression of her pants elastic.

We did that. I sensed that there was more. I don't know what the Parrs thought. They were intoxicated and it seemed to be enough for them.

When I grew bored of them I'd slip away. They'd find me again, inevitably, expressing dependence, submission, emotional captivity, but not before I'd had time to scout about and see the things I wanted to see.

I saw my parents hold court on the street-level balcony. They seemed to fill the space, to command the attention of the brown-skinned husbands and wives who drowsed around wrought-iron tables crammed with iced drinks, lipsticked cigarettes, magazines fingerprinted with tanning oils. My parents were risky, arbitrary, careless, a little callous. They made people laugh. They made people want them. The adult Parrs were there somewhere, in a paralysis of gentility.

Once I followed them all to the beach. If the balcony was full of promise, here was a chance to express it. They were very brown and agile in the water. The water frothed and seethed around them. They were a different race from the shoulder-strapped and jacketed people who sawed with steak knives in The Trusthouse dining room. I saw my mother and Mrs Parr relieve Mr Parr of his bathing suit in the shallows.

I saw Diana. She took Jess to swimming lessons, pushed Jess on the swings, turned Jess's sandy feet under the tap on the seawall. She liked to stretch out on a red towel, cocking her hip to get comfortable, hooking a finger inside some chafing strap or band, while Jess dug moats in the tidal sand nearby and youths paraded. She was aware of their smiles, their supple blood. Or back in The Trusthouse she'd straddle the edge of the bed and paint her toenails while Jess slept on the next bed and I watched quietly in the shuttered light. She would murmur to me from behind a blinding curtain of corn-gold hair, her mouth muffled against her long, drawn-up bare leg.

It was at about this time that I first saw the stranger.

My memory of seeing him has the hazy configuration of a dream. I am alone. Bored with the limited needs and wants of the Parrs, I have escaped The Trusthouse and ventured into the backstreets. The sun is high, silent, burning from windshields, from chrome, beating off brick walls, melting the tarry streets. Nothing can be seen clearly in air as hot as that. The man on the corner seems to be smouldering at the edges. I don't know if he has a sad or a hateful face, only that he doesn't smile, is still and watchful, watching me pass by on the other side. He starts after me. I turn around twice to confirm that. This is a power better than any power I have over the Parrs. I can scarcely breathe. Then when I turn two more corners and stop, watching for him down a long, heat-blurred street, and he doesn't come, I retrace my steps, my heart hammering at each corner and recessed doorway, back to where he had first materialised—but the streets are silent and empty.

I went back the next day. He was there. He followed me. He disappeared again.

The power I felt didn't last. I went back twice more at the same time, knowing he'd be waiting for me—but then, he knew I'd come. I deliberately didn't speak, didn't pass on his side of the street—but he didn't encourage it. Also, the sun was always blinding; I couldn't read him. And I couldn't help but turn to see that he was following me. I had to know. To that extent he controlled me. He always was there behind me, and his pace was unhurried, controlled, incurious.

So, next time I went early, to catch him unprepared. He wasn't there. I tried again later. He merely watched me pass, then started after me. He hadn't been anxious at all. If there was an expression on his face, it was knowing and elusive. And he always vanished in some alley or through some door.

I wanted a miserable declaration from him. I wanted to see guilt, misgiving, desire. Anything, even the Sunday papers' brand of child-snatching evil, would have been better than this remoteness and inaccessibility.

I wanted him to crack.

The next day, Diana handed Jess into my care. It was the day the authorities drained the boat basin.

She was there with Jess, I with the Parrs, and we were among the hundreds gathered at the rail to watch a line of policemen sweep up and back, treading high in the muddy residue. We waited, scarcely moving. I remember the absolute silence. Now and then a young cadet stopped, bent down, tugged something free, but it was always an inner tube, a fruit tin. Then one man brought up a beer bottle, someone called from the seawall: 'No drinking on the job,' and the spell was broken.

I turned away. They wouldn't find anything. It was a page one story, they'd been digging and combing the seafront for days, but they hadn't found even a sandshoe or a cotton singlet.

Besides, I was more interested in Diana. Someone was with her and I could sense her heartbeat. He lived at The Trusthouse, the son of the Italian owner, dark and always smiling. I wanted to see what would develop. I wanted to watch the change in her, and so I said yes when she started to push Jess on to me each morning, saying she had things to do.

Not that the Parrs noticed anything. One night Diana and her fellow took us to a western double at a drive-in. We went in the glossy Jaguar that always stood in The Trusthouse's private courtyard, the Parrs and I in the back seat, Jess in front with Robert and Diana. After he had parked the car, Robert hooked the tinny speaker to his window, where it crackled like a badly tuned radio, and we settled back to watch. The screen glowed dully. Slides flipped by, advertising local funeral parlours and grocers. No-one looked twice at the two likenesses up there, the words *Have you seen these children?* blazing beneath them. Everyone knew those faces from the newspapers, the bus-shelter posters.

Then the features started and a queer kind of darkness settled over everything. Now and then a nearby car heaved once on its springs or I heard sudden, cut-short cries. A bottle rolled slowly and stopped. There were the red eyes of cigarettes all around me. I took all of this in. The Parrs sat open-mouthed before the images on the screen, Jess fell asleep, but I took in the night sounds and the soft, minute, almost soundless motions of Diana in thrall on the front seat.

The days passed. Soon the Parrs would be gone. I was pleased; they'd grown tiresome.

'What if she tells on us?'

I looked at Jess. 'She won't tell.'

This time we were in my room. Jess and I had already stripped the clothes from our bodies, Jess tossing her shorts and shirt away with a kind of victorious expansion. Now she was treating my bed like a trampoline. I laughed. I liked her spirit. It was a family spirit and the leaden Parrs didn't have it.

Trevor undid a button. Lorraine turned her back. I heard the meek scrape of fabric on skin. I waited patiently. It didn't take long. The doubts and modesty disappeared and the Parrs were bloated and heavy lidded again.

Jess bounded about on the edge of things, incurious after a few minutes. She sang and talked to herself. But I had sneaked two cigarettes from our mother's bag and she stood still long enough for me to plug one into her mouth, grin at her and tell her to puff. She was like a little rubbery creature arrested in movement, her eyes wide in concentration, gulping in the smoke.

Trevor snatched it from her mouth. 'Don't waste it on a kid.'

I'd been noticing this thuggish kind of confidence in the Parrs. I didn't like it. It was unappealing and it assumed a levelling. By the time we'd finished and made our way down the staircase for lunch, I knew how I would shake the Parrs again.

'Not allowed.'

This expression sprang automatically from the damp mouths of Trevor and Lorraine Parr. They seemed to say it as one word, a gobbled sound meaning 'no', and I believe it was the first expression they had ever learnt.

I pointed out that they'd been doing a number of things that were not allowed. 'We'll be three against one,' I said. 'We'll just see what he does.'

I talked long and hard that afternoon. I gave them ten shillings each, I made dizzy promises, until my plan seemed less perilous, assuming a shape that would fit the itch they felt.

'Just walk past him?'

'And see what he does,' I said.

They looked at Jess. 'What about her?'

'Wait here.'

I took Jess by the hand and we began the long journey down through the slumbering corridors of The Trusthouse. It was home and we were made to feel welcome in it. The brass and the wood panels gleamed, the air was scented with wax, cables snickered quietly in the liftwell. Mr Delgado bowed to us; wide smiles split open the faces of the maids.

On the balcony they were dozing with trays of drinks, newspapers and oily paperbacks. My father had propped the hotel's mantel radio on the dining-room windowsill. The Third Test had started; the parents of The Trusthouse children wouldn't be budging until the last ball of the day. My mother saw us, threw open her arms, clasped Jess to her in an extravagant display of love—extravagant to the glum Parrs at the next table, not to me. 'I'll be back soon,' I said.

Five minutes later I had Trevor and Lorraine with me against a grimy brick backstreet wall. 'There,' I said.

They peered around my shoulders at the stranger. They giggled, partly because they were apprehensive, but mostly because the stranger I had planted in their minds was not the stranger who had been playing some elusive game with me. After all, I didn't want them to be scared before we'd begun. The stranger I had created for them was untidy, a little grubby, a half-mad muttering man who exposed himself and whom they could safely sneer at. I wanted the truth when it hit them to rattle their teeth.

We set out along the footpath, enveloped in heat that had been stored for days in the bricks. Once or twice the Parrs let out a snuffling laugh. We drew adjacent to the man. The sun was in our eyes; all we could see of him was a dark outline on the opposite side of the narrow street. Then we were past him. I could hear our footsteps and the excited breathing of the Parrs, nothing else. I don't know what we looked like—a roundchinned, red-faced girl, two thin knobbly-kneed boys with short, decent hair?

Anyway, the man began to follow us and I told the Parrs to look. They turned, saw the implacable shape pacing us, and immediately came undone. One of them squealed, infecting the other, and they ran squealing and giggling down the street.

Disgusted, I ran after them.

I thought at the time that we must have seemed too stupid to bother with, for the man wasn't there the next day, or the next. In fact, it was the Parrs' last day at The Trusthouse before we saw him again.

I remember that we were idling in the dunes near the breakwater. I couldn't be bothered with the Parrs by that stage but they continued to find me scheming and foreign and they would not give me up. Jess was with me, so I couldn't slip away from them.

We were in a windless hollow. The sand was gritty, riddled with shell chips and desiccated seaweed, but it was better there than on the shoreline itself where the wind had uprooted umbrellas and driven sand like needles into our eyes and against our arms and legs. Cloud shadows chased over us. Now and then both Parrs looked reproachfully at me, as if waiting for me to say something—that I would miss them, perhaps; that I looked forward to next year. On Lorraine's face was the awful bloat and pucker of a face close to tears. But I had nothing to say to them; I had stopped taking them to the third floor; I simply wanted them to go home.

The reprieve came when Trevor said, 'What's he want?'

He was frowning at the seawall behind my back. Thinking it would be his father, I turned without interest or curiosity and looked straight into the eyes of the man from the backstreets. This time there was no transfiguring sun behind him, no air of reserve and stealth. Instead, he hadn't shaved, he hadn't washed, he was missing buttons and half his wits. I could see nicotine on his forefinger when he beckoned to us, and I could see the privation in his eyes. He wanted us badly. He opened and closed his mouth once in a kind of hunger.

The man seemed to restore the Parr children. They grew crafty and aspirant, leaning toward me to whisper, 'Let's follow him.'

I remember that my attention was sharp and absolute from that moment. I had made the man crack, now I wanted to see the true shape of his decline, and I was not going to let the Parrs take control. I stood up and I led the way to the seawall steps.

The stranger was half a block ahead of us on the esplanade. We had to hurry. We didn't want to lose him. The jetty, the kiosks, the beachfront shops were thronging with people who had been driven up from the beach by the wind. We dodged through knots of them, bumping their heavy hips, and we heard their futile shouts, but you could not stop us.

The man was waiting at his corner. Before we quite reached him he was on the move again, leading us into a region of fetid lanes. Drains ran down the centres of them. Thin cats with weeping eyes crouched low to the ground as we passed. A woman slept on a cement step and on the other side of an alley fence I heard the slash of heavy urination in a lavatory bowl.

It was no place for Jess. The man was waiting at a wooden gate, I had him where I wanted him, but this was no place for Jess. I began to look back over my shoulder, searching for her.

Trevor passed me first, exultant, knowing that he would beat me now.

Then Lorraine.

Then I was alone there, and I remained alone, and it made my heart stop.

What's not clear is whether or not the man would have done more than simply show his grubby photographs. Apparently the Parrs got nervous when I failed to appear. At the inquest they said his room smelt. He made their skin crawl. They couldn't make sense of the photographs.

But it is clear that he didn't take Jess. We were his alibi. No-one knows who took her. I remember the clamp of fear I felt, my useless, frenzied search of the dazed streets. She was the third. No-one found her, just as no-one found the first two—or the fourth, eighteen months later. All this happened thirty years ago. That there has been no trace is the hard part. There have been other incidents—this wide, slow, principled city has an underbelly—but there was always evidence: the drowned man in the river, a skin-stripped torso, the slit throats of the creatures in the zoo. But we have nothing, which means we can't put Jess to rest. We tried a Dutch clairvoyant, just as the first family did. He said he could see a garage floor. Once we got a letter, but it was a hoax.